Good
for You

OTHER BOOKS BY CAMILLE PAGÁN

Good for You

Camille Pagán

a novel

LAKE UNION
PUBLISHING

Published by Lake Union Publishing, Seattle

www.apub.com

Amazon, the Amazon logo, and Lake Union Publishing are trademarks of Amazon.com, Inc., or its affiliates.

ISBN-13: 9781542038034 (hardcover)
ISBN-13: 9781542038010 (paperback)
ISBN-13: 9781542038027 (digital)

Cover design by Eileen Carey
Cover image: © MR. BUDDEE WIANGNGORN / Shutterstock;
© Oks_K / Shutterstock

Printed in the United States of America

First edition

AUTHOR'S NOTE

This novel includes grief over the loss of a sibling. It also briefly describes child abuse from an adult survivor's perspective. As a person who doesn't like reading graphic or extended depictions of abuse, I was careful to mention it only where I felt it was absolutely necessary. However, I believe books that include abuse as but one aspect of a character's life can help remind survivors that they're not alone, and that nothing's wrong with them. And in my experience, that can make all the difference.

For Laurel Lambert, my lifeline

ONE

Sometimes it takes such a terrible amount of effort to be normal.

After thirty-four years of practice, Aly Jackson nearly had it down to a science. But as her boss frowned at her, she had to remind herself to plaster on a smile. Yes, he'd just announced that he was going to have to cut her staff's already-anemic pay. But her can-do spirit was why she'd been named the youngest editor in chief in the history of *All Good*. And she had no intention of making James Fox, the magazine's publisher and the owner of Innovate Publishing, think he'd made a mistake in hiring her.

"Well, kiddo," he said from one of the identical leather sofas they were seated at. He furrowed his brow. "I know this isn't ideal."

Aly was roughly the same height as a sixth grader—and not a tall one—which was why she slipped on heels soon after she awoke and didn't kick them off again until right before she crawled into bed. If anyone else had called her *kiddo*, she would've been seething inside. But James was as much her mentor as her employer, and his guidance had helped her ascend the masthead so quickly.

Admittedly, she *was* the tiniest bit annoyed at the bomb he'd just dropped on her. But the secret to breezing through tough conversations was deciding in advance to keep your cool. And Aly'd been preparing herself for a doozy of a chat since James texted her at six a.m. to say he wanted to have coffee as soon as she got into the office. An early-morning missive from James wasn't unusual, but he didn't actually *drink* coffee; that was his genteel way of informing her he had bad news. (The good kind was delivered as an invitation for cocktails, regardless of the time of day.) Which was fine. When it came to publishing, Aly thought of news as the weather report. You might not like the forecast, but you couldn't dress accordingly without it.

"It's not ideal," she allowed, "but I'll handle it."

"I knew you would," James said warmly. "Which brings me to our second item of business. The pay cut alone isn't enough. We needed to slash nearly another hundred thousand to make up for a shortfall in advertising revenue."

His navy suit probably cost what some people spent on tropical vacations—not that Aly would know. Because in addition to hyper-competency and James' mentoring, the other reason she'd landed the top slot at the magazine was because she'd been willing to accept less than a third of what the previous editor in chief made. For her, the job wasn't about the money. It was about fulfilling the dream she'd had since picking up a copy of *All Good* in a doctor's office when she was in elementary school. Every time she walked into the steel and glass tower that was home to Innovate Publishing, she thought about how all her planning and perseverance had paid off. Money would come later, or not at all. What really mattered was that she'd made it: she hadn't let her childhood keep her from living her dreams.

"Got it. What are you thinking?" she asked, hoping to buy a few seconds to come up with some suggestions of her own. The magazine had recently reduced pay for freelance writers (again), and the pages had grown progressively flimsier, to the point that they easily tore when turned. After four decades of helping women create effortlessly organized lives, *All Good* had a brand reach of more than twenty million and was valued at nearly half a billion dollars. Yet there they were—running on fumes and a prayer.

"Whittle the masthead. I need you to shave that hundred thousand from staffing," said James.

Aly gripped the cup of dark roast she'd bought herself and tried not to let her keen expression give way to the frown lurking just behind it. The two editorial assistants already did the work of four people. The executive and managing editors were essential, and the middle of the book, as they called each issue, wouldn't exist without her three remaining senior editors. Production and Design were already stretched thin. Then it came to her.

"We'll cut someone from the research department," she told him. Fewer fact-checkers meant more errors, but at least there would *be* a magazine to mess up.

"Great," said James. But she could tell by the way he nodded that he was about to say just the opposite.

"I need the rest of the team," she said quickly. "But we can write more of the September issue in-house."

"It's the twenty-first century, Aly. Less is more," James said with a *we're-in-this-together smile*. "*Sporty* just got rid of their executive editor, and they're doing fine. Your exec—what's her name again? Regardless," he said before Aly could volunteer that it was Meagan, "she has to go. It's the only logical choice. Don't worry, I'll have Linda from Human Resources handle it."

Learning that she wouldn't have to personally escort Meagan to the corporate guillotine did little to ease Aly's mind. They'd both been at the magazine for twelve years and had shared a cubicle for much of that time. Would they have been friends if Aly had not been there to witness every salad Meagan scarfed down over her keyboard or overhear the teary phone conversations she'd had with whomever she was dating? Doubtful. But Meagan was the only person who knew about . . . well, what had happened last September.

Sure, Meagan had been a bit brittle since Aly became editor in chief six months ago. But *fire* her? There was making strategic decisions, and then there was being a monster.

Suddenly Aly had an even better idea. "James," she said brightly, "I'll take the cut. Slash another thirty-five from my salary. That, plus cutting the other salaries and letting a researcher go, should just about get us to a hundred."

Thank goodness she lived with Seth now, because after her student loan payments were deducted from her bank account at the end of each month, she barely had enough to buy groceries. But to Aly, a magazine job that offered dental insurance and a steady paycheck would never not feel like winning the lottery.

James snorted. "That's ridiculous. You're barely making more than your senior editors."

"Right, but we both know that'll change if I get a chance to fully right the ship. Circulation's up by three percent since last year, and digital advertising is on a steady rise," she said proudly. "I'll ask for that thirty-five back with interest the minute we're out of the red."

She'd expected James to agree to her suggestion. Praise her, even, for her dedication and long-term vision. Instead, he leaned forward and said in a too-gentle voice, "Aly, I know you've been through a lot."

This was the problem: James knew her too well. In addition to mentoring her, he had set Aly up with his son, Seth. Founded by James' great-grandfather, Innovate Publishing was a family business, and Seth was the head of the company's sales department. He and Aly had cleared their relationship with HR, and they maintained firm boundaries at the office—but things still got a smidge personal at times. As such, James knew more about Aly's life than she'd prefer.

"I'm doing great!" Then she softened her lie with the truth: "Work keeps me sane."

"Well, kiddo, you're the absolute gold standard, and I mean it." Before she could thank him, he added, "And, Aly? New salaries go into effect on the thirtieth. Please let your team know."

It was the second of June. Which meant her staff would have one more paycheck before the cut. Then what? Just the month before,

All Good's most talented senior editor had left to work at a nonprofit because—and this really killed Aly—it paid "way better" than publishing. Who would decamp next? She didn't even want to think about it.

James was looking at her, so she pushed the corners of her lips back into position. But even though the magazine had recently published an article about research showing that fake smiling tricked you into feeling happy, she still felt like her heart had been dipped in cement.

Then her gaze shifted to the floor-to-ceiling window just behind James' desk. Eight stories below, Midtown Manhattan pulsed with life. Wasn't she lucky to be here—exactly where she always wanted to be, doing what she'd always hoped to do?

Not everyone could say that.

"Absolutely," she said to James, who beamed his approval, and while this did nothing to warm her, she at least felt like she'd accomplished something.

Aly's brother, Luke, had once called her a shark. "You'll die if don't keep moving," he'd said, winking at her, and though she'd pretended to be offended, she'd actually been incredibly pleased that he'd described her so perfectly. It was a gift, to have someone know you that well and love you even more because of it. In her experience, it almost always went the opposite direction.

Yes, Aly just needed to keep moving, and eventually she'd swim her way back to normal. Except as she marched out of James' office, a fleeting but awful thought surfaced in her mind.

What was the point now that Luke was gone?

TWO

With the September issue just around the corner, Aly would've preferred not to spend precious time at that morning's editorial meeting explaining the pay cut. Still, the announcement went as well as it could've. Sure, she caught nearly every editor around the conference table exchanging subtle glances with each other. But no one shouted or stormed out—or even protested, which surprised her. Usually staffers spoke freely at her meetings, which had not been the case when Ellen, the iron-fisted editor in chief who'd hired Aly fresh out of college, had been in charge. At one point, Aly shot a *help-my-hands-are-tied* expression at Meagan, who sat directly across from her, but Meagan just looked away.

Oh well. Meagan was distant sometimes, but she more than made up for it with her snappy cover lines and ability to artfully rearrange even the sloppiest copy. And Aly certainly wasn't going to tell Meagan that she'd personally yanked her pink slip out of James' hand. After all, taking charge without taking credit was how she'd gotten ahead in the first place.

It was past noon when the meeting adjourned, and because she hadn't had anything but coffee, her stomach was on its way to self-digesting. The pile of page proofs on her desk would double by the time she returned from getting food, but *All Good* was hardly *The Devil Wears Prada*; Aly didn't have an assistant to go fetch lunch for her. She grabbed her bag, dashed to the elevator, and headed downstairs.

The building's lobby was directly attached to the salad chain next door, which meant that even though the food wasn't particularly good, the place was always packed. Today was no different, so Aly got in the queue. She figured she could practice the *All Good* principle of doing more in less time and answer some of her unread texts while she waited.

Two were from her best friend, Harry. *Ground control to Major Bomb,* he'd written in the last one. *Send proof of life so I know you haven't fallen in a sinkhole. P.S. Chicago > New York. Wish you were here xo*

As much as the Second City remains second best, I wish I were there, too, she wrote back. *P.S. Alive and well—will call tonight or tomorrow x*

She had a message from Seth, telling her that he was heading to the gym after work and that she should get dinner without him. She hearted his message, even though she didn't feel loving about eating alone.

Unfortunately, the other five texts were from Aly's mother. She skimmed them and vowed to write her back at some unspecified date in the far-off future.

She'd just looked up from her phone when Meagan's voice came floating through the air. She glanced around the man standing in front of her, who was built like a football player, and saw Meagan a few spots ahead with Ashleigh, the senior health and beauty editor. She was about to call to them when Aly heard her name. And although it took her a few seconds to fully process what she was hearing, she must have somehow known Ashleigh was not speaking to her, but rather *about* her, because she immediately stepped out of sight, behind the linebacker again.

"I mean, ugh." Ashleigh was using a stage whisper. "You know *she's* not taking a salary cut."

Aly waited for Meagan to defend her, or at least change the subject. Instead, Meagan said, "Totally."

"You have to give her credit—dating Seth is a serious strategic decision, and it looks like it's paying off. Literally!" said Ashleigh, who was no longer pretending to keep her voice down.

Nearly all of Aly's decisions were strategic, but Seth was that rare exception; not only was he almost everything she wanted in a partner, she actually liked him. And James himself had introduced them! But that fact didn't keep blood from rushing to her cheeks. They were right—it did look bad. She might as well have handed extra ammunition to her own firing squad.

"For now," said Meagan. "They won't last. Then what?"

What other people think about you is none of your business: that's what Luke always said, and although she was pretty sure he stole that line from someone famous, the advice had served her well. *Get out of here*, she commanded herself. *Slip out the door before you overhear something worse.*

But her feet refused to move. And that's when she really began to panic.

"Then the gig goes to someone who can actually handle it."

Meagan didn't respond this time, and Aly wanted to believe she was frowning at Ashleigh to encourage her to stop while she was ahead. But for some reason she could only picture Meagan smugly flipping her honey-highlighted hair away from her face.

Ashleigh kept going. "Did you see how she smiled like a crazy person when she said that she'd figure something out?"

Okay, maybe Aly *had* been smiling like a crazy person. She'd be the first to admit that she might've taken the whole cheerleader routine a smidge too far. If she had, though, Meagan was the one person on staff who knew why she sometimes became blindingly sunny.

It was either that or give in to the dark side.

Except Meagan didn't tell Ashleigh to cut Aly some slack or hint that she'd been through an awful lot recently. "She never should have gotten that job," Meagan muttered. "Not with the funk she's in. It won't be long before she destroys what's left of the magazine and takes us all down with it. What a *beach*."

Aly flinched. Her father used to call her a *beach* all the time. Of course, he'd used a stronger word than that, and so had Meagan. But Luke claimed that cursing was the lazy man's thesaurus. Though Aly wasn't sure she agreed with him, she had taken his claim to heart because he always was the smartest person in the room.

Or at least he had been.

It occurred to Aly that her real mistake was not thinking through what would happen *after* the editorial meeting. Because for all that's been said about the best-laid plans, the real danger was having none at all. While Aly was busy bargaining and budgeting with James, she'd forgotten to decide what she'd do if someone got upset about the news . . . or agreed with her secret fear that maybe she didn't actually deserve the one job she'd been obsessed with since she'd learned it existed.

Aly's hands and feet were tingling. And then, though her heart pounded so hard she could feel it in her throat, she suddenly rushed at Meagan and Ashleigh. "Yeah, hi," she said, glancing back and forth between them with bulging eyes. "I was right behind you. I heard *everything*."

"Al—" began Meagan, but Aly interjected before she could continue.

"I kept you from getting canned!" she squawked. If she seemed unhinged, it's because, well—she was. Like a grizzly bear after a very long winter, something primal and ferocious had just emerged from deep within her, and it was becoming readily apparent that she was powerless to stop it. "I won't even say that's what friends do, because clearly we're not. But I'm a great editor and I care about our magazine more than almost anything. You, on the other hand—" She pointed an index finger at Meagan, jabbing the air for emphasis. "*You're* the beach."

Except instead of saying *beach*, she'd pulled out the poor man's thesaurus—which made her think of Luke, and how disappointed he'd be if he could hear her.

And then . . .

Well, and then Aly had no recollection of what happened next.

THREE

Crap. Not this again. It had been years—decades, even—since Aly'd had one of her little memory incidents. There were parts of her childhood she literally couldn't remember, but since they were the worst parts, she'd never had a problem with that.

Well, there'd been that fight with her closest friend in high school, Jill, that she completely spaced on. Afterward, Jill had accused Aly of lying when she confessed that she didn't know what they'd squabbled about, and they never really talked again after that. Aly had been mortified, but she'd told herself it was a one-off.

Except now it clearly wasn't. Aly's ears were ringing as she made her way through the lobby, but her thoughts were clear. *Shouldn't I feel dizzy or something?* she wondered as she stepped into the elevator. *Because obviously something's wrong with me.*

As the elevator ascended, it occurred to her that there *had* been another incident fairly recently. She and Seth almost never fought, but last fall, they'd gotten into an argument before bed. And when he brought it up the next day, she had to pretend she knew what he was talking about until she could patch together that they had fought about how he felt like she never wanted to sleep with him. But that was not long after Luke died, and in addition to being numb from her navel to her knees—as she still kind of was, truth be told—she'd felt like someone had filled her head with gravel. Now, nine months later, she could hardly chalk today's memory lapse up to grief.

Which meant the stress of the job was officially getting to her. In fact, the conversation with James was probably directly responsible for her brain short-circuiting. If this had happened at any other point in her career, she would've taken a vacation, or at least a few days off, to get her head on straight.

It was a shame that was neither financially nor logistically feasible right now.

Well, whatever Aly said at the salad place—whatever she did— couldn't have been *that* bad, she reasoned as she strode to her office. She'd speak to Meagan and Ashleigh as soon as they got back to their desks. Okay—maybe at the end of the day after everyone had time to cool down. And if they couldn't own up to their role in this little kerfuffle, she was willing to take one for the team and move on.

But what, exactly, was Aly apologizing for? And why did her mind refuse to rewind and show the footage between when she volleyed Meagan's insult back at her and when she fled the scene?

It couldn't have been more than some quick venting. An angry sentence or two; nothing more. Aly had to believe that. Because otherwise something was seriously wrong with her. She'd been stone-cold sober (she hated feeling even slightly out of control, so neither drugs nor alcohol held any appeal). And her everyday memory was usually airtight—she always remembered where her keys were, and she could usually recall where Seth had set his, too.

She wondered how many people in the restaurant had overheard her. No more than fifteen, she calculated as she turned on her computer monitor. Maybe twenty, twenty-five tops. Most of them probably had no idea who she was, anyway.

Her head had that gravel feeling again. But whenever you couldn't think straight, you could still read—that was another Luke-ism. They'd spent many a miserable afternoon cuddled together in the corner of their small, shared room—him reading to her before she could read herself, and later poring over their books "alone together," as her favorite *Frog and Toad* book described her ideal state of being. So Aly pulled a printout from the top of the wire basket on the corner of her desk, grabbed her red pen, and began to review the August pages.

She quickly lost herself in the gloriously tedious process of editing. Cut this sentence, swap that photo, use this headline instead—the work required a clear vision, a gimlet eye, and a true passion for producing copy that, if you got it right, actually improved readers' lives. Though she sometimes felt she'd walked into a party she hadn't been invited to, Aly was born to do this work. And as much as she enjoyed fashion magazines shilling clothes that she would never wear, and gossip rags filled with celebrity fan fiction, *All Good* had always been her favorite. With its photo spreads of serene spaces, articles offering simple solutions for everyday problems, and scrumptious recipes that somehow managed to mostly be good for you, the magazine showcased the sort of life that was the exact opposite of the first eighteen years of her existence.

She was so engrossed in her pages that she started when her phone vibrated on her desk. She knew it wasn't Harry—as a corporate lawyer, his insane hours meant he was text-only until around eight every night. She sort of hoped it was Seth. Maybe talking to someone would jog her memory.

But it was her mother. And though she'd repeatedly asked Cindy not to call during her workday, Aly answered. "Mom, I'm kind of in the middle of something. What's up?"

"Finally. I was starting to think I'd have to send a search party to find you."

"Ha. You're welcome to come to New York any time." This was a lie and they both knew it. Then again, it was more likely that Cindy would visit Manhattan than Aly return to Michigan. To her, the state was one big unhappy memory. And now that Luke was gone, she was never going back there again.

"I'm busy, too, you know. They're working me to the bone at the supermarket," said Cindy. She paused, and Aly braced herself for what was coming next. Sure enough: "And it's way past time for us to deal with the house."

"*Us?* You don't need to do anything." What was it about her mother that made Aly revert to the absolute worst version of her teenage self? She closed her eyes, took a deep breath, then said coolly, "It's my problem, and I'll deal with it."

"You've been living in a city for too long, Miss Fancy Pants. Because where we come from, having an entire house in your name is hardly a *problem*. And it's almost been a year."

Aly wondered if Cindy had been drinking. She'd allegedly been sober for a while now, but as the years had gone by she'd gotten better at disguising her relapses, and sometimes the only way to know for sure was to wait and see if she'd pass out midsentence.

"Actually, eight months and twenty-seven days," Aly said, gazing out her office's one small window, which looked out at an airshaft. Although it was no corner office, it was better than where most of the other editors sat—a cube city lit with overhead fluorescents and completely devoid of sunlight, practically a prison—but Aly's office was still so dark. "Who's counting, though, right?"

"Don't be like that. If you're not going to put the house on the market, I'd like to move in there."

"I *am* putting it on the market in the fall, after I get through the busy season at the magazine. And for the record, you *have* a home, Mom." Cindy had bought a tiny bungalow just outside of Grand Rapids a few years earlier. Aly was pretty sure Luke had helped her buy it—and by *helped*, she meant bought it for her—but he'd never fessed up.

And now Cindy wanted his home. The one that had technically become Aly's.

"Things with Billy aren't going so good," Cindy said quietly.

Billy was her sometime boyfriend. Unfortunately, they were happiest together when they were both off the wagon. So maybe she *was* sober.

"Yet the house that you and Billy live in belongs to *you*. Unless you signed the deed over to him in some misguided romantic overture?"

"No, Allegra. I did not. And don't use your big words on me."

"I've asked you a million times," Aly said through gritted teeth. "*Please.* Don't call me Allegra."

"It's on your birth certificate."

"It's an allergy medication." It was also the name of the person best known for the bruises she used to show up with at school before Luke ran their father out of town. She'd officially switched to Aly, which Luke had called her since she was little, the minute she'd arrived in New York as an ambitious twenty-two-year-old, ready to forget almost everything that had come before that.

"Well, it wasn't a pill when you decided to welcome yourself into the world. Your brother—"

Aly's brother was dead. And the last person she wanted to discuss him with was their mother. "I'm going to stop you right there," she interjected.

Cindy exhaled loudly. "I've been trying to pin you down about this for months now."

Admittedly, she *had* been trying to bring it up for a while. But Aly had no legal or ethical obligation to speak with her about it. And she'd decided not to deal with the issue of Luke's house until a full year had passed.

Just then James appeared in the doorway to her office. *Thank goodness,* she thought, waving him in. Now she didn't have to lie to get off the phone. Anyway, she wanted to tell him that she'd already executed their plan. "I'll call you later," she told Cindy, and hung up.

"Am I ever glad to see you," she said as James strode toward her desk. Her stomach chose that particular moment to growl loudly, reminding her that she'd now missed not one, but two meals. That wasn't unusual—sometimes Aly got so busy that she ended up eating 90 percent of her daily calories when she got home at night (which definitely broke all the *All Good* rules). But forgetting that she hadn't eaten was strange. Obviously, her mind *was* a mess.

"Sorry about that—never did make it to lunch," she said, pointing to her stomach as she smiled sheepishly.

But James barely returned her smile, and Linda from Human Resources had just walked in behind him. They stood in front of Aly's desk, even though there were two perfectly comfortable Ikea chairs they could have sat in, and Linda held a manila folder that struck Aly as highly suspicious.

She suddenly regretted getting off the phone with her mother. Which was how she knew something was seriously wrong.

"About lunch," said James softly. "Aly, we need to talk."

FOUR

"Seth? Seth, is that you?"

Aly was still crying hard enough that she couldn't really make out the figure that had just walked in the apartment, but it was safe to assume it was her boyfriend of three years. After all, no one else had a key. But why wasn't he calling out to her? Didn't he see that she was in distress?

She wiped her eyes on her sleeve and slowly rose from the sofa, where she'd been semicomatose for the past several hours. "Seth?"

"I'm here," he said from the kitchen. Their Gramercy Park one-bedroom was small by most standards but practically palatial compared to the closet-sized Chinatown studio Aly'd lived in before. She loved being a stone's throw from Union Square. She'd been instantly smitten by the farmers' market and Union Square Park when she'd first visited on a trip to the city during college. Now she lived just next door.

Seth must not have seen her; otherwise he'd have immediately realized something was amiss. Not just because she was crying, but because never, during the year they'd lived together, had she put on sweats at six o'clock on a weeknight—to say nothing of the fact that she'd made it home before dusk and wasn't hunched over her laptop.

Come to think of it, why was *he* home so early?

"Weren't you going to work out?" She clipped her shin on the edge of the coffee table as she started in his direction. "Ouch," she said, folding over in pain. She rubbed her leg and tried to blink away the fresh tears that had sprung to her eyes. She finally got Seth in focus when she stood again. He was at the counter, suit jacket discarded, and shirt sleeves rolled up, already a third of the way through the beer he'd just cracked open.

"I decided to swing by the apartment first," he said with an unreadable expression. "Are you okay?"

She sniffled. What humiliation! What a complete disaster of a day! But Seth would help her unpack what had happened and help her determine her best next steps. He was nearly as strategic as she was; that was one of the things she liked best about him. "No," she admitted. "You won't believe what happened."

"Oh, I heard," he said, meeting her eye.

She startled. "What?"

"All of upper management knows you're on leave."

"Oh." Well, that did make sense. "What else did you hear?"

Seth arched his brows, which were nearly identical to James' but not as bushy. It occurred to Aly, not for the first time, that at some point the Fox genes would fully kick in, and the hair sprouting from Seth's orifices might get out of hand. *All Good* would be putting the holiday gift guide together in a few short months. Maybe they could feature electric razors with nose hair attachments. Freebies were one of the few remaining perks of working for a magazine, and although Aly usually let the rest of the staff have dibs, she could ask for this one small item for Seth. "I know you had a meltdown," he said.

She frowned. Someone, presumably a junior staffer at *All Good* or one of its sister magazines, had pulled out a phone and recorded her at the salad place, then promptly uploaded it to YouTube. She knew this because James had started to show her the video on his phone when he and Linda came to her office. And she'd told him—perhaps more sharply than she should have, given that he was being awfully nice to her about the whole thing—to turn it off. *Immediately.* Unaware that she had no recollection of the events that were now digitally memorialized, James had complied.

Only actors, narcissists, and freakishly beautiful people liked seeing themselves on film. But Aly had been on several morning television shows to share *All Good* household hacks and product recommendations, so seeing herself onscreen was hardly new to her. And while she didn't love the way her nose often wrinkled as she spoke, she'd been able to sit through the footage. How else would she figure out how to improve for the next time? Yet she hadn't been able to bring herself to ask James to send her the link so she could view it later, privately. She wasn't sure why.

Okay.

Yes, she was.

She'd taken one look at the wild-eyed woman who had clearly lost control of herself and understood that she couldn't watch a single second more. Not then, not ever. Because she sounded entirely too similar to the way she had on the worst day of her existence—

When dreadful Wyatt Goldstein called her and informed her that his sailing trip with Luke had not gone as planned, and now the one person she needed most in life was no longer in it.

Well, what was done was done. Aly had told off two of her staff in public, and according to Linda from Human Resources, this was in violation of Innovate's code of conduct. Now Aly was on a month-long unpaid leave while the company conducted an "internal review." Whatever that meant. She couldn't get over the unpaid part. Here she'd volunteered to slash her own salary for the sake of the magazine, and this was how they thanked her?

"Complete meltdown?" she bluffed. "I wouldn't exactly call it that."

"I don't know, Al." The buttons on Seth's shirt strained as he shrugged; what free time he had, he mostly spent working out. "I kind of *would* call it that. It wasn't a good look for you. And it was weird." He regarded her with what seemed like a mix of suspicion and reverence. "I had no idea you were even capable of using the F-bomb, let alone lobbing it more than once."

She cringed. Bad enough that she'd called Meagan a beach, but the *F word*? Luke would've been horrified.

Now her eyes pricked with new tears. It was too bad she'd never have a chance to talk to Luke about what happened, because he would have helped her shed the shame. Assuming she remembered the incident at some point. And she would. Wouldn't she? She didn't have dementia or head trauma, and her cruddy childhood was in the past. Memories didn't just go *missing* indefinitely.

Did they?

Seth continued. "I still think you should see someone. Don't you think this has something to do with . . . you know, Luke?"

Of course it did. Everything had to do with Luke. That didn't mean she could afford to see a therapist she had to pay out of pocket for. As she'd discovered while trying to find someone after Luke died, the in-network options for Innovate's health plan were booked into the next century. "Am I not allowed to have an off moment?" she asked quietly. It occurred to her that no one would mistake her for normal now. Normal adjacent: that had a decent ring to it. Maybe that could be her goal until she had this whole mess sorted out.

Seth coughed and looked past her.

"Wait a second," she said, narrowing her eyes. "Did you *watch* the video?" James had told her they were already working to get it removed from YouTube.

Still not meeting her gaze, he nodded.

"Who else saw it? I thought it was supposed to be gone already. James said . . ."

"It was just me," Seth said quickly. "Aly, he's my dad. *Of course* he was going to show me. This is kind of a big deal for *All Good*—you know the magazine is the company's biggest revenue-generator. And . . . well. We have to figure out how to run damage control, not to mention figure out who posted it in the first place." Someone had anonymously forwarded the video to James mere minutes after it had been posted.

"Jeez," she muttered. *We?* Seth headed up sales, not corporate communications. And *damage control?* All this, because she found the courage to tell her subordinates to stop undercutting her, and by default, the magazine they worked at? Now who would handle the September issue, which was the biggest revenue generator of the year? What about the *Good Morning America* announcement she was supposed to make about their new line of kitchen products for Target?

Meagan would end up at the helm, she realized at once. The very editor whose name James could not even remember, who had been on the verge of being unceremoniously deposed, would fill her shoes for four whole weeks.

This was *not* the plan.

At once, Aly realized that her previous plan was no longer in effect. She needed to come up with a new one that would turn this debacle into a victory. And like the Macy's balloons she watched get filled before the parade each Thanksgiving, she felt her spirits slowly begin to rise.

"I'm going to fix this, Seth. If there's one thing I know how to do, it's fix things. I'll call another team meeting, clear the air. We'll start anew."

"Um. That's going to be hard to do when you're not allowed back in the building, no?"

She hadn't thought of that. "I'll do it remotely, then."

"Without your laptop?"

Her cheeks burned as she recalled Linda taking her keycard, badge, and computer, watching her retrieve her personal belongings from her office like she was a white-collar criminal. (Aly'd half expected Linda to escort her out of the building, but she'd been spared that humiliation.) No matter. While humiliation may have been a natural response to what had happened to her, it wouldn't get her out of this. She needed to tap into her good old-fashioned grit—perhaps the one thing she had her parents to thank for. "Fine. I get it: no meetings. I'll take the month to reflect and reorganize, and I'll come back stronger than ever. I'll come up with a plan for scaling *All Good* so it's the most valuable brand in the history of magazines." She glanced around. "Do you think I could set up a small office in the corner of the living room? Laptop or no laptop, I have business to attend to."

"Aly," he said flatly.

"The bedroom?" It would be a tight squeeze, but she could make it work.

"*Aly.*"

"What is it?" Why hadn't he hugged her yet, or at least put an arm around her? Sure, they'd never been particularly touchy-feely, but did he have to stand there looking at her like she was a stranger?

He was going to break up with her, she realized. Which was *really* not the plan.

"I think we should spend some time apart," she announced.

He was visibly startled. "*What?* Are you leaving me?"

Aly considered this. Yes, she supposed she was. She nodded.

"Where will you even go?" he asked.

"Somewhere other than here," she said.

"And why would you do *that?*"

He seemed so surprised that she wondered if she'd misread him. Well, even if she had, she'd still just seen the crystal ball that was his body language; better to rip off the Band-Aid now and get this relationship over with. "Because it's not good for the company for me to be with you right now," she told him, thinking of what Meagan and Ashleigh had said at the salad place. "And I really need to focus on work."

"Where are you going to go, Aly?" he asked again. Because "their" place was actually his. Though he'd never said as much, she was pretty sure his family had bought it outright for him; he didn't even have a mortgage. The reason she could afford to live there was because he only asked her to split the expenses and monthly maintenance fee with him.

"Somewhere." Under different circumstances, she would've called Meagan to see if she could crash at her apartment. "Maybe I'll get a hotel room."

"I'll get the hotel," he said quickly. "I'll rent a room tonight, maybe tomorrow night, too—give you some time to come up with a plan. I know you're . . . not in a great financial position." He said this with the most tenderness he'd shown all night, and it was almost enough to make Aly blurt out that she hadn't meant any of it. Then he added, "I can give you some money to tide you over."

She shook her head vigorously. "I don't want your charity. I want my job back." And she would do whatever it took to get it—including but not limited to making it abundantly clear that she wasn't using Seth to get ahead.

He grimaced. "Are you okay to be by yourself?"

Was she? She honestly had no idea. "I'm not going to hurt myself, if that's what you're asking."

"Well, good. Um." He grabbed his suit jacket from the coat rack and turned toward the door. "Will you let me know where you end up?"

"So that's it, then?" she said to his back. Aly wasn't sure what she wanted from him, especially since she'd just dumped him.

Actually, she did know. She wanted him to beg her to reconsider, to tell her that he didn't want to be without her—that together, they would figure out how she could bounce back stronger than ever.

Instead, he spun around and said, "Don't you think it's weird that neither of us has mentioned love once in this entire conversation?"

She stared at him. It was kind of weird. Because she *did* love him. Not passionately, it was true—but she wouldn't have gotten through Luke's death without him. And she certainly wouldn't have spent three whole years of her life with him if her initial fondness—she could still remember the warm, welcoming smile he gave her on their first date—hadn't blossomed into love after she got to know the good, generous man he was.

So why couldn't she say it now?

"Goodbye, Aly," he said quietly. "I'll see you at work next month."

Seth was gone before she could tell him that his predicting her return to *All Good* was the most loving thing he could have possibly said to her.

FIVE

Job. Home. Relationship. In less than twelve hours, Aly had lost most of the primary markers of her identity.

But as she stood in the shower after Seth left, letting the water beat down on her so long that her skin turned red, it occurred to her that it could've been far worse. There had been a time when she believed she and Seth would go the distance. Lately, though, he'd seemed less like Mr. Right and more like Mr. Right Now; while their coupled-up friends were starting to get engaged and married, and even have children, she and Seth had been perfectly happy to maintain the status quo. Which didn't bode well for their future together.

And so, although she tried not to think about it too often, she'd suspected that at some point she'd have to find a place of her own. It was just that she'd expected that time would come later in her tenure as editor in chief, when she was making the kind of salary that could land you in, say, a true one-bedroom with a tiny balcony, or at least somewhere within walking distance of a park. Now she'd be lucky to rent a room in a far-flung corner of Queens.

Aly's ultimate goal was to become one of those publishing legends whose name was synonymous with the magazine they ran. She'd eventually retire to do something meaningful, like speak at journalism schools. (She had an image of herself gray-haired, clad in ostentatious eyeglasses and long, flowing linen apparel, gesturing animatedly before a class at Columbia.) Or maybe she'd wander around Italy—she'd not been yet, but she hoped to go one day—eating carbs and soaking up the sun. A husband and children never featured in Aly's future fantasies. It wasn't that she didn't want them; Harry and his husband, Tim, had recently welcomed a son, Beckett, and they were so blissed out (if exhausted) that she couldn't help but be envious. It was just that it was hard to envision being a member of a happy family when she'd never had one before.

Regardless, although her leave was temporary, she would still have to re-prove herself as worthy of her job in order to keep it. Though Aly frequently questioned whether her ascension was a fluke—she didn't have a master's degree in journalism like Meagan did, nor Seth's publishing pedigree—she knew deep down that magazines were a dinosaur, and her real job was to dodge the asteroid as long as possible. And she was devoted to doing that in a way few others were.

Now she just had to remind James of that. "No need to apologize," he'd assured her earlier that afternoon after she'd said *sorry* for the fifth time since he and Linda appeared in her office. "We've all had our moments. I'm just sorry yours was public." But publishing was a very, very small world, and the last thing Innovate needed was gossip about rancor in their ranks.

Ugh—she would need to make nice with Meagan and Ashleigh. Though poking herself in the palm with a flaming toothpick sounded more appealing than groveling, Aly knew she had to act like a leader so she could return to being one.

The water finally began to run cold, so she reluctantly got out of the shower and slipped into her pajamas. It was still technically too early to call Harry, but she couldn't wait any longer.

He picked up on the first ring. "Babe? Everything alright?"

Her face crumpled. Of course, he knew it wasn't; otherwise, she wouldn't have called before the late-night talk shows were on. "No," she said, and oh no—here came the tears. She cried for a few minutes while he made soothing noises and told her it was going to be okay, and eventually she managed to tell him what had happened.

"It wasn't exactly like I blacked out," she explained. "It was more like . . . I couldn't hear the words coming out of my mouth."

Harry gasped. "That does not sound great, babe."

"I know," she said miserably.

"Did she clap back?"

"Meagan?" Aly frowned, trying to remember, but in her mind's eye, the only thing that appeared was the other patrons parting as she speed-walked out of the salad place. "I'm pretty sure she didn't say boo in response."

"Pretty sure, or sure?"

"I have no idea, Harry," she admitted. "And I thought it would come back to me . . . but it hasn't."

"How long did this go on, exactly?"

"No longer than a minute." Aly's internal clock was rarely wrong; although she was guessing, she was willing to put money on her recollection of the timing, at least, being fairly accurate.

"And did you tell James what really happened?"

"Of *course* I didn't! Why would I give him a reason to think I truly wasn't competent to do my job?"

"Well, maybe he would've told you to see a doctor rather than telling you to take a month off."

This was a good point. *Did* she need to see a doctor? Probably, she conceded. And she would—just as soon as she figured out how to undo the mess she'd made.

"Al, why didn't you text me earlier?" asked Harry gently.

"I knew you had a crazy week, and you'd drop everything to talk to me."

"Every week is a crazy week, and this is an emergency."

"Is it really, though?" she said.

Harry and Aly had met as freshmen at Michigan State. They lived in the same dorm, and as they admitted to each other while hiding out in the study lounge one evening, neither of them liked their suitemates—hers were a trio who knew each other from high school and who didn't see the point in acknowledging her existence, while his were a bunch of "bros," as he referred to them, who took one look at slight, nerdy Harry and decided to make his year miserable. It wasn't long before Harry practically moved into Aly's room; he often even slept in her bed with her. Harry wasn't out yet, so everyone thought they were a couple, and neither of them cared to dispute that. Other than the whole swapping bodily fluids thing, they practically were. Aside from Luke, Harry was the best person Aly had ever known.

"Aly," said Harry, "I don't mean to be dramatic, but you can't remember what happened. That's kind of a big deal."

"I guess," she said, though the truth was, the more time that passed, the more it seemed like the whole matter had been completely blown out of proportion. She knew enough to understand she'd lost her temper. Yet how many editors in chief before her had been hailed as visionaries despite the fact that—or perhaps because—they terrorized their staffs? How many Hollywood hotshots and politicians had been given one pass after another after exhibiting truly egregious behavior?

But Aly wasn't those people, she suddenly realized. Here she'd been, faking her competence and hoping it was enough, when lo and behold: she hadn't fooled anyone. Still, she was down but not out. There had to be a way to reframe this setback as an opportunity.

"Can you ask James to send you the link, so you can at least forward it to me, so I can see how bad it was?" asked Harry.

And have Harry see her behaving . . . well, from what she'd managed to see, like her mother at her very worst? Because those wild eyes, the waving hands, the cursing—they were classic Cindy, hollering on a bender. *Absolutely not,* she told him. "Even if it wasn't getting taken down—which it is—that is not going to help me. Just the opposite, in fact."

"Standing offer if you change your mind."

"I appreciate that, but you can put me down for 'never' on that one," she said, nestling into the corner of the sofa, away from the dent in the center where she and Seth usually watched television together or worked side by side.

"Fine. I can't say I'm sad to hear that Seth is out of the picture, though." Harry'd never liked Seth, even though he was unable to articulate why, exactly. When pressed, he simply told Aly that he thought she could do better. But how could she possibly? Seth was polished, precise, and completely obsessed with publishing. *Why* had Aly broken up with him? She should have just blurted out that she did love him and hadn't meant any of it.

She was starting to get depressed again.

"Babe?" said Harry. "You still there?"

"I'm here," she said glumly. "How am I going to make this right?"

"I don't know, but you always find a way. I'm not worried about you. Except, where are you going to live?"

"That's the million-dollar question. As you know, I'm kind of broke. And before you say anything, that's not me asking for money."

He gasped in mock horror. "Do you think your old friend Harry doesn't know you at all? You'd probably go wait tables at Hooters before accepting a single dollar from me."

She had to smile.

"I can hear you grinning," he said, and she smiled even wider.

"I love you, Har."

"And I love *you*. Now, keep that in mind as I gently remind you that now is the perfect time for you to go deal with Luke's house. You will never again have such an ideal window to do this."

The corners of her mouth immediately fell. "It isn't September yet."

"I know," he said gently.

"And the plan was to go back at the year mark."

"I know," he said again. "But Aly, sometimes the only way to move forward is to let go of the plan and live. That's how the best things happen. Just look at what happened with Beckett." Harry and Tim had hoped to adopt, but not until they were in their late thirties. But when Tim's teenage cousin contacted him to say she was pregnant and would be pursuing adoption and couldn't think of better parents for her child than him and Harry, they didn't think twice before saying yes.

She frowned. "I get that. For the record, though, I'm living." Granted, she didn't *feel* particularly alive lately, but that wasn't the point.

"I wasn't saying you weren't, babe. But given that you need to be out of Seth's place ASAP, and whether you do it now or in September, you do need to put Luke's house on the market, well—two birds and all that."

"Hmph."

Harry continued. "I'd invite you to come stay with us, but with Beckett being up half the night, I promise you'd have the most miserable time. Still, Saugatuck is only two and a half hours from Chicago," he said, referring to the lakeside town where Luke had lived. "We could at least drive in for a night to see you. Wouldn't that be fun?"

She'd rather go to them. She'd flown to Chicago soon after Beckett was born, but that was nearly half a year earlier. He was probably already an entirely different baby now.

"You're always welcome to visit," he added when she didn't respond.

Now she felt guilty. "I know, and I love you for saying that—but I'm not going to crash with you when you have your hands so full. Maybe I'll get an Airbnb or something. And you're right; I do have to deal with Luke's house at some point."

"But . . . ?"

But it felt gross to her, to have inherited something of value as a direct result of her brother's death. And she wasn't ready to deal with it yet. "I don't feel good about it," she admitted. "I don't want to go there." Luke was four years older than her, but he'd been wise in a way that made it feel like he had decades on her. He'd gone into banking after college—not because he loved it, but because he wanted to make a bunch of money quickly, invest it, and then cash out and "go have a life," as he put it.

Aly had assumed this would involve him traveling the world; after putting in fourteen-hour days at work for nearly a decade, what better way to have a life? Instead, he'd done the most bizarre thing she ever could've imagined: he sank almost everything he'd saved into a home on the shore of Lake Michigan, not twenty miles from the crappy little farm town where they'd grown up, and became a sailing instructor. It was like escaping from prison and immediately asking to have handcuffs put on.

Then, less than a year and a half after Luke bought the house, he died unexpectedly.

"You don't have to stay long. You've been planning to sell, anyway," said Harry. "And wouldn't now be a good time to do that?" He meant because she was broke.

"Yes. You're right."

"Of course I am," he said, and she smiled a little. "Besides, when's the last time you had a vacation?"

"Never," she said, and he laughed because it was practically true. For a long time, Aly didn't have enough money to travel farther than New Jersey. Even when she started making a little more, her student loans still devoured the bulk of her paychecks. Seth had taken her to the Bahamas right after they moved in together, but they'd both worked through most of the trip. She'd end up working through this one, too, and she was probably the only person who didn't think that was a problem.

"I don't know, Har. I don't think I'm ready." Actually, she knew she wasn't. But a spark of an idea was taking shape in the back of her mind. She would find an inexpensive place in southwest Michigan, or even Chicago, to rent for a week or two. Then she'd sell Luke's house without setting foot in it. She'd have to hire someone to box up his things. And that might require taking out a small loan, or—ack—even borrowing from Harry, since a few missed student loan payments in her midtwenties meant her credit wasn't exactly stellar. But Harry was right: the timing *was* good. If she could simply manage to arrange a few workarounds for the sale, it was doable. And once she sold the house, she would return to New York, find an apartment, and turn *All Good* into such a phoenix that it would become the model for all other magazines struggling to survive.

"Maybe not," Harry conceded. "Is there anything I can do?"

"No," she said. In spite of her excitement over her new plan, she was getting choked up again. How lucky she was to have such a true friend. "You've already done more than you can know. Thank you for being here for me."

"Anytime, and I mean that in the most literal way. You're going to be okay, Aly. I promise."

If he'd been anyone else, she would've assured him she already was. But this was Harry, the only person other than Luke who'd never needed her to sugarcoat the truth.

So she said, "It's entirely possible that I'm never going to be okay again. And somehow, that's going to have to be okay."

SIX

That night, Aly dreamt she was on a boat. She hadn't been on one in more than a decade. Although she'd grown up near the shore, and she and Luke had made up dozens of stories during their childhood about a brother and sister who sailed around the world, she didn't like the water—or at least not how powerless it made her feel. But in her dream, she was in the middle of a vast lake, or maybe it was a sea, and the waves were crashing over the side of her dinghy.

In Aly's dreams, she was always aware of her real-life limitations and constraints; she was always herself. And so, in this dream she was all too aware that she had no idea how to sail.

"Luke!" she cried out, frantically glancing around for him. She knew, the way you just do when you're dreaming, that he was there with her on the boat—or at least he had been very recently. Luke had taken up sailing in his late teens and had immediately become obsessed with it. He could help her. "Where are you? I need you!"

Above her, lightning split the sky and the boat lurched sideways. Then, suddenly, she was overboard.

I'm wet. Aly could actually feel the water around her, pulling her under. She was a decent swimmer, but she was no match for these waves, for this storm. *I'm going to die,* she thought as water filled her nose and mouth, and then her lungs. *Just like my brother.*

Suddenly she was at the shore; she was dragging herself up the beach; she was in front of Luke's house.

And he was there.

"Did you save me?" she gasped. "How did I get here?"

Luke flashed her his crooked smile. "You swam, you crazy shark," he said, wrapping his arms around her. He was so warm and welcoming that she didn't even care that she was soaking his shirt. "You saved yourself. I was just watching to make sure you knew how."

Aly's eyes flew open. She was drenched in sweat; no wonder she'd felt water on her skin in her dream. The clock on the bedside table read 4:04. Outside, Eighteenth Street was as silent as it ever would be.

According to an *All Good* article about sleep, though dreams are often interpreted symbolically, they're really nothing but an opportunity for the brain to problem-solve and form new memories. Anyway, Aly didn't believe in signs.

Or at least she hadn't. Because as she threw off her soggy covers and got out of bed, she could not deny that this particular dream seemed like far more than an expression of her overanalytical mind, or even her latent sorrow.

It was the first time she'd dreamt of Luke since he'd died, and he'd spoken directly to her. It had to mean something; it just had to.

Aly spent the rest of the day packing and preparing. Early the following morning, Manhattan disappeared behind Aly as her cab sped into the Queens Midtown Tunnel. A few hours after that, clouds swallowed the city as her plane rose in the sky. She didn't want to leave; she didn't want to deal with the house now, when she needed to focus on getting her career back on track. But even in her subconscious, Luke was right, just like he'd always been. She *was* a shark, and she needed to keep moving.

And at this juncture, the only way for Aly to keep moving was to do the one thing she dreaded most.

SEVEN

"Denied?" Aly looked at the woman at the car rental desk with surprise and horror. "Are you sure?" Yes, she'd put the last-minute plane ticket on the credit card she'd just handed to the clerk—but she'd covered half the fee with the airline miles she'd accumulated while racking up debt over the past couple years. Had the occasional takeout order here and box of tampons there really added up to that much money? How did anyone even manage to *live* anymore?

"I'm afraid so," said the woman kindly, even though she probably had this exact conversation several times a week. "Do you have another card you can try?"

Aly swallowed hard. Her American Express was already maxed out, so that wasn't an option. The only other choice was her debit card. Her bank account contained enough cash to get her through three weeks of expenses, at best—never mind that she would be without a paycheck for four. Well, she'd made do with less before. Maybe she could spend part of the next month editing assignments and admission essays for students, like she'd done to make ends meet when she was in college. Or she could try to sell the designer purse Seth had gotten her for her birthday last year. It didn't match the rest of her wardrobe, and she'd always felt like a phony carrying it. Or . . . something else, something that didn't involve borrowing even more money that she wouldn't be able to pay back this decade.

As she rifled through her overpriced bag for her wallet, she tried not to focus on how much she hated herself for telling James she'd accept a lower salary, even if it was only until the magazine was doing better.

"Do you take debit?" she asked, and the clerk nodded. "Great—but I'm going to have to change my reservation. How much would it be to just rent the car for twenty-four hours? Is there a place in Saugatuck where I can drop it off tomorrow?"

"Hmm." The clerk frowned and began typing rapidly on her keyboard. After a moment, she said, "The nearest drop-off location is in Grand Rapids."

"That's forty-five minutes away," said Aly. She'd tried to book a flight to the Grand Rapids airport, but they'd been nearly twice the price of flying into Detroit. "How can I get from there back to Saugatuck?"

"There might be a bus you can take, or a car service. Changing the reservation to tomorrow afternoon will save you about a hundred and ten dollars." She smiled apologetically. "You'd lose the discount for renting more than a week."

A hundred and ten dollars would only cut down the total fee by about a third. And in addition to getting back to Saugatuck tomorrow, she'd still have to find a way back to the airport in ten days. "Leave the reservation as is, please," she said, trying not to wince as she passed the card to the clerk. Maybe someone would offer cash for Luke's house. Having been a renter her entire adult life, she didn't know much about real estate. But the search she'd conducted while waiting for her plane to board indicated that Western Michigan was a hot market, especially waterfront properties; places often sold in a mere day or two. *Fingers crossed,* she thought as the clerk handed her a clipboard with a stack of papers to sign.

The drive from the airport to Saugatuck wasn't unpleasant, especially after she made it through the Detroit-area traffic. Winters could be long and cold and gray in Michigan, but in June the fields were green, and the trees practically sparkled from either side of the highway. Still, with every mile that passed, Aly felt the invisible weight on her chest grow heavier and heavier.

"You need to separate the place from the past," Luke had told her the one and only time she'd visited him after he'd moved back to Michigan. He'd lived in New York for years because that's where the financial firms he'd worked for had been located. He'd never meshed with the city the way she had, though. And seeing him practically bound around his new house made her realize why. She may have been the shark, but he needed to be near water. It enlivened him in a way that few things did.

Luke's house perched on the top of a hill at the south edge of town, not far from where Saugatuck abutted its sister city, Douglas. Two stories high and about two thousand square feet, the place wasn't a mansion like many of the nearby houses. But with its cedar shakes, big picture windows, and nearly panoramic view of Lake Michigan, Aly had to admit that it was incredibly charming.

Still, as she'd confessed to Luke as he gave her a tour, she didn't understand. He could've lived anywhere. Why *there*? Where he was so much farther from her—and closer to their mother? Luke had always been far more generous toward Cindy than Aly thought he should've been. It certainly wasn't to be closer to their father, who'd moved down to Florida, or so he'd claimed when they'd last heard from him a decade earlier. Luke made friends wherever he'd gone, but like Aly, he hadn't really kept in touch with anyone he'd grown up with. So truly, she didn't get it.

"I just like it here." He shrugged as they stared out at the lake. The sun was setting, painting the waves in sherbet shades. "The water calms me. And it feels like home, don't you think?"

Home to Aly was the sound of horns bleating and ambulances wailing—sweet music compared to the yelling and the subsequent sounds of her own crying that had so often filled her ears as a child. Home was the unintentional jostle of a fellow pedestrian, rather than the deliberate sting of her father's hand. It was the incongruent odors of food carts and perfumed air wafting out of expensive stores, rather than the smell of cigarettes and cheap booze. "Suit yourself," she'd told him. "New York is my home now and always will be. I just wish you'd come back."

Luke had looked at her then, questioning and perhaps even a bit hurt. "Always is a very long time, Aly," he'd said softly, then put his arm around her. "I know you're the word person, but you might want to pick another one."

Her eyes blurred with tears as she pulled off the highway and headed toward town. Now that Luke was gone, the only word worse than *always* was *forever*. For a person so good at knowing the right thing to do, why on earth hadn't Luke stayed away from the water? Why hadn't he remained on dry land, where human beings were meant to be? Why hadn't he used his stellar judgment and taken Wyatt with him on the sailboat—hadn't that been the point of inviting his best friend to Florida? Or why hadn't he at least turned around the minute he realized a squall was approaching?

Damn it, Luke.

She was nearly to his house. Before her, the horizon was a gray-ish blue. June was high season, and the homes on the lakefront were abuzz with signs of life—children running around on the lawns, adults hauling groceries and suitcases inside, cars zipping down the winding lakefront drive.

When she reached the front of Luke's house, she considered driving around for a while longer, but she'd been up since the crack of dawn and felt a bit woozy. As much as she hated to admit it, it was probably best not to stay behind the wheel.

She took a deep breath as she pulled onto the long gravel drive-way. The house was set back from the road, behind a thicket of trees.

As she got closer, she saw that the Craftsman looked exactly as it had when she'd last visited: weathered shakes, low boxwoods bordering the perimeter, the brass bell that Luke had hung over the door. But then she spotted a small SUV on the side of the house.

That's weird, she thought. It was probably a cleaning crew or gardener. Luke had pressed a set of keys into her palm when she'd last seen him. "My place is your place," he'd said. "You're welcome anytime, even if I'm not here. Everything will be taken care of for you." As a child, Aly had longed to hear these words from her parents; they were no less impactful coming from her brother as an adult. She'd had no interest being in Michigan, of course, but just knowing she had somewhere to go where the fridge would be stocked and she had a warm bed and where she'd be safe meant everything to her, as she tearfully told Luke.

So in that way, it wasn't really a surprise that Luke's will included plans for his house to continue to be tended to. His lawyer had confirmed that someone was taking care of the place when he'd sent over the papers, which Aly still hadn't been able to bring herself to read. At least she'd thought to tuck the thick folder into her suitcase on her way out of the city; she'd probably need those documents to legally sell the place.

She parked her compact rental car beside the SUV, then sat there for a few minutes with her forehead pressed to the steering wheel as she tried to prepare herself. Instinctively, she knew the place would smell like Luke. It wasn't like he had a signature scent or anything—mostly he smelled sort of *clean*, like soap and fabric softener. That was notable because growing up, their parents both smoked, and their washing machine had been perpetually broken, which meant their clothing usually announced their presence before they had a chance to. And of course, Luke had personally chosen every item of furnishing in his home. The total effect was a bit nautical for Aly's taste—lots of navy blue and big framed maps of the Great Lakes, with model sailboats and anchors for decor. But it was undeniably *him*.

And it was going to hurt like hell to have to see it.

As she fished around in her purse for the keys, which Luke had attached to a small compass key chain, it occurred to her that maybe she shouldn't have resisted this visit so much. It might be exactly what she needed to get past her weird mental blips and be more present at work. Besides, she didn't have to dip a single toe in the lake. She could walk along the dry sand and stroll through town, and maybe read some of the novels Luke had lined his shelves with. ("No boring business books," he'd told her with a wink as she combed through his vast selection. "Those days are behind me.") She *did* need to regroup before returning to the office. This might be just the place for that.

And maybe—just maybe—being at Luke's house would help her understand why her preternaturally intelligent brother would do the dumbest possible thing and get himself killed.

Okay, she told herself, finally stepping out of the car. *You can do this. You can. You know how to do hard things.* First, she would walk to the door. Then she would place the key in the keyhole, twist, and turn the doorknob. And . . . step inside.

If she could just get that far, it would almost be alright.

But when Aly reached the door, she discovered it was slightly ajar. *Really?* she thought with irritation. She'd have to have a word with these cleaners.

"Hello?" she called, tentatively sticking her head into the house.

Oh no, she immediately thought as her eyes swept the room. The house was mostly open concept, with a spacious kitchen that led directly into the living and dining areas, which looked out at the patio, and beyond that, the lake. But rather than the clean, tidy space she'd expected, there was . . . stuff.

Everywhere.

Piles of clothes in the middle of the entryway. Empty cereal boxes and open cans strewn across the counter. Bedding on the sofa, food wrappers on the floor. A blizzard of books on the dining room table.

Luke had been robbed! And—Aly nearly gagged—what was that *smell?* It was like someone had forgotten to take the trash out for months.

Trash. A burglar didn't leave trash behind. No, this was even worse than she'd imagined. Someone had broken in and was living here. She'd read about renegade squatters who took over people's homes while they were out of town. Then they used some archaic law to justify their occupation, and it took forever for the authorities to force them to leave.

Oh, this was very, very bad indeed.

Without turning around, she began to slowly back up. The main thing was to leave silently, so the intruder—*intruders*, she quickly corrected herself; judging from the mess, there must be several of them—didn't hear her. She would creep back to the car, and since she wasn't strong enough to put it in neutral and push it down the driveway before turning the engine on, she'd have to manage to peel out extremely fast.

But as she took another step back, she hit something. Something solid and . . . stinky. Like, really rank. Without thinking, she pivoted.

And then she screamed bloody murder.

Because a man stood there. A very tall, very shirtless man with a disgusting unkempt beard and wild dark eyes, staring right at her. *So this is how it ends,* she thought, her own scream ringing in her ears. She'd made more than a bad decision—she'd made the worst one.

Or maybe it was the best. As the man eyed her like a psycho, the ground beneath her began to sway. That was probably what Luke had been trying to tell her in her dream. He was waiting for her at the beach house because he knew—as the dead must, she decided, even as another voice in her head told her she was quickly losing her already-tenuous grip on reality—that she was about to join him, wherever he was.

The floor crumbled beneath her before she could think anything else, and then everything went black.

EIGHT

Ugh, there it is again, Aly thought as her eyes slowly opened. That terrible, tangy, seven-days-without-a-shower stench. Who knew that a man's overripe odor could double as smelling salts?

But as soon as the hairy pecs she'd slammed into came into focus, she immediately squeezed her lids closed again. Best to play possum. Maybe if he thought she was unconscious, he would leave her alone long enough for her to dash out the door. Why hadn't she thought to bring pepper spray—or better yet, a machete? Oh, Meagan and James were going to feel *so bad* when they heard she'd been strangled and tossed into Lake Michigan. It almost made her forgive them for putting her in this position.

Almost.

Okay, the smell wasn't the worst thing she'd ever come across. Somewhere under the not-so-subtle notes of BO lingered something she couldn't put her finger on. Wood, maybe? Anyway, she was definitely awake now, and that counted for something. Then again, maybe it was best not to be conscious for her own bitter end.

"Aly?" grunted the man.

The intruder knew her name? He must have gone through Luke's papers, seen the photos of her on the fridge and in frames around the house, and made the connection. Sneaky squatter. She forgot about playing possum and scrambled off the sofa, only then realizing that the madman hadn't left her on the floor where she'd fainted. *Ouch.* Her head hurt—a lot—and she felt weak.

But not so weak that her fight-or-flight instinct didn't kick in. She immediately began bear-crawling toward the door.

"Aly. Stop."

She froze.

That voice.

It was deep. Unhurried. And *extremely* exasperating. No . . . it couldn't be.

But of course it was. "Motherclucker," muttered Aly, still on all fours.

"Nice to see you, too," he said coolly from above her.

"Stop looking at me, Wyatt," she snapped.

He immediately spun around. "This better?"

Of all the beach houses in all the towns. "Why didn't you tell me it was you?" she seethed as she attempted to stand. Her elbow ached. Had she hit something on the way down?

"I grabbed your arm to break your fall," he said.

Her eyes widened. Was he pulling some freaky mind-reading trick on her?

"Here," said Wyatt, who'd just turned to face her again. He extended his hand, and although it was calloused, entirely too large, and undoubtedly filthy, she reluctantly accepted it. At least he wasn't a squatter—well, not a random squatter—and yes, he'd probably kept her from flattening her face on the floor. Still, what the heck was he doing here, and why did he look like he'd been living under a bridge for the past several months? His beard was such an unkempt mess that she wouldn't have been surprised if a couple of birds flew out of it.

"Why aren't you wearing a shirt?" she asked. No wonder she hadn't recognized him—the one time she'd seen him before, he'd been in a suit and tie, shaved, and looking like a productive member of society.

He shrugged.

"Is all this—" She gestured to the tornado that had torn through the first floor. "Is this your doing?"

He tilted his chin, nodded.

She was growing more irritated by the moment. Was he preverbal? Was it so difficult to form a full sentence and tell her what was going on?

"The real question is, why are you *here*? This is . . ." She didn't want to say it, but she had to. "This is my house."

Now he opened his mouth, but instead of speaking, he began to laugh. "Your house?" he finally managed.

"What's so funny?" she said, trying not to let her eyes linger on his bare torso. It wasn't as though he was running around in his underwear— he had shorts on, though no shoes—but since he was mere inches from her, it seemed entirely too intimate.

"He said you probably had no idea."

"He? He who?"

"Roger," he said, referring to Luke's lawyer. "He said you wouldn't answer him."

It was true that Roger had tried to get her on the phone. Maybe more than a few times. He'd emailed her, too. And after she confirmed that she didn't need to deal with anything immediately, she'd told him to mail her the paperwork and she'd call when she was good and ready. Which was supposed to be September, at the earliest.

"What's to answer?" said Aly, putting her hands on her hips. She needed to stay angry; it was either that or fall apart, and she couldn't afford to do that when her plan B was already so clearly in danger of turning into plan C. "Luke left it to me. He told me he was going to, right after he bought it, and everything would be taken care of."

"By *me*," said Wyatt in a low voice. There was a slight sheen on his shoulders and stomach, probably because he hadn't bothered to turn on the air-conditioning. Still, had he no shame? Did she really have to stand there and bear witness to his sweaty skin?

"What do you mean, 'By me'?" she demanded.

"Luke left me this place, too," said Wyatt, waving his arms around. The man had the wingspan of a condor. How tall was he, anyway?

"That's . . . not possible."

"It's not only possible, it's true, and whether you like it or not, it's what happened. If you'd picked up the phone when I called you last fall, or even last winter, none of this would be a surprise to you."

"But . . ." Now she was the preverbal one. Wyatt had called her at least once, maybe even two or three times, but she'd been so upset with him for going on that stupid sailing trip with Luke that she immediately deleted his voice mails. He and Luke had been in the Florida Keys, not on Lake Michigan, when it had happened. It was a last-minute vacation, and Luke had invited Aly to join them. Practically begged her, really, but she'd just applied for the editor in chief position and didn't feel she could take time away from work. Also, she hated Florida, if only because that's where their father was rumored to be.

And she would never forgive herself for that choice.

But she wasn't letting Wyatt off the hook, either. He was the one person who could've told Luke not to go out when a storm was approaching. Or he could've gone out with him; Luke would've had a better chance of surviving if someone else had been there. Why would Wyatt go all the way to Florida, only to not get on the damned boat?

"I don't believe you," she said weakly. Luke had no reason to leave the house to both of them. Though she'd only met Wyatt once, he and Luke had been close friends since college, and Luke talked about him all the time. Because of this, Aly knew he came from money—like, stupid money, even more than Seth's family—and what's more, he'd gone into banking, which made her think he was not just privileged, but also greedy. So he didn't *need* this place. He didn't need anything.

And what Aly needed was for him to leave.

"Who do you think has been paying the taxes, the electricity bill, the water?" he said.

"Luke," she mumbled. "I figured . . ." She hadn't really figured anything because she'd been avoiding it. "I guess I thought he'd left something in his will and Roger was handling it."

Wyatt had the nerve to bark another laugh.

Aly could now clearly see how deeply she'd stuck her head in the sand when it came to her brother's death. She couldn't afford to hire a lawyer, but she could have at least handed the papers to Seth to look over, or maybe used one of those online legal services. Then she would've saved herself the trip to Michigan.

She was starting to freak out, and not just because Wyatt's presence had ruined everything even more than it had already been ruined. Was her avoidance somehow connected to her memory loss, and maybe her passing out after she was scared by Wyatt, too? She'd heard about couples who died within a year of each other. Luke was her brother, not her partner, but he was still the person she loved more than anyone else in the world. Maybe her body decided to up and quit on her. If so, she could hardly blame it.

"You should drink some water," said Wyatt, looking her over.

Goose bumps danced along her arms, even though it was nearly eighty out and Wyatt was apparently morally opposed to central air. *Of course you're freaked out,* she assured herself. *This was not what you were expecting.* "Aren't you going to ask me what I'm doing here or how long I'm staying?"

He shrugged again. "It's your place, too. You can do whatever you want."

This was the first reassuring thing he'd said to her. She might hate him for the part he played in her brother's death, but he was a semi-reasonable person. Or at least he had the potential to impersonate one after he took a shower and shaved the rug off his face. There was no way a guy who grew up on Chicago's Gold Coast wanted to live in this moderately sized house, no matter how beautiful the view. He was probably only here for a short while—just like her. So they would sit down like two rational adults and come to an agreement about putting it up for sale. Maybe he would ask to buy out her half, and that would be fine, too.

She just needed to get in, get out, and get back to her life.

Except while she was thinking all this, Wyatt had started strolling across the living room toward the French doors that let out onto the deck.

"Wyatt! We need to come up with a plan!" she called, but the sound of wind and waves, which were high this afternoon, drowned out her voice. Still, he'd paused outside the door momentarily, which told her that he'd heard her.

Yet he continued making his way down the sloping hill toward the beach . . . away from her.

And that's the point at which Aly realized that fainting and forgetting were the least of her problems.

NINE

It wasn't that Aly couldn't imagine living in squalor. She could, because she had. Cindy'd cared far more about her next drink than the condition of her home, and Dan, her father, had believed that housework was for women. So unless Aly and Luke decided to clean their small bungalow—as they often did, though only when their parents were out, because to be in their presence was to inflame them—it was inevitably messy, grimy, and in various states of disrepair.

As adults, both Aly and Luke prioritized cleanliness. No matter how cramped their dorms, rented rooms, or apartments were, they were always organized and welcoming. In fact, one of the reasons Aly's then-supervisor had promoted her from editorial assistant to associate editor after less than a year at the magazine was because her immaculate desk was "on brand" for *All Good*.

This was precisely why the state of Luke's home—Aly knew she'd have to eventually stop calling it that, and she would, just as soon as someone else bought it—was so appalling to her. With his dirty clothes and wet towels and discarded food, Wyatt had defiled the place. He might as well have crapped all over her brother's memory.

As Aly watched him amble down the beach, she realized that she'd have to make him either pull his act together or leave. Immediately. Because she had ten days to get the house spotless and sold.

She was starving, and though she hated to agree with Wyatt, she probably was dehydrated. So she quickly downed a glass of water and devoured the chalky protein bar she'd grabbed from the cupboard at Seth's early that morning. Then she went to retrieve her suitcase from the rental car, so she could get settled.

Knowing that more mess awaited her, Aly steadied herself as she climbed the stairs to the second floor, where all three bedrooms were located. And still she gasped in horror as she entered the first of the two smaller guest bedrooms. Wyatt had left his two suitcases wide open beside the bed, which didn't even have sheets on it, and the entire floor was covered with blankets and clothes. There were empty chip bags on the bedside table and a dirty plate that had begun to resemble a science experiment. It smelled almost as bad as the kitchen had.

Filthy, she thought, closing the door behind her. How had Luke possibly been friends with this hurricane of a human being?

The two guest rooms were side by side, connected by a jack and jill bathroom. Aly'd just started for the second bedroom when she suddenly had an urge to get it over with. Before she could talk herself out of it, she crossed the hall and flung open the door to Luke's bedroom.

She braced herself for more of Wyatt's destruction. But aside from a gray wool rug, the floor was completely bare. The books and photos on the shelves remained neatly arranged, and the duvet on Luke's large four-poster bed was unwrinkled. The room still even smelled like him.

In fact, judging from the dust on the dresser, the room hadn't been touched since . . .

Before.

Though it was the largest of the three bedrooms and the only one that had its own bathroom, Aly'd known that there was no possible way she'd ever sleep in there. How could she, when it was still so very Luke?

And it appeared that Wyatt felt the same way.

Something in Aly shifted then. For the first time since she'd arrived—since last September, really—it sank in that Wyatt had lost

Luke, too. She didn't really know much about how men's friendships worked. Seth's inner circle had been together since elementary school, but they were impermeable and clammed up whenever she walked in the room. As for Harry, he and Aly were entirely too attached; though they both had a decent number of acquaintances, neither had ever made other close friends. And Luke—well, though he'd always been popular and well liked, Wyatt was the only person he'd remained close to year after year after year. Yet she'd been kind of thinking that it was . . . different somehow, for him, than if he'd been a woman who'd lost her best friend.

Maybe she was wrong about that.

Her empathy for Wyatt evaporated the minute she stepped into the second guest room. Though free of empty containers and moldy plates, it was nonetheless filled with moving boxes and bags, and random pieces of what she assumed were Wyatt's clothing. "Really?" she muttered, kicking an errant pair of boxers out of her way.

The sole silver lining of all the clutter was that it gave Aly something to do—which was better than ruminating about how her brother should still be alive and how she'd come perilously close to imploding her carefully crafted career. After rolling her suitcase into the closet, which was blessedly empty, she picked up a box to haul to Wyatt's room. It was heavy—what was *in* it, anyway? But she was determined to tidy up quickly, so she could move on to more important things. Like salvaging her career.

An hour later, the room was clean, and Aly was tired to the bone. Still, her mind was abuzz. Because with every surface she scrubbed and box she hauled, she'd become more and more convinced that Wyatt was wrong. There was no possible way Luke left the house to both of them. After all, Wyatt didn't need the money. Nor had Luke made a promise to take care of him. (That would've been weird, she decided, not to mention unnecessary.) He probably told Wyatt he could crash there whenever he needed to, and Wyatt had gotten the details mixed up.

Yes, this was all just a big misunderstanding.

Aly retrieved the folder with Luke's will out of her suitcase, but when she pulled out the thick stack of stapled pages, the words might as well have been hieroglyphics. So she opened the contacts on her phone, hit Roger's number, and left a message with his assistant.

Less than two minutes later, her phone lit up.

"Aly? It's Roger," he said.

"I know," she told him. "Caller ID."

"Oh. Right. I'm guessing you reached out about Luke."

"I did," she said. This was the first time since before her episode at the salad place that she sounded like herself, which was to say calm and in control. "I'm at Luke's house."

"Good."

"And Wyatt Goldstein is here. At the beach house."

Roger cleared his throat. "Yes."

The only reason Roger didn't sound surprised was because Wyatt had spoken with him recently, Aly told herself. Not a big deal. "He's under the impression that the place is half his."

"Aly, do you have the paperwork I sent you?"

"I do. But I'm . . . having some trouble focusing right now," she admitted. "I was hoping you could just tell me what I need to know. I'm sorry I didn't get back to you sooner—I had a lot going on at work."

"It's okay. I can't say I'm used to having my calls not taken for nearly nine months, but grief is complicated," said Roger.

Aly knew he was trying to reassure her, but she'd really have preferred if he'd told her she was behaving like most people did under these circumstances. The last thing she needed was someone pouring more gasoline on the fire of her fears about her addled brain.

Roger continued. "Long story short, your brother left both you and Wyatt the house. By which I mean you each have fifty percent ownership and share fifty percent responsibility for all that home ownership entails."

"But . . ." Was Wyatt going to bill her for the utilities he'd covered for the last nine months? Maybe she could sell a kidney on the black market. Or harvest one of Wyatt's while he slept, she thought, a smile appearing on her lips for the first time that day.

"I know," said Roger. "It's not the decision I advised Luke to make. But it's perfectly legal. In fact, it happens all the time, but usually with family members rather than strangers."

"Oh, Wyatt's strange, alright," she said, wiping her brow with her arm. She really needed to turn the air-conditioning on, which meant she'd have to find the thermostat. "Here's the thing: I need to sell this place," she said, walking into the hall. "Like, yesterday. So what do I need to do?"

"That's a bit complicated," said Roger. "Not the paperwork—that's fairly straightforward. But both parties have to want to sell. And it's my understanding that Wyatt does not."

"What?" Aly was downstairs now and had just located the thermostat. Eighty-four degrees! No wonder she fainted. "That makes no sense. He couldn't possibly want to live here."

"You'll have to talk to him about that. In fact, I'm surprised you haven't already—he's the executor of your brother's estate."

Aly shook her head. But why? Sure, Wyatt worked in banking, but she wasn't incapable of dealing with money and paperwork.

But even as she was thinking this, she knew why. She'd avoided so much as opening the files Roger had sent her for the better part of a year. She was clearly in no position to execute Luke's estate—whatever that involved. Knowing Luke, he must have understood that she'd be overcome with grief and had wanted to make things as easy as possible in the event of his death. And so he put Wyatt in charge.

Except based on her interaction with Wyatt, he was in just as bad shape as she was.

"If things become contentious, I can put you in touch with a mediator," said Roger.

Aly sighed and looked out the glass door. The sun was just beginning to lower in the sky, and the beach was empty. Well, almost empty. Because Wyatt sat at the water's edge doing . . . nothing, from what she could tell. "I don't think it'll come to that," she told Roger. "I'll talk to him as soon as he gets back."

But Wyatt didn't return that night, or at least not before Aly finally crawled into bed, nearly delirious with exhaustion but still furious that he couldn't be bothered to finish their conversation.

You just need to get through the next week and a half, she assured herself seconds before sleep pulled her under. *Then you'll never have to see him again.*

TEN

Aly felt like she'd run a marathon in her sleep when she awoke the next morning. Her arms and backside were sore—probably from hauling nearly a dozen overstuffed boxes from her room to Wyatt's—but it was more than that. She was . . . *soul tired*, she realized, recalling the phrase Luke had used when he retired from banking at the ripe old age of thirty-six. She'd had no idea what he meant then. Now, staring up at the timber beams that spanned the ceiling and seemingly unable to so much as push the duvet off her body, she got it. *This* was why sharks didn't stop. Objects in motion remained in motion, but those that weren't . . . Well, they were in serious danger of staying that way.

But wait—was that the scent of coffee cutting through the stale air? Maybe she'd wait another day to harvest Wyatt's organs. Still sluggish but newly motivated, she slipped into a T-shirt and a pair of shorts, then began down the stairs.

"Hello?" she called as she entered the kitchen.

Once again, Wyatt was nowhere to be found. And although there *was* fresh coffee in the pot, the counter looked even worse than it had before. She didn't want to clean up his mess, but she couldn't stand to leave it like that—especially not when she knew it would've driven Luke crazy. So she put the dirty dishes in the dishwasher and began throwing out the empty containers.

"This is what happens when you let a toddler loose in a frat house," she muttered, tossing an empty can into the recycling bin.

"I've never been in a fraternity," growled a voice from behind her.

"Would you *please* stop sneaking up on me?" she hissed, spinning around. But as soon as she saw Wyatt's face—at least, the part that wasn't covered with hair—she remembered that she was supposed to be convincing him to sell. Which meant she needed to at least *pretend* they were on the same team. "I'm kind of skittish these days," she said in a more apologetic tone.

"Yeah. Well."

She waited for him to finish, but he just stood there.

Looking at her.

At least he was dressed today, albeit in a T-shirt that looked like it was auditioning to be a rag and a pair of jeans with holes in the knees. His beard was still—well, offensive, to be honest, but his hair, which was dark brown and threatening to curl, was kind of nice. And she needed to try to think nice-ish things about him. After all, they were roommates, at least for the time being. *Co-owners*, she corrected herself, but then another voice in her head whispered, *cellmates*.

This was going to be harder than she thought.

"I was hoping we could talk about the house," she said, staring up at him. Aside from a pair of wedge sandals, she hadn't packed heels, and at once she understood what a mistake that had been; he made her feel impossibly small. And Aly *hated* feeling small.

"Huh," he said, turning to retrieve a mug from the cupboard. He glanced over his shoulder at her. "Coffee?"

"Always."

He nodded, poured some into one mug, then handed it to her. "Cream's in the fridge."

"Thanks," she said. "Is it in date?"

He shrugged.

Same team, Aly, she told herself, pulling the carton from the back of the fridge. Miraculously, the half-and-half was potable. She tried not to feel self-conscious as she poured some, but the burning sensation on the back of her neck told her that Wyatt was still watching her—probably studying her for weaknesses and devising ways to get rid of her so he could go back to turning the house into a hoarding hut.

She took a sip of her coffee, which was warm and strong and so good that she loathed Wyatt at least 3 percent less than she had a minute ago. "So as I was saying, I'd like to talk to you about this place."

"Why?"

She cocked her head, instantly on edge but also sort of confused. "What do you mean?"

"Why are you here now?" he said bluntly.

"Why are *you*?" she volleyed back.

"Asked you first," he said from behind his mug.

He was nothing if not direct, and while she normally would've respected that, the irritation she'd felt yesterday was starting to simmer again. "Because . . . I realized I'd put this off long enough." But her cheeks burned from the lie, and even though Wyatt seemed preoccupied with pouring coffee down his gullet, she suspected he could tell she was fibbing. "I had a break from work and decided to take advantage of it." There. That was better.

He set the mug on the counter. "You could've given me a heads-up. Then maybe I wouldn't have made you pee yourself yesterday."

Without thinking, she glanced down at her crotch, as though it could tell her if she'd had a tiny accident right before fainting and, as with her outburst at the salad place, had immediately forgotten about it.

"I'm kidding," he said.

Not funny, she thought, even though some demented part of her was threatening to mirror the smile he'd just cracked. "I had no idea you'd be here—and before you mention it, I'm aware that that's on me. Don't worry, I won't be here long."

"I'm not worried," he said, reaching for the carafe again.

"That's a lot of coffee," she said as he refilled his mug.

He arched an eyebrow. "I had a late night."

She flushed. She didn't need to know, nor did she care, what Wyatt did after dark. Or maybe she should, actually. "I hope you locked the door when you came in," she said, tilting her chin with indignation. "It was wide open when I got here yesterday."

"*Wide* open?" he questioned. "Or just unlocked? Because this isn't Manhattan. It's pretty darn safe here."

Ugh, he was the absolute worst! "Whatever. The point is . . ." What *was* the point, again? Oh, right. "I want to sell the house," she said, folding her arms over her chest.

Wyatt's eyes met hers. "No."

"Pardon me?" she said, willing herself not to break his gaze. Why wasn't he blinking? Was this some sort of negotiation power play that men in finance liked to use?

"I'm not interested in selling."

"But I *need* to," she said.

"No, you don't."

How dare he make assumptions about her! "Yes, I do. I'm kind of in a situation."

"Whatever it is, you don't have to sell," he said evenly.

"I *do*," she said. Uh-oh—she needed to calm down, lest her brain decide to go and bury its memories in her mental backyard again.

"No one has to do anything," he said calmly. "And selling when you've been here one whole day is reactive, if not borderline impulsive."

Now she turned away, fast, so he wouldn't see the tears that had just sprung to her eyes. Reactive! Impulsive! How she hated him. "Nothing about me is reactive or impulsive," she said in a low voice. "And if you knew me at all, you'd understand that."

"Maybe so," he conceded. "But I know Luke. And he didn't leave you this place so you could immediately sell it."

Knew, thought Aly. *You* knew *him.* But as she turned back around, she had the weird urge to hug Wyatt . . . because she made the same mistake all the time. Fortunately, her urge passed as quickly as it had appeared.

"So what do you propose we do? Because I'm broke, and you—" She glanced at the counter. "You're turning my brother's dream home into a giant petri dish. And I'd prefer not to spend the next nine days dealing with the havoc you've been wreaking."

If he registered her insult, he didn't let on. "First of all, you're not broke."

Just because her wardrobe was no longer secondhand didn't mean she wasn't right up against the edge of being unable to feed herself. But of course, Wyatt had probably been diapered in hundred-dollar bills as an infant; he wouldn't know a struggle if it socked him in the stomach. "Okay, you just keep thinking that," she spat.

His eyes landed on the microwave behind her. "Gotta go."

"What? Where are you going?" she said.

"Out," he said, grabbing his keys from the hook beside the door. "Later."

Neanderthal, she thought angrily. Did he even know how to use more than two words at a time?

He left the door open—again—as he left the house, and Aly stuck her head outside as he was climbing into his SUV.

"You are so exasperating!" she yelled.

Wyatt didn't turn around, but once again, he paused—just for a moment, but still—before pulling the car door closed and starting the engine, then peeling out of the driveway.

Aly knew she shouldn't have hollered at him, as it was counter-productive. But this time, she didn't really feel ashamed or even guilty. Because Wyatt was asking for it. Practically begging, really.

And if he wasn't willing to work with her on selling the house, she'd simply have to find a way to work around him.

Now what? she wondered as she wandered around the rooms. She didn't have her computer. While she *had* planned to use good old-fashioned pen and paper to brainstorm a new strategy for the magazine, it seemed like an exercise in futility, with her head still so fuzzy. Harry was at work, and she didn't feel like reaching out to anyone at the magazine—not yet. And as filthy as Luke's place still was, it would probably only take another two to three hours to clean it.

Which meant that most of this day, and the nine more that would follow it, stretched endlessly before her.

But through the double doors on the far side of the living room, the water glittered in the morning sun. And although she hated the water—she really did—somehow it seemed to her that Luke would've wanted her to at least go say hello.

Tall grasses flanked the wood stairs leading from the end of Luke's yard to the sandy, dune-like hill that let out onto the flat beachfront. The sand was warm beneath Aly's feet, but it was still early enough that it didn't burn her soles. In fact, she was surprised to realize that it felt . . . not unpleasant, really.

The water was clear, and waves lapped at the shore. She could see a lone boat in the distance, but it was a big one, the kind with a motor rather than a sail, and maybe that's why the sight of it didn't tug at Aly's heart.

She'd intended to walk down to the shore and turn right back around. Instead, she sat at the dry spot just beyond the water's reach, as Wyatt had done the day before, and stared out at the lake. It was so vast that she could not see the other side.

Luke had been with her the last time she'd been in this spot. And though she knew it was just her mind playing tricks on her, it was almost like he was sitting right there next to her.

Once upon a time, a boy and a girl got on a boat and sailed far away, she heard him say. This was how he'd started all the sailing stories he'd spun for her. She couldn't have been more than two or three years old when he'd begun telling her these tales—they hadn't had many books, and library trips were few and far between, so Luke had simply begun making up adventures for her. In some, they sailed all the way to India or the Arctic; in others, they fought off pirates or found treasure or rescued talking dolphins. No matter what misery awaited them at home the rest of the day, Aly felt like everything was going to be okay while Luke told her a story.

But that voice—Luke's voice—did not keep speaking. Instead, she heard the rush of the water and gulls crying overhead; and after a moment, the sound of her own crying, too.

"Why, Luke?" she whispered, wiping her eyes.

Maybe if he'd picked a different sort of story—about princes and princesses, perhaps, or fairies and trolls, or anything other than a boat and a great big body of water—he wouldn't have become infatuated with sailing and ended up on that foolish, fateful trip.

And then Aly would not be sitting by herself on Luke's beach, wishing for a voice in her head to help her forget—if only for a moment—that she would have to go through the rest of her life alone.

ELEVEN

A watched phone never buzzed: Aly knew that, even as she couldn't resist her compulsion. And each of the dozens of times she flipped her phone over, she was greeted by the photo of her and Luke as children that she used as wallpaper . . . and not a single message or missed call. It had been four days since the Incident, as she and Harry had begun referring to it. She wasn't expecting to hear from Seth so soon; before she left, she texted him to say she was going to see Harry, and he had said he was glad to hear that and to let him know when she wanted to get the rest of her things. But why hadn't anyone from *All Good* reached out to her?

Well, it was early Friday afternoon. Everyone was probably checked out mentally, although probably not literally. Summer Fridays, the seasonal publishing tradition of letting employees leave early to extend their weekend, hadn't been officially discontinued—but more often than not, staffers simply had too much work to do to take off before the afternoon. Maybe Helena, the production manager, would call on her way out to the Hamptons to check in. Or perhaps she'd get a text from Jada, the senior recipe editor. No, Aly decided. Jada had looked upset when the salary cuts were announced, and anyway, she'd been kind of quiet since Aly's promotion.

Even a short while ago, Aly would've expected to hear from Meagan at least once or twice while she was out of the office. But that was before she'd found out what Meagan really thought of her. Eventually the memory of what Meagan had said—or at least the part that hadn't been wiped from Aly's mental hard drive—wouldn't sting quite so much. But for now, Aly cringed every time she thought of it. How long had Meagan felt that way about her? Had she been faking their friendship all along? Aly couldn't help but feel like her fifth-grade self, sitting alone at lunch because her classmates said she was too stupid and stinky to join them. Except now Aly was nearly eight hundred miles from the cool kids' table (which was to say Manhattan).

She'd been trying to work on her strategy for revitalizing *All Good*— but focusing was nearly impossible. So she'd been passing the time by cleaning, and because Wyatt seemed intent on immediately undoing her efforts to keep the place remotely habitable, she had plenty to do. And yet straightening and sanitizing weren't enough to fill all the hours. *What did people do when they didn't work all day?* she wondered, scrubbing an unidentified sticky substance off a refrigerator shelf. A few brief days untethered from her computer, and she'd already decided that she was never, ever going to retire. This was awful.

Or maybe, she admitted as she tossed a decaying head of lettuce into the trash, she was just lonely. She'd put a call out to a few Realtors, and several were coming by that weekend. Maybe once she got that sorted out, she'd drive to Chicago to see Harry and his family.

Aly'd just finished cleaning the crisper drawer when she caught a whiff of something. It took her a second to realize said something was . . . *her*. Because in spite of her best intentions, she hadn't actually showered since she'd arrived two days ago. Argh, Wyatt was already rubbing off on her! It was yet more evidence that she needed to get him to sell—but first, she had to convince him to have a conversation with her, as the last time they'd spoken was the previous morning when he'd made his stupid joke about her bladder. After ensuring that the fridge was no longer harboring *E. coli*, she headed upstairs to give herself the same treatment.

She liked to listen to music when she showered, though she hadn't had much opportunity recently. Seth claimed the sounds of the city overstimulated him enough, so he preferred the apartment quiet (crypt-like, Aly thought in less charitable moments). But Seth wasn't there to surreptitiously turn the volume down, so she hit the "Good Vibes" playlist on her phone and cranked it all the way up. Then she peeled off her clothes and stepped into the bathroom.

She was already making her way across the tile when she realized she wasn't the only one who'd decided it was finally time to shower.

"Ahhh!" She quickly turned and pulled the door closed, but it was too late—the sight of Wyatt's south side was burned into her brain. Granted, she'd seen worse things. And she had to admit that unlike Seth, he'd been genetically blessed with an un-hairy back. Also, when did bankers find time to work out? Then again, he hadn't once mentioned banking, nor had she heard him on the phone or seen him on a laptop. Maybe he, like she, was on a sabbatical—though his was likely voluntary.

Her cheeks flamed hot as she grabbed the duvet off the bed and pulled it around her body and switched the music off. *He wasn't facing you,* she reminded herself. *He didn't see you.* But that did little to make her feel less . . . naked. "Sorry!" she yelled in the direction of the bathroom.

She heard a knocking sound. It took her a moment to realize it was coming from the other side of the bathroom door. Did he plan to harass her about her mistake? Berate her, even? He was the one who chose not to use the lock.

"What is it?" she said loudly.

"You decent?" he called back.

"Yes," she said, at once indignant. "Are you?"

"Born that way," he said, flinging the door open. He had a towel wrapped around his waist, and he still hadn't done anything about his Tom Hanks–in–*Castaway* beard.

"Don't you want to put some clothes on?" she said, as though she wasn't wearing a comforter.

He looked down. "I'm covered. And now who's sneaking up on who?" he said, looking up at her with an arched eyebrow. "You at least get a good look?"

Her blood boiled. What was *wrong* with him? "Ugh! As if I'd even want to! There's a lock, you know. And we clearly need to do something about this." She glanced away, eager not to give him the impression she was spending any time observing his . . . flesh.

"This?" he questioned.

"Us." She knew she sounded angry. But she *was.* "We need a schedule for the bathroom. Or you can use Luke's."

He stared at her, but it was a different kind of stare than before. This one radiated irritation. Maybe even fury. "A *schedule*?!"

"Yes. I can shower at night and use the downstairs bathroom at all other times," she suggested, as she knew that neither of them would use Luke's bathroom. "And you can—"

"No," he interrupted.

She shook her head so hard it was a wonder she didn't wrench her neck. "What do you mean, 'No'?"

"Last time I checked, that word only had one meaning."

Rude! "What's wrong with a schedule?" she said, frowning. "I'd prefer not to walk in on you. Ever again."

"I'm thirty-seven years old," he said, but the way his eyes were burning, she could almost imagine him as a young child on the verge of a temper tantrum. "I don't follow other people's manuals for how to live."

"It's a *plan*, not a manual. To make both of our lives easier." *And less cringe-inducing,* she added mentally. "And while we're on the subject, this difficult living situation is one more reason we need to sell this place. Or . . ." She'd been hoping to have a longer, at least slightly more thoughtful, conversation about this, but it was readily apparent that Wyatt was not going to make himself available to her for such a thing. "You can buy me out."

"No," he repeated.

"Why not?" she said.

"We can talk about it later," he said obtusely.

"Fine," she said, because he didn't look any less stubborn than he had before she'd seen his butt, and she was done fighting with him. "I'll call Roger and figure out my options for getting what I need so I can get out of here. He mentioned mediation."

"You sound like you're threatening to call your dad."

It was her turn to give him a death glare. "My dad is a jerk who never expressed one iota of interest in helping me with anything. So no, *Wyatt.*" She hissed his name like a curse. "I sound like I'm threatening to call my brother's lawyer. If you knew anything about me, or Luke, you'd know we haven't spoken to our father in years. Now leave me be."

"Aly, I'm sorry . . ."

His face was all twisted up. But it was too little, too late, and she raised her hand. "Please. I'd like to be alone."

His eyes met hers briefly. Then he pivoted and closed the bathroom door without another word.

Less than a minute later, Aly heard the door on the other side of the bathroom close, which told her Wyatt had returned to his room. But she remained perched on the end of the bed, seemingly unable to budge, long afterward.

Focus, she commanded herself. *You need to focus, so you can fix this.*

How, though? She was beginning to understand that there was no "same team" where Wyatt was concerned. The man was a vagabond who couldn't tell the difference between a plan and a plantain, and he had no interest in even attempting to help her out. Maybe he hated women or had forgotten that his best friend would've wanted him to treat his younger sister with consideration, if not kindness. Regardless of Wyatt's wound—which probably had much to do with his mother, she reasoned, because didn't it usually?—whatever was broken in him was not hers to fix.

She had no choice but to play hardball. Yes, she'd call Roger immediately, and a mediator if she had to. She'd forge Wyatt's name on the real estate documents if it came to that. And if he protested, she would post all over social media about how this so-called friend of her brother was such a monster that he was making her declare bankruptcy. (Could she declare bankruptcy when she had no assets aside from the one that yoked her to Wyatt? She had no idea how that worked and made a mental note to ask Harry, who knew everything.)

But after she'd finally showered and put clean clothes on, she emerged from her bedroom to discover . . .

Tape?

Bewildered, she stepped over the blue painter's tape just outside her door. While she'd been bathing and trying to get her head on straight, Wyatt Fricking Goldstein had run a line down the center of the hallway. And apparently the stairs, too. And the entire living room and kitchen, including the fridge, and even the patio.

The man had literally split the house in half.

She screamed in exasperation, hoping that wherever he was, he could hear her. And maybe she was hollering at the heavens, too, because now she was as angry at Luke as she was at Wyatt. What had he been thinking? The last thing she needed in her life was someone who was unreliable and unpredictable and quite possibly unstable.

She found a message scribbled on a sticky note on the counter. It took Aly several seconds to try to decipher Wyatt's chicken scratch. *Here's the plan,* he'd written. *Do whatever you want with your half of the house. Don't touch mine.*

"Fine," she muttered, balling up the note even though she wasn't going to throw it out—she needed it as evidence for the mediator, or maybe even court. "I get it, Wyatt."

And she did. This wasn't hardball.

It was war.

TWELVE

Aly didn't see Wyatt that evening, or at all the next day, which made her wonder if he had a girlfriend nearby. Because as much as she loathed him, she'd rather he was sleeping over at someone's house than camping out in his car, as the latter would only make him even more ornery. Regardless, he was *definitely* avoiding her as a result of their little bathroom blowup. So she fully expected her next interaction with him to be unpleasant, and perhaps even combative.

But when she came downstairs Sunday morning, she discovered that he'd already poured her a cup of coffee.

"Thanks," she said, resisting the urge to ask him if he'd slid the mug over on her half of the kitchen island, or his. Because he hadn't labeled the sides, and she'd removed all the tape before the Realtors had come by the day before.

"Morning," he said. Then, apropos of nothing, he asked, "When's the last time you ate something other than a protein bar? Do you want some eggs or something?"

She blinked furiously. This was another trick, wasn't it? Because why else would he push her secret button—the one that got triggered when someone tried to do anything that remotely resembled caring for her?

"I'll have you know that I had a banana," she retorted. It had actually been her dinner the night before, and she'd woken up with a gnawing feeling in her stomach. Maybe she'd make some oatmeal for breakfast, or rice with milk and cinnamon. She and Luke used to joke about writing a cheap-foods cookbook one day; they knew all the budget-friendly staples, and the myriad ways to combine them.

"Suit yourself," he said, shrugging. "What did the Realtors say?"

Three agents had come and gone the previous afternoon, each practically begging to rep the sale. The first was an older man who seemed dubious that the house could possibly be hers; he kept inquiring about her parents. The next was a pleasant woman in her forties, but the minute she'd asked when Aly's "husband" would be joining them—never mind that Aly's left ring finger was bare—Aly had rushed her out of the house and told her she'd call her if she wanted to work together. The last agent, Luis, was about her age and didn't ask a single leading or inappropriate question. In fact, he told her as much about the house as he asked about it—pointing out that it was built on a particularly solid location at a safe distance from the ever-eroding waterfront, and that it had only had three owners in its eighty years of existence. Luis, Aly decided, was her agent.

Or at least he would be if Wyatt stopped being so incredibly stubborn.

"How did you know about the Realtors?" she asked, eyes narrowed. "I thought you were out."

"I was," he said. "But every time I drove by, I saw a different luxury car in the driveway. It's not rocket surgery."

"Oh," she said, somewhat impressed that he'd pieced it together so easily. Maybe that's why she decided to tell him the truth. "They said the house will sell in a hot second—but that if we want an all-cash offer, we need to put it up for sale this month. Apparently, June is when the best deals get made. The further into the summer, the less hot the market," she said, parroting what Luis had said.

"We?" questioned Wyatt.

Aly stared at him, momentarily confused. Oh. She *had* said that. "I guess I was being optimistic," she admitted.

"Fair." He shrugged. "Listen, I've gotta run."

He always had to run. And even though she didn't *want* him there, it was getting kind of annoying.

Then he surprised her. "But you're right—we need to talk. I'm planning on going over to the Mermaid tonight," he said, referring to a local bar and grill. "Six-ish. Why don't you swing by, and we'll chat?" He looked her up and down in a way that said he found her wanting. "I'm buying, so you're eating more than a banana. And that's not a question."

"Hmph," she said, but then she had to look away, so he wouldn't see the tiny smile that had surfaced.

"Hmph yourself," he said and strolled off.

Aly looked down at the coffee he'd handed her and saw that it already had cream in it—exactly the right amount, too. *Darn it,* she thought as she took a sip. Of course it was perfect; maybe even better than the last time, and she found herself blinking back tears. It wasn't just the random act of kindness or his sudden acquiescence to have a conversation about the house. It was the fact that she had softened so fast that she barely recognized herself.

If this was war, then she was forced to admit that Wyatt was winning.

THIRTEEN

It wasn't a big deal, meeting Wyatt for dinner. That's what Aly kept telling herself, but the positive self-talk *All Good* espoused didn't make a dent in her jitters. Seth had been in the habit of "pregaming" with a drink or three before he went out to meet colleagues or friends. While Aly sometimes wondered if his secret social anxiety fueled an unhealthy, if sporadic, relationship with alcohol, she found herself wishing for a similar coping mechanism. At least she had Harry, who she called as she pulled out of the driveway. *Please pick up,* she prayed. His Sunday schedule was ever in flux; she had no idea if he was at the office, playing tennis, or out for a walk with Beckett.

To her relief, he answered after the third ring. "Horatio Medellin, Esquire. How may I assist you?"

"Oh, thank goodness," she said. "There's no time for humor, Harry. I'm on my way to meet Wyatt for drinks." She gripped the steering wheel so tightly that her knuckles went white. "Well, dinner. Or something."

"*That* escalated quickly."

"Ha. It's not like that. He wants to talk about the house."

"Progress! Has he agreed to sell?"

"No, and he doesn't want to buy me out," she said, recalling the conversation they had after their bathroom run-in. "But he hasn't explained why, yet. I feel like I'm walking into a trap."

"There's no reason to be nervous, lovey."

"I'm *not* nervous."

"I know you're not," cooed Harry. "Which is definitely why you sound like you just finished running a 5K."

Aly exhaled. So maybe she had been a little short on oxygen. "Alright, I'm nervous. I just . . . don't know how to win."

"How about not trying to?"

"Do you *want* me to stay broke? I need to settle this so I can get the heck out of this barren wasteland, find an apartment that's not a two-hour commute from the office, and go back to being an editor in chief." Even now, six months into the gig, she could barely believe she'd earned the right to say that. (Or had she, given the episode with Ashleigh and Meagan? Maybe not, she conceded.) "Remember that?"

"Oh, I do. Any word from your coworkers?" asked Harry. She'd texted him the afternoon before to tell him about the radio silence.

"Nothing. Weird, right?"

"Not really. They're probably on edge. Give it a few days. Once the dust settles, and everyone's back in the office, I bet you'll start hearing from people."

"I hope so." She'd just reached the downtown area. "Ack, I'm already here. I've got to find a place to park, and you know I need full concentration to pull that off." Aly could never understand New Yorkers who complained about taking the subway. You couldn't read in a car, nor could you blatantly people-watch. Eyes on the road, hands on the wheel, full focus on surviving—driving was pretty much the worst.

"Oh, do I ever." He laughed. "I still remember the time you took out my parents' mailbox when you came to visit."

"Let's never speak of that again," she said, grinning at the memory. But then her face fell. If only time rendered all accidents funny. "Wish me luck, okay?"

"Not that you need it, but good luck. Hey, Aly?"

"Yeah?" she said, watching a middle-aged couple walk down the street holding hands. Had her parents ever been affectionate with each other? She truly couldn't recall. Just as well, she decided. Aside from her adventures with Luke, who'd sometimes teased her but never tortured her the way some kids' older siblings did, most of her early years weren't worth remembering.

"Just let things unfold the way they're going to, okay?"

"You make it sound like I'm a control freak," she remarked, but as she heard herself say this, she realized that Harry, in his gentle way, was making that exact point. "Noted. I'll report back."

"Please do. Love you!"

"Love you, too," she told him.

Luke's house was a mile from central Saugatuck as the crow flew, but the city was divided in half by the Kalamazoo River, which fed into Lake Michigan, and crossing the bridge more than doubled the drive time. As it was a tourist town, summers were incredibly busy, and Aly had to park in a cozy residential neighborhood referred to as "up the hill." She picked up her pace as she made her way toward the stretch of waterfront that composed the downtown area. It was only a few minutes after six, but she had a feeling Wyatt wouldn't have a table yet—not on a night like tonight, when the air was warm without being oppressive, and nearly every restaurant had a line down the sidewalk. He didn't strike her as the punctual type; he probably hadn't even arrived yet. She wanted to put her name on the list right away so they wouldn't have to wait together any longer than necessary.

Because what were they even going to talk about? No matter how it went, the conversation about the house couldn't possibly take longer than a few minutes. Then what? Would they discuss the weather until one of them feigned an emergency and fled the premises? After arriving at college and discovering that everyone except her seemed adept at navigating social situations, Aly had read a slew of books on small talk and likeability. But now her mind refused to recall how to make friends and influence vagabonds. *Crap,* she thought as she approached the restaurant. *What now?*

She didn't see Wyatt in the line of patrons waiting to speak to the hostess, so she stepped behind the last person waiting. She'd barely been there a minute when she felt a hand on her upper back.

"Hi," said Wyatt.

"Um, hi," she said. He wore a pair of aviators, but she still found herself glancing anywhere but at his face. This was so awkward! It was *such* a bad idea! He was going to tell her she was stuck with the house—and by default, him—forever. In fact, he probably brought her here because he assumed she wouldn't make a scene in public.

If only he knew, she thought, suppressing a smile. It was the first time she'd made light of the Incident, if only momentarily, and it was a welcome improvement.

"I have a table," he said, nodding toward the outdoor seating.

"Really?" she said, following him toward the far end of the patio.

"Don't sound so surprised," he called over his shoulder.

"I'm not. I just didn't think you'd be . . ."

"On time?" he questioned, pulling out a chair. She'd just started for the other side of the umbrellaed four-top when she realized he'd pulled it out for her. "Old habits die hard."

She mumbled her thanks and sat down across from him. The patio looked out at the gray, placid river, and her eyes trailed a small speed-boat for a moment before she looked at him. "By 'old habits,' you mean banking?" she asked. Luke had told her that in finance, punctuality was nonnegotiable.

"Yes and no," he said vaguely.

So he was back to incomplete sentences. *We're just going to have the most riveting conversation.*

"You look nice," he said.

Aly glanced behind her.

"I meant you."

She tried to disguise her surprise as she turned back to him. She'd opted for a T-shirt and shorts, and although she had brushed her hair—which she'd not done regularly since arriving at Luke's—she was hardly in her best state. This was more of his trickery. "Oh. Uh. Thanks."

"Sure."

Wyatt turned and motioned for a waiter while Aly sat in silence. *Say something,* she thought, though even in her own mind, she wasn't sure whether she was imploring herself or him. *Anything.* Now he was looking at her again. Was he waiting for her to speak? "What's with the beard?" she blurted, then cringed. What was wrong with her?

He seemed nonplussed. "What do you mean?"

Long beards were bacteria magnets—there were *actual studies* proving this! But what did she care? Wyatt could be as filthy as he wanted to be. It didn't impact Aly in any way. "Nothing," she said. "Sorry, I shouldn't have said anything. It's just that you look . . . different from the last time I saw you." *And unlike then, you're actually speaking to and looking at me now.*

"Yeah," he said. "I never thought about it before, but I guess that's the point."

Before Aly could ask him what he meant, she heard her name. "Aly Jackson, is that you?"

Aly couldn't identify the voice, but her cheeks were aflame all the same. Anyone who recognized her here, in southwestern Michigan, knew the person she used to be. The person she had no interest in so much as thinking about, let alone being identified as. Why hadn't she put on a wig and glasses to go out in public? A few days away from the city and she'd already lost her street smarts.

With reluctance, she swiveled in her seat. Then her eyes widened, and her heart rate slowed. "Ms. *Perez*?" With her dark curls and smooth, tan skin, Aly's high school guidance counselor had barely aged since Aly had last seen her more than a decade ago. Except, why was she wearing a black apron and a name tag?

"Oh please, call me Mari. It's so great to see you! Are you here on vacation? I heard you were living in New York these days."

"Yeah," said Aly, immediately overcome with guilt. She should've reached out ages ago—if not to update her, then at least to thank her for everything she'd done. Were it not for Mari Perez, Aly would probably be . . . Well, she didn't actually know where she'd be, but certainly nowhere good. "Do you work here?" she asked, trying not to sound surprised or judgmental.

"Yep," said Mari, smoothing her apron. "I'm a server. Just during the summers. Teaching doesn't pay as much as it used to."

"Did it *ever* pay much?" asked Wyatt curiously.

"Wyatt," hissed Aly.

"No," said Mari, unfazed. "No one goes into teaching for the money. But it hasn't kept up with the cost of living, and I have bills to pay, which *is* the goal. So," she said, smiling. "Can I bring you two something to drink? Maybe an appetizer to get started?"

"Oh," said Aly, because she hadn't realized that Mari was *their* server. "Um, water's fine for me."

"You don't want a glass of wine or something?" asked Wyatt. "Remember, it's my treat."

Mari looked back and forth between them, and Aly realized she probably thought they were on a date. "I'm sorry—how rude of me not to introduce you both," she quickly said. "Wyatt, this is Mari Perez, my high school guidance counselor. She helped me get into college." Mari had done far more than that, but even if she'd wanted to tell him—and she didn't—Wyatt wouldn't understand. His parents had no doubt hired tutors and college coaches and financial planners to ensure he reached his full potential. "Mari, this is Wyatt." Before she could consider the consequences of doing so, she explained, "He's Luke's friend. Er, was."

Mari's smile dissipated. "Oh, Aly, I heard the news. I am so sorry. Luke was an amazing person. I still remember how he'd go out of his way to make all the other students feel seen."

"Thank you," mumbled Aly, staring down at the cross-hatching of the metal table. This was precisely why she hadn't told her coworkers, and why she avoided seeing anyone who'd known her brother. She much preferred interacting with people who only knew the alternate version of her life—the one in which she had not suffered catastrophic loss. Because the moment others learned the truth, they looked at her differently. They *treated* her differently. Wasn't that what had happened with Meagan? Right after Aly broke down and admitted why she was weeping in the women's bathroom, Meagan had stopped sharing any bad news with Aly. Really, she'd quit being honest with her, as though the only things Aly could handle were kittens and rainbows.

Then again, Meagan might have had a point.

"It's nice to meet you, Wyatt. Any friend of Luke and Aly's is a friend of mine," said Mari.

He's not my friend, thought Aly, looking away.

"Thanks, Mari," said Wyatt.

"You got it. So, drinks?"

"Could you bring us a couple of margaritas?" he said. "Strong, please."

"I don't really drink," said Aly.

Even from behind his sunglasses, she could tell Wyatt was regarding her quizzically.

"Water and one margarita?" said Mari.

"No, it's fine," said Aly, sighing. "I'll have what he's having."

"Then we'll also have the cheese puffs to start, and two burgers, medium, with cheddar, and fries. That sound alright?" Wyatt asked Aly.

"Yes," she said, her mouth all but watering. Maybe she was even hungrier than she'd realized. "Thank you."

"It's the least I can do," he said, and although he was probably just saying it, goose bumps went scrambling up and down her arms. Did he feel responsible for Luke's death? Truth be told, Aly *had* blamed him.

But as infuriating as Wyatt was, now that he was sitting in front of her, she didn't feel that same pure, uncomplicated hatred toward him.

Which made the situation a lot more difficult to parse.

"What did you want to talk about?" she asked after Mari left. "You mentioned the house?"

Wyatt took his sunglasses off and placed them on the table. Aly gulped. Clearly, he was preparing to tell her something terrible. Otherwise, why would he make a point to look her in the eye? "Yeah, so, Luke left you money." He said this offhand, like he was mentioning that he was allergic to shellfish.

"Is your sole mission in life to shock me?" said Aly. Why was she just hearing about this now? And why didn't she know how to feel about it? On the one hand, maybe she could afford something other than a banana for her next dinner. On the other, she didn't want anything associated with Luke's death.

"Like I said, I tried to call you. As Roger probably told you, Luke made me the executor of his estate. I think there are terms on the inheritance—you don't get it all at once. It's not a ton."

A ton, she thought, bitterness seeping back into her thoughts. Wyatt Goldstein had no idea what a ton was for her.

"That's because most of Luke's money went into the house—it cost him nearly two million," he continued.

Two million dollars? Aly could barely comprehend that number. So if she sold . . . she'd be a millionaire? She wanted to be excited, but the lump in her throat felt a lot more like dread.

"Still, to your comment the other day about being in a tough financial situation, you're probably not," said Wyatt. "Or at least not the way you think you are. Because there's also some kind of life insurance coming your way, but apparently that takes forever to process, and I . . . Uh, I got a late start on it. I'm sorry."

He did look sorry, if not sheepish, but the ground beneath Aly felt like a waterbed. None of this should have come as a surprise to her.

Luke had money, and he was good at making plans; of course he'd taken out an insurance policy.

And yet.

"Are you okay?" asked Wyatt, reaching forward and touching her arm. "You look kind of funny."

"I'm fine," she said, pulling away from his touch. "And how I look is none of your concern."

"Okay," he said evenly as he put his hand in his lap. "Sorry."

"What does this have to do with selling Luke's house?" she asked after a moment.

He reached into the back pocket of his shorts, then slid a check across the table. "This is for you."

With some reluctance, Aly unfolded the check. *Thirty thousand dollars?* "For the record, that's a *ton* of money," she said, shaking her head with disbelief.

"Maybe it is," conceded Wyatt. "It's at least enough that now you don't have to do anything sudden about the house. I don't know why you decided to come now, and obviously you don't have to tell me. But I know Luke wanted you here—he made that clear in his will. And though I don't really get it, he wanted me here, too. I know it's not right for me to stay long-term, but I'd like to be here for the summer, at least."

So Wyatt was fully admitting that his only plan was to not have one. Aly met his gaze across the table, then quickly turned away. So many emotions swirled inside of her, but the only one she could name was overwhelm.

"I just think you should at least stay through July," he blurted. "You have to give it a chance."

Hadn't that been exactly what she'd been trying to do the past several days? What's more, she had a job to get back to. A *life*. And now, with thirty thousand dollars she'd have enough money to find a new place to live. Anyway, why did he care what she did?

"Luke never did anything without thinking it through," added Wyatt.

Before Aly could respond, Mari reappeared, a tray balanced on her left palm. "Two margaritas and some cheese puffs. And Aly—we should catch up while you're in town."

Across the table, Wyatt looked at her steadily.

"I'd love that," said Aly, glancing away from him and up at Mari. "We'll have to do it sooner than later, though, because I'm leaving next Friday."

Except . . . what if Wyatt was right, and Luke had wanted her to be here?

FOURTEEN

"Aly? You there?"

"Jada?" Aly could have wept with gratitude as she put her phone to her ear. More than a week had passed since she'd been involuntarily placed on leave, and now, finally, one of her coworkers had reached out. "How amazing to hear from you!"

"Yeah, you, too. I've been meaning to call. How are you?"

Aly had always thought that phone conversations were inherently awkward, but she swore she could hear something . . . tense in Jada's voice.

"I'm good. Really good. Taking care of some family business," she said cheerfully, stashing the vacuum in the closet. "And of course, actual business, too." The truth was, she'd struggled to work on her plan for the magazine and had taken to deep-cleaning the house instead. But talking to Jada would help get her back on track.

"I'm so glad to hear that," said Jada. "It's been a weird time for everyone. You didn't hear it from me, but there's talk that they're considering making the website a full-on shopping portal. Like, every single thing featured would be for sale. Can you even imagine?"

"No way!" As horrifying as this prospect was, how wonderful it felt to talk shop! "James would have told me if they were thinking about something like that," she said. But then it occurred to her that maybe he wouldn't have if he didn't intend to keep her on.

For the first time, Aly allowed herself to fully imagine the worst-case scenario: What if her leave of absence became permanent? A chill ran down her spine.

She was going to have to buckle down and make sure that didn't happen. "Other magazines that have tried that ended up folding right away. It would basically be announcing the end of *All Good*."

"I *know*," said Jada. "Let's hope it's just a rumor, right?"

"Oh, I'm going to do more than hope," said Aly. "I'm going to render any discussion of turning the magazine into an endless advertorial completely irrelevant." She'd resisted the line of home products that James had insisted on creating. But now she saw the value of *All Good* selling its own items, rather than hawking other companies'. The latter compromised editorial integrity—and that was the backbone of their brand. So step one of her comeback tour would be to expand the *All Good* product line. What about hair care, or supplements? Or—

"Aly," said Jada, breaking through her thoughts. "The reason I'm calling is because . . . well . . ."

Aly's optimism vanished as quickly as it had arrived. "What is it?" she said.

"The video's up again."

Aly squinted; suddenly the sun seemed entirely too bright. "The video?" On the day of her meltdown, James and Linda said they'd have the footage down by that afternoon; no one was supposed to know about it. If Jada was throwing around the word *again*, then everyone knew about it. "They were supposed to remove it."

"Girl, you know that's not how the internet works—you can check out anytime, but you can never leave. By the way, I don't think I've ever heard you curse like that. Or at all, actually. Nice job."

Crap. The entire staff of *All Good* had probably already seen it. This was a problem. "When you say 'up,' do you mean the whole team has seen the video?"

"I'm not sure, but that's probably a safe assumption."

Stay calm, she instructed herself. *The last thing you need is to lose your mind again.* "Isn't that a massive violation of privacy?" she said. "I could sue whoever posted it."

"Pretty sure because it was taken in a public place, they have the right to post it. That doesn't make it okay, obviously." Something about the way Jada said this gave Aly the sense it was not the first time she'd discussed it. No doubt the staff had been talking and had probably watched the footage on repeat. Now Aly'd have to launch a redemption campaign from Michigan. She hadn't cashed the check that Wyatt had given her, but now she would need to so she could buy a laptop. Because she had work to do.

"Do you know who took the video? Or at least who put it online?" she asked Jada. She was going to fix this. She *was.*

But first, she needed more information.

"I don't, but James has already sent a company-wide email condemning it. He basically said that whoever posted it is violating Innovate's policies and will be fired. The whole thing is a bad look for Innovate."

Yes, yes it was. And that was on Aly.

"Listen," said Jada, lowering her voice, "from where I stand, Meagan and Ashleigh are the real losers in this situation."

Aly had put Jada on speakerphone, so she could open up the inbox on her phone. She didn't see James' email. Actually, there were *no* new emails awaiting her. She hadn't looked in a few days, but how had she not registered that when she'd last checked?

Her heart seemed to skip a beat. Was she already halfway to being canned?

"Thank you for letting me know, Jada. I'm so glad you told me all this. It's going to make it much easier to make things right."

"Of course," said Jada. "Listen, I'm really sorry about your brother. I wish you'd told us."

Ugh. Of *course* Meagan had told everyone about Luke. She'd already proved she had zero loyalty to Aly, and she'd flat-out told Aly she didn't think she should be "hiding" it from the team. As Aly had tried in vain to explain, it wasn't a secret; it was private. There was a big difference—one that Meagan was apparently incapable of discerning.

"Thanks," said Aly. She knew she was supposed to say something else, like she was doing as well as she could under the circumstances, or how she was taking it one day at a time. But her tongue was a stone in her mouth, and her lips were blocks of wood.

"Listen, my best friend runs a content marketing firm in Newark," said Jada. "They're doing really amazing work for places like the Natural History Museum, and the pay is pretty darn good."

She swallowed hard and forced herself to speak. "Jada, I appreciate your concern, but I'm not looking for another job." Not yet at least. Not before she tried to turn this situation around.

"Aly—" began Jada.

"I've got to go, but thank you for reaching out. I really, truly appreciate it. Tell everyone that I said hi and that I'll be back soon," said Aly and hung up.

Outside, the lake was choppy, and dark clouds loomed in the distance. Aly unlocked the French doors and went to sit on the edge of the patio before it stormed. Then she sighed deeply, but it only made her think of Meagan doing downward dogs in the middle of their shared cubicle back in the day. They used to talk about opening their own magazine together—after they'd taken over *All Good*, of course.

Had Meagan posted the video?

In her heart, Aly knew that the video was never coming down. Even if she or one of Innovate's legal eagles had it removed from that platform, it would end up on another one, and then another, or emailed or texted from person to person. Anyone who ever looked her up online would, with a very small amount of digging, come across her meltdown. Sure, she could hire one of those pricey reputation management firms to bury it beneath more flattering search results—and maybe after selling Luke's house, that's exactly what she'd do. Still . . .

No one would ever mistake Aly for normal ever again.

How on earth would she come back from this? Because there was no scenario in which she would not want to return to New York and get her job back. Who would she even *be* if she wasn't a magazine editor?

The old version of herself. And that was simply not acceptable.

Which meant she'd have to learn to live with this.

Wyatt stood behind Aly now. With the wind continuing to pick up, she hadn't heard footsteps, yet she could just *sense* his presence. But she didn't turn around; instead, she waited for him to announce himself.

A few seconds later, he sat beside her on the stairs—not shoulder-to-shoulder, like Luke used to, but close enough that she could smell that he'd showered. She nearly smiled: she might have been a thorn in Wyatt's side, but at least she'd upped his hygiene game.

"Hi," he said.

Aly'd barely seen him since their dinner. But no matter how late he got in—if she heard him come in at all—he always had fresh coffee waiting for her the next morning. And unless her eyes were playing tricks on her, he'd been making less of a mess, too. Sometimes he actually put his dirty dishes in the dishwasher, and she nearly fell over when she realized that he'd *run* the machine. She wasn't sure what his objective was, and she wasn't convinced that this wasn't all some sort of long con to get what he wanted out of her . . . which was probably to keep lazing about the house for the rest of the summer. But at least for now, her life was a little bit easier than it had been when she arrived.

"Hey," she greeted him.

"Hey. I didn't mean to eavesdrop, but that didn't sound good," he said.

"Oh," said Aly, still staring straight ahead. "You heard."

"Just a little. Did your ex put up a video of you or something?"

She snorted. "No, my ex would love for the video in question to not exist. He works for the same company I do, and . . ." Should she spill about the rest? She had no idea if she could trust him. Then again, anything she was about to say would soon be public knowledge, if it wasn't already.

"You don't have to tell me if you don't want to," said Wyatt, stretching his long legs out in front of him.

She expected his feet to resemble a hobbit's, but they were clean and normally shaped, even sort of elegant looking. What a strange mix of contradictions this man was.

Oblivious to her scrutiny, he continued. "I just wanted to see if . . . I don't know. If you wanted to talk or something."

Maybe it was spending most of the past week in silence, but she kind of *did* want to talk.

So she did. She told him about how she'd been named editor in chief less than three months after Luke's death, and how it was the only thing that had gotten her out of bed each morning at a time when her instinct was to simply rot into oblivion. She told him about how working at *All Good* had been her lifelong ambition, and how she'd never in a million years imagined that she'd achieve it so early. And then she told him what had happened at the salad place.

Wyatt nodded as she babbled on, frowning at times, yet seemingly nonjudgmental about her brain blip. But when she finally came up for air, he put one of his mitts on her back and said, entirely too gently, "Let me get this straight: You don't actually *know* what you said to your coworkers?"

"No," she said. His hand felt kind of nice, which told her just how starved she was for physical contact. "And I don't want to."

His brown eyes bored into her. "How can you come up with a strategy if you don't have all the facts? That's what you normally do, right?"

She couldn't hide her surprise. So he *had* been paying attention. Or maybe she was just an open planner in large print.

"Well, yes," she admitted. "This is different, though." *Because I don't want to see myself acting like my mother,* she added internally, though she was hardly going to confess this to him.

"Hmm," he said, clearly unconvinced. "Would it help if I watched the video for you and gave you a summary?"

"Please don't. I seriously don't want to know."

"Aly, what do you have to lose?"

Everything, she thought. Her dignity. The ever-tenuous shred of self-regard she'd managed to cultivate. Her belief that she'd become the woman she'd always wanted to be, rather than the bratty, dumb, worthless girl that her parents had convinced her she was. *You just never learn,* her father often said before cracking her across whatever part of her body was within reach.

She could not bear the thought that he might be right. That for all her trying, she'd never really learned to be someone other than a person who provoked anger and abhorrence in the two people who were supposed to love her most.

"I need to keep acting like someone who deserves this job. And if I see that video, I might not be able to anymore," she said, blinking hard. But it was no use; a tear escaped, only to evaporate on the hot wood patio. Then another fell, and three and seven and ten more.

"Here," said Wyatt, pulling a packet of tissues from his pocket. Why did he have tissues in his pocket? How long had they been there? As she whispered her thanks and took them from him, she had to admit she didn't care.

"Why are you being nice to me?" she said with a sniffle after she'd managed to mostly turn off the faucet attached to her face.

"Do I need a reason?" he asked, looking at her curiously.

"Well, you did divide the house in half with tape," she said, wiping her cheeks with a tissue. "I thought you were mad at me."

"I was irritated, sure, but mostly I was just trying to prove my point."

"Well, you did," she said, smiling a little.

"Good." He grinned. His teeth were orthodontic ad–straight, save for a crooked canine, and she found the whole effect oddly charming.

"At least now you know why I'm here. I wanted to wait until September. I knew I wouldn't be ready before then, and—" She glanced around. It wasn't as though the beach itself, or even the house, was so triggering. But even after almost a week, she kept waiting for Luke to walk through the door or come strolling across the sand. Instead, there was only Wyatt. "Turns out I was right."

"You were waiting for the one-year mark." They both knew he meant the anniversary of Luke's death, which was the sixth of September.

"Yes," she admitted.

"Then you *weren't* planning on selling the house this summer. That was impromptu."

Well, when you put it like that. "That's one way of looking at it."

"So if it wasn't part of your plan, that's another vote for not selling right now."

For once, she wasn't exasperated; she just didn't understand why he cared. "Seriously, Wyatt, you're not fooling me with the whole thrift store vibe you've got going on," she said, and his bottom lip popped out in protest. "I *know* you have an insane amount of money, and you could live anywhere. Why here?"

"I don't know," he said, meeting her eyes again. "I mean, I guess I sort of do, but if I tried to explain to you, it would probably come out wrong."

"I'm used to that by now."

"That's fair," he said, smiling at her. "Let's just say you're not the only one who's unemployed. And before you start protesting, I know—"

he said, holding up a hand. "You're only *temporarily* off the job. But I'm permanently no longer a banker. Because I secretly hate banking—I always did—and after what happened last September, I didn't want to keep doing something I hated for a single second longer than I had to. So I quit, and it turns out that almost everyone in Chicago thought that my ditching the status quo was akin to having a mental breakdown. Which is how I ended up here, away from everyone who insisted on judging me. But I still don't get why Luke left me half a house that should be a hundred percent yours. Do you?"

"No," said Aly. She was so stunned—not just by his confession that the house shouldn't have been his, but by the fact that Wyatt was speaking so freely, when their conversation at the Mermaid had been stilted—that she didn't know what else to say.

Also, she saw something in his eyes, a particular type of pain that she recognized as her own. But how could that be? He was a proton to her neutron, the tropics to her tundra, a vaulted fortune to her purse full of pennies. He couldn't possibly know how she felt.

"I don't plan to keep the house," he added. "I don't deserve it, so if you want to sell, that's going to have to be okay with me. But I'm not ready to go back to real life yet, Aly. So I guess I'm asking you to let me have a little more time here if you can. And like I said the other day at the restaurant, I think you should give it more of a chance, too. Luke wanted that for you, even if I don't know why."

Aly spoke before she could think not to. "Okay."

"Okay?" he said, like he'd misheard her.

"Yeah. I'm still planning on leaving on Friday—I have to get back to New York. But you can stay until fall. I'm going to need to cash that check, which I'm not really geeked about, but if I'm rational, whether I cash it or sell the house, the money's coming from the same place."

"Thank you," said Wyatt. He sounded sincere, and he touched her again—so lightly she wondered if she'd imagined it this time—before standing. "We should head in," he said, gesturing to the dark clouds gathering over their heads. "It's going to storm."

"I need a moment," she said.

"I get it." But then he visibly startled.

"What is it?"

"Uh—I think I just spotted your mom."

"My mom? Where?" said Aly, confused. Granted, Cindy's hair *was* a shade of orange not found in nature, but how could Wyatt see the driveway from the patio? Besides, why would she be here when she didn't know Aly was in town?

"Yeah." Wyatt grimaced. "She's inside our house."

Aly was too busy jumping up to notice he'd used the word *our*.

FIFTEEN

"Alllllllleggggra! I've been looking for you!"

Cindy stood at the counter, watching Aly as she reluctantly let herself through the French doors.

"Looks like you found me," she said, unable to keep the sarcasm out of her voice. "What are you doing inside the house, Mom? And how did you know I was here?"

"Is that your fancy editor look?" asked Cindy, ignoring her questions.

"What do you mean?" said Aly, glancing down at herself. She wore a threadbare T-shirt dress—hardly the kind of thing she'd wear into the office.

"You're wasting away."

This, coming from a woman who was all of ninety pounds soaking wet. Food had never been a priority for Cindy—not for herself, nor for her children, and beneath her oversized T-shirt and sweatpants, she appeared withered to the point of frailty. In fact, now that Aly thought about it, it was strange that her mother even noticed her figure; she was usually too worried about herself to pay much attention to Aly. "I'm good," she said.

"Well, you don't look it," said Cindy, who made it sound like Aly's appearance had personally offended her.

You're not looking so hot yourself, she thought, though years of biting her tongue made it all but impossible to voice her true feelings to her mother. Cindy *did* seem to be sober. But age and alcohol had not been kind, and the deep grooves in her leathered skin gave her away as someone who'd smoked nearly her entire life. "Did you let yourself in?" asked Aly, looking through the window for Wyatt. Where had he disappeared to?

"The door was open. Not the safest," said Cindy, glancing around the house. Her deep gray irises were the same color Luke's had been; to her dismay, Aly resembled her father, who had dark hair and eyes, and skin that shifted from practically translucent in the winter to golden in the warmer months.

"No, it's not safe," agreed Aly, making a mental note to have another word with Wyatt.

"I do have a key, though," added Cindy.

Forget Wyatt—Aly needed a locksmith. "And why is that?"

"Oh, your brother wanted me to have it," said Cindy, but Aly had spent too many years with her mother to mistake her darting eyes for anything other than a sign she was lying.

"What's the real reason, Mom?" she insisted.

Cindy sighed and walked into the living room. "Billy and I were having trouble one day, and Luke wasn't home, so he told me where to find the key out on the patio, so I could let myself in. I forgot to give it back."

"I'm happy to put it back for you," said Aly, extending her hand.

"Why are you here now, Allegra?" said Cindy, who made no motion to approach Aly, let alone offer her the key. "I thought you had no interest in Luke's place. But from the looks of it, you've been here a while," she said, staring pointedly at the pile of laundry Wyatt had left on an armchair.

Which was when Aly realized her mother had no idea that Luke had left the house to Wyatt, too—and not to Cindy. There was no way this wouldn't crush her mother—and maybe even send her into a booze-filled spiral. Moreover, she would want an explanation, and Aly couldn't provide her with that.

"Why are *you* here now?" she asked, hoping to distract Cindy from the fact that every item of clean clothing she was looking at belonged to a man.

"I told you that me and Billy are on the outs. I've been staying with my friend Jean over in Fennville and decided to go for a drive to clear my head. Somehow ended up over here." She shrugged. "When I saw a car in the driveway, I thought I'd investigate in case something sketchy was going on. But never did I imagine that my own daughter wouldn't tell me she was in town."

Now it was Aly's turn to lie. "I was going to."

"Well, you didn't," said Cindy, jutting her chin out. Then her expression shifted. "But since I'm here, how about letting me stay in one of those guest rooms? I like the one that looks out at the water. Or I can stay in Luke's room, unless you're already set up there. I don't want to wear out my welcome at Jean's, and you don't need this whole big house to yourself."

What? No. *No.* There was no scenario in which Aly wanted to be under the same roof as her mother, and certainly not now. In one breath, Cindy would be poking at Aly, trying to get some sort of reaction out of her so she could inform her that despite her highfalutin degree and snooty job, she was still just like the rest of the Jacksons. In her next breath, she'd be pretending like their past was picture frame–worthy. Dan had never hit Cindy—he prided himself on not being "that kind of man"—but he'd always behaved as though he'd made a mistake in marrying her. Yet Cindy had the audacity to act like he'd been father of the year before he went on his "walkabout," as she referred to his disappearance after the night Luke told him he'd literally kill him if he ever laid a finger on Aly again. Aly knew one person couldn't be responsible for another's addiction, but Cindy hadn't become a blackout drinker until Dan took off. It was almost as though her new reality was so intolerable that she decided to opt out of it entirely.

But what most enraged Aly was that her mother wanted to return to the time when her husband had unloaded all of his frustrations on his own children.

"Hey, Aly," said Wyatt, strolling in through the side door.

Aly startled. He was smiling like a crazy person, or at least someone who seemed thrilled to see her. Then he put his arm around her, and despite her incredulity, Aly somehow knew not to turn and address him like the nutter he obviously was.

"Didn't know we had company," said Cindy, addressing Aly.

"This must be your mom," he said, pulling Aly in closer. She barely reached his armpit, but suddenly she didn't hate feeling so small—not when Wyatt was a giant human shield. She looked up at him, at once grateful and questioning.

"Play along," he mouthed.

"I *am* her mom," said Cindy, and Aly couldn't tell if she was proud or irritated—probably both. She glanced at Aly. "What happened to . . ."

It was not lost on Aly that even after three years of dating, her mother could not remember Seth's name. She hadn't liked to involve Cindy in her personal business—but *still*. Had everyone but Aly recognized that she and Seth were not built to last? "We broke up."

Cindy swapped her frown for a smile as she turned back to Wyatt. "And you are . . . ?"

"Wyatt," he said, extending one hand without letting go of Aly. "Wyatt Goldstein."

"It's nice to meet you, Wyatt," said Cindy, who was now clearly charmed. "I'm Cindy."

"I take it Aly didn't tell you about me?" Wyatt glanced down at Aly with a bemused look. "You're full of surprises, aren't you?" he said, touching the tip of her nose with his finger.

In spite of herself, she laughed—she wasn't the only one who was full of surprises.

"If I'd known you were here, I wouldn't have barged in," Cindy said to him apologetically. "I just had no idea."

"Oh, it's pretty new," said Wyatt.

"*Very* new," said Aly.

"And yet you're living here together," said Cindy, who didn't appear to disapprove.

"When you know, you know," said Wyatt.

Aly could feel heat rising to her face. He was taking this a little too far.

"You want to wait to take a nap?" he said, winking at her mischievously before looking back at Cindy.

"Oh. Well," said Cindy, looking back and forth between them again, "I don't mean to interrupt. Allegra . . ."

"Who's Allegra?" said Wyatt, winking again at Aly, whose stomach backflipped in response.

"I meant Aly," said Cindy quickly. "Maybe the three of us can do dinner or something."

Aly stiffened; the relief she'd just felt immediately revealed itself as an illusion. "I'll call you, Mom," she said woodenly.

"Please do," Cindy practically twittered as she made her way to the door. "Because I want to hear more about you, Wyatt. Aly's been quiet as a church mouse about you. Last I heard she was dating some suit in the big city. You're a breath of fresh air is what you are."

"Thanks—I get that a lot," said Wyatt, smiling beatifically at her as she stepped onto the stone path leading to the driveway. "Bye now, Cindy," he said, closing the door.

"What was *that*?" said Aly, staring at him with newfound reverence. "And who even *are* you? I had no idea you were capable of snake-charming."

"That was me making sure that your mother didn't wiggle her way into an endless overnighter," said Wyatt matter-of-factly.

"But how did you know . . ." *That I can't stand to be around her for more than a few minutes,* she added mentally. *That her face reminds me of the worst part of my life. That my own mother triggers me and makes me feel like I'm ten again, hiding under my bed listening to my father holler about what he's going to do to me once he finds me and knowing she's sitting in the next room and doesn't care.*

"Luke and I were close, Aly," he said quietly. This simple sentence told her everything. He knew about their childhood. He'd known all along. "I've actually met your mother before, when I came out here to see Luke's new house. I could tell from her expression she didn't recall it. Makes sense—she was a bit tipsy at the time," he added. "I figured I'd use that to our advantage to get her out of here."

For once, Aly didn't feel embarrassed that someone had seen her mother drunk. Maybe because he didn't seem to be judging her for it. "Thank you."

"You don't have to thank me." He was doing the no-blinking thing again. But why? This—this *kindness,* it was the opposite of a power play; Aly could not pretend otherwise. "I owe you for letting me stay the summer," he said.

"Right," she said. But she hadn't remembered that, and she wished he hadn't said it. As she excused herself and practically ran up the stairs to her room, she was awash with confusion. She didn't need Wyatt. She didn't even really *like* him.

And yet she was desperate to hit the invisible "Rewind" button in the sky and return to the moment in which she believed he'd done something nice for her—not because he owed her, but simply because he wanted to.

SIXTEEN

The following morning, a mug of hot coffee waited for her on the counter. Wyatt had left two keys beside it, and a note scrawled with what she now recognized as his handwriting. *Changed the locks,* he'd written. *Don't tell Cindy.*

She smiled for a second, only to remember that he was helping because he thought he had to. Even the coffee was probably an obligation. If Luke had told Wyatt about their childhood, then he'd probably shared how he'd been the one to care for Aly: stashing Band-Aids beneath his bed so he'd have them to put on her cuts and scrapes after she fell. Making inventive snacks for her out of the scant contents of their fridge and cupboards. Hiding her when they heard the door slam or angry footsteps in the hall. She hadn't realized it until she was nearly out of elementary school, but Luke routinely provoked their father so he would redirect his anger at him, rather than at Aly. He'd saved her life, maybe even literally, more times than she could count.

Yet in the end, karma had proved itself to be a cosmic joke, because no one had saved his.

No wonder Wyatt was being nice to her. He felt sorry for her. Whether she sold the house or not, she really did need to get out of here before she started feeling sorry for herself, too. After all, moods are contagious.

Aly took the keys but left the coffee, then got into her car and drove downtown.

There was a charming café a block from the water that she'd been meaning to try. It was still early so she parked across the street and ambled over. There was a line out the door, but this time Aly didn't scroll her phone or check her text messages as she waited. For once, she didn't want to distract herself from her sadness. Her brother wasn't here and that was unfair and awful, and she was not going to pretend otherwise. She stood there, feeling miserable but not caring if anyone thought she had resting beach face or noticed that she kept wiping the corners of her eyes. Until she got back to New York, she would stop worrying about looking normal and just . . . be.

She'd just ordered a latte and a muffin when she spotted a tall, scruffy man hunched over a laptop at one of the small tables on the other side of the café. For someone who'd probably attended the best prep school, Wyatt had awful posture. She hid behind a post while she waited for her order, silently observing him. What was he even *doing*? She'd never seen him on a computer before, and she couldn't help but watch with amusement as he laboriously typed using the hunt-and-peck method. *Serves him right for dictating missives to a secretary for years,* she thought, but then she remembered what he'd said about banking. He was lucky that he could just up and quit without having to worry about where his next rent check would come from. Still, she felt sort of bad for him. For all its faults, she loved publishing and couldn't imagine doing something she despised. In fact, she'd told Luke that very thing. And now that he was gone just two years after he'd ditched his soul-sucking career, she felt doubly convinced that no job, no matter how wealthy it made you, was worth wasting your life on.

The barista was approaching the counter with her muffin and her drink, so she rushed over to retrieve them before he could call out her name. Then she carefully tiptoed behind Wyatt, leaned down, and whispered, "Boo!"

She laughed when he nearly fell off his chair.

"You're lucky it's you," he growled, but now he was laughing, too. "I deserved that, huh?"

"My little shower surprise was probably worth several of your sneak attacks. But yeah, you had it coming." As she heard herself, she realized her dark mood had disappeared. But she was supposed to be avoiding him so he wouldn't take pity on her!

And yet.

"What are you up to?" she asked.

"Working," he said, but he'd just closed his laptop.

"I can go," she volunteered, as he obviously didn't want to tell her what he was working on. "I was planning to grab a quick bite and head over to Oval Beach. I'm only here a few more days, and I figured I should see it before I take off."

"You're leaving?" he said, frowning.

"Well, yeah." Though the days had seemed to drag on forever, the past week had somehow flown by. "That was always the plan."

"The plan," he repeated. "Always with the plan."

"You say that like it's a bad thing," she said, mirroring his frown. "How else am I supposed to get my job back?"

"I thought you said you had the whole month off work."

"I do, but I still need to get back to the city. I have to buy a laptop."

"Definitely can't do that in Michigan. Or, you know—on the internet," he deadpanned.

She rolled her eyes. "Okay, fine. But I still need to find a place to live and hopefully get my boss to meet with me, so I can show him that I've used my time away to think about how to improve the magazine." Her confidence rang hollow. Where would she even tell her taxi driver to *go* after she arrived at the airport? She could get a hotel room while she searched for a new apartment, but this seemed like a wasteful way to spend the money Luke had left her. Perhaps she could ask Seth if she could crash at his place for a few nights—a week, max. Aside from the suitcase she'd taken to Michigan, her few belongings were still at his apartment, and it would be a good opportunity to pack everything up, and maybe get closure with Seth; although she didn't regret having broken up with him, she did feel bad about the way it had played out. After three years together, didn't they owe each other a proper goodbye?

"I see," said Wyatt, whose phone had just started vibrating on the table. He immediately flipped it over, but not before Aly saw *MOM* written across the screen.

"Do you need to get that?" she asked.

"Nope." He drained his coffee.

"You sure?" she said. "You have a weird look on your face."

"Are you saying I'm ugly?" he said, pretending to be hurt.

She laughed. "Don't try to change the subject."

"Fine—then I definitely won't ask you if you've been to the Dunes."

"At Oval Beach? Of course, though it's been years."

"I meant Warren Dunes," he asked, referring to the state park an hour south of Saugatuck. "I've never seen them, but I was just reading that they dwarf these dunes."

"Oh—yeah, I've been. But not since . . ." Her voice trailed off, and tears pricked her eyes before her brain had even registered the memory.

Not since she'd gone with Luke more than a decade earlier.

Wyatt slipped his laptop into his bag, then stood and folded his arms over his chest. "We should go."

"We?" she questioned.

"Yeah. You and me—unless you want to bring Cindy," he said, smirking.

"That's a hard no," she said, laughing. "And by the way, thanks for changing the locks."

"Don't mention it. Anyway, I've never been to Warren Dunes, and apparently, you're leaving any day now. It might be fun. Unless my beard offends you too much for you to spend two hours in a car with me," he added.

"Oh," she said, sheepish. So he was aware that his facial fur made her want to do rude things with a pair of scissors. "It's fine."

"Good. Then how about this afternoon, after lunch? Unless you have *plans*," he said, arching an eyebrow.

She blushed. "I don't." *I never have plans anymore,* she added mentally. *And I seem incapable of making any, which doesn't bode well for my future.*

"Then I'll meet you at the house around one," he said.

Now she smiled. "It's a plan."

Panic didn't fully set in until she was nearly home. *SOS,* she texted Harry the minute she got into the kitchen. *I'm going on a beach outing with Wyatt*

Blinking dots immediately appeared, then text: *The plot THICKENS!*

Nothing is thickening, Harry

Tell that to your rugged roommate

Her ears were burning. *You've never even seen him,* she typed, grateful they weren't on FaceTime.

It's called Google, babe

You're certifiable

Harry didn't write back right away—he was probably in the middle of emailing a client or tactfully informing a junior associate that they'd bungled a brief. She was about to tell him she'd check in later when he texted her a photo of what was clearly Wyatt's banking headshot. But Harry had scribbled a scraggly beard on his chin and had written *HOT* over his head.

Now her face was officially on fire. *Harry! This is Luke's best friend we're talking about. Ew. No*

I'm incorrigible (a word I can't actually spell without the help of autocorrect). And you're going on a DATE. Tell me how it goes! More soon xx

I'm NOT. You're the worst and I can't believe I love you xo

Aly sighed and sank into her bed. The mattress Luke had chosen was nice—expensive, no doubt, and soft on top while solid enough that she didn't roll into the middle. She wished she could take it with her to wherever in the five boroughs she ended up. She was tired, so very tired; it was a shame she couldn't nap. She'd never been able to, even if she'd stayed up half the night studying in college. Luke hadn't, either. "I think it's from years of being on high alert," he'd said to her when they'd discussed it over dinner one night when they both lived in the city. "Because of Dad, you know?"

She did.

She hadn't seen or heard from her father since she was fourteen, but the memory of him followed her like a shadow. Sometimes she felt sorry for him—how broken did you have to be to take out all your anger on a child? Mostly, though, she hated him for what he'd taken from her. Besides her childhood, he'd stolen her belief that she was inherently lovable. And yes, the sense of safety that allowed a person to fall asleep midday.

She laid there for nearly half an hour, wishing for unconsciousness. Then she went into the bathroom and splashed her skin with water. She had bags under her eyes that no amount of concealer could correct, and she was badly in need of a haircut. She swiped on tinted gloss, and then decided to add waterproof mascara in an attempt to appear slightly less exhausted. Photo-ready she was not, but it was just Wyatt, and it would have to do.

"Hey," he said when she came downstairs. She must have looked as spent as she felt, because he said, "We can go another time if you're not feeling up to it."

But Aly didn't respond. Though the man sitting on the counter was wearing a worn Lake Michigan T-shirt she'd seen plenty of times and a beaten-up pair of swim trunks, it took her several seconds to process that it was Wyatt. Because his jaw was no longer covered with fur. And now the whole effect was . . .

Well, she wasn't going to admit this to Harry, but he had not been wrong.

"Where . . . is . . . your beard?" she uttered.

"Gone," he said with a shrug. "You ready?"

She hoped he couldn't see her swallowing hard from across the room. "Ready as I'll ever be."

SEVENTEEN

Luke had taken Aly camping at Warren Dunes the summer between her junior and senior years in high school. He had one more year at Notre Dame and had come home for a week before heading to Manhattan for an internship. He'd always liked to introduce Aly to the wider world, as he put it, whether it was having sushi for the first time or volunteering at a soup kitchen or browsing at expensive stores along Chicago's Magnificent Mile. Aly had attempted to explain to Luke that she didn't need to *try* camping to know she wasn't a camping person, but he'd insisted that she at least give it a night before deciding. So he'd packed a cooler full of food, borrowed a tent from someone, and rented a spot at the campground adjacent to the Dunes.

In some respects, Aly had been absolutely right. She'd felt every lump and bump of the ground through her sleeping bag and struggled to fall back asleep after a thunderstorm woke them at three in the morning. Hot dogs *did* taste better when roasted over an open fire, but somehow sand had ended up in her bun and watermelon and even her water bottle. After a single afternoon, she'd gotten so grimy that she questioned whether she'd ever get truly clean again.

And for all that, she'd loved it. The Dunes, which stood more than two hundred feet above the lake and stretched nearly as far as a person could see, looked more like the Middle East than the Midwest. "It's the kind of place where a person can think bigger thoughts," he'd remarked after they'd hiked to the top of an especially tall dune. They were sitting beside each other under one of the few trees in the area, gulping down water and mopping their brows with their shirts. Lake Michigan looked so large that it took up the entire horizon, and the water was bright blue that day—nearly turquoise, really. Although she'd never been to the ocean before, Aly remembered thinking the lake looked like the photos she'd seen of it.

"Yeah," she agreed. "It is."

"What are you going to do with yourself, Al?" Luke asked. "I mean after high school. You only have a year to go."

"I don't know. Go into nursing, maybe," she said, squinting beneath her straw hat. The local community college had a good program, and nursing paid a decent wage.

"Correct me if I'm wrong, but somehow I don't see a word nerd's true heart's desire as poking people with needles and taking their blood pressure," said Luke with a wry smile. "What do you *want* to do?"

He sounded like Ms. Perez, who'd encouraged her to take advantage of her natural talents. "I want to be an editor in chief of a magazine?" she said, as if she was asking him for permission—and maybe she was.

"I like it," he said. "Which one?"

"*All Good*," she said, wrinkling her nose because she might as well have just said she hoped to sprout a set of wings. "Or something like that," she quickly added.

Luke bumped her lightly with his shoulder. "Don't water it down, sis. Get specific."

"Fine," she said, smiling out of both pleasure and embarrassment. "I want to be the editor in chief of *All Good* one day. That seems impossible, since I'll barely be able to pay for community college, let alone the kind of school where I could land a job like that. I've never even been to New York, and, well—" She motioned from left to right. "I have no idea how I'm going to get from here to there."

"You don't have to know the way," said Luke, who'd been watching her with those wise gray eyes of his. "You just have to want it, and to start thinking it's possible. I know you can do it. So even if you don't believe that yet, borrow my belief."

Aly adored her brother and his unshakable faith, and that's why she didn't tell him how unrealistic his advice was. She *definitely* needed to know the way. Without clear directions, she was sure to get lost. "Let's just pretend that's true," she said. "Then what do *you* want, Luke?"

He didn't say anything right away, and she wondered if she'd offended him by using the word *pretend*. Then he said quietly, "You're going to think this is stupid."

"Have we met?" she said, incredulous. "Sometimes you've got lofty ideas, but I'm the last person to think anything you say is stupid. I don't even think you could pull off stupid if you tried."

"Thanks." The left side of his mouth lifted upward. "The thing is, Al, I don't have an ideal career in mind like you do, and that's kind of tricky at times. But I do know that I want to make enough money to make a difference in other people's lives. Sounds cheesy, huh?"

Aly wrapped her arms around him. He was lean but solid, and she remembered thinking he felt unbreakable. She wanted to be unbreakable one day, too. "Not at all," she said, hugging him. "If anyone can figure it out, it's you." She could still remember him, no older than eight or nine, making her a delicious dinner out of a can of tuna, a packet of Saltines, and some cheese that she was pretty sure he'd hidden in the freezer so their parents wouldn't find it and eat it. He'd wiggled his way into a job at twelve, so he'd have money to buy them both new shoes and the occasional movie ticket. He'd managed to get a full ride to Notre Dame, even though he'd struggled with science. If he didn't know how to do something, he worked at it until he did.

Now, as Wyatt sped down an open country road toward the Dunes, Aly wished she'd told Luke that he *had* made a difference, and not with his money. Yes, Mari had helped her with the nuts and bolts of getting out of town and onto the next big step toward her dream. But Luke's conviction had given her the courage to try, even when she was convinced (as she often was) that she wasn't the kind of person who could have the kind of life she wanted.

"You okay?" asked Wyatt from beside her. They'd spent most of the drive in silence, and Aly had vacillated between finding it perfectly comfortable and wanting to fill the quiet between them. But she hadn't made small talk, or even turned on the radio. Just as she'd not pushed down her sadness in the coffee shop, she didn't try to disguise her discomfort now.

"I'm fine," she said, trying not to glance at his newly shorn jaw. It was . . . sort of chiseled, to be honest, and it irritated her. She'd just barely gotten used to his mandible mullet.

"Okay." But the way he said this told her he didn't believe her.

"I was just thinking about Luke," she admitted.

"I see." They entered the state park grounds, and he paid the attendant the fee and continued to the parking lot. Aly didn't expect him to elaborate. But after they'd parked, and as he pulled his backpack from the trunk, he said, "That happens to me a lot. Thinking about Luke, I mean."

"Oh," she said, adjusting her crossbody bag, then falling into step with him as they made their way toward the closest dunes. "You two were close."

"We were," said Wyatt. "He was easy to be around."

Luke *was* easy to be around. That was one of the reasons people flocked to him. They never flocked to Aly like that, not even after she read all those self-help books. You couldn't fake charisma; you either had it, or you didn't. Aly wished she did, but at least she had a brother who brightened everything around him. That had always been more than enough for her.

"That sounded dumb," said Wyatt. City life had turned Aly into a champion speed-walker, but she could tell he was shortening his stride so she could keep up with him. "Luke was a hell of a lot more than just easy to be around."

"It doesn't sound dumb. And for the record, he was," she panted; she was getting winded. The dune they'd begun scaling was at least ten stories high; she'd be drenched in sweat by the time they reached the top, and that was *if* she reached the top. Yes, she routinely walked from Union Square to the Upper West Side and back, but she'd forgotten how steep the Dunes were.

"He didn't want me to be someone I wasn't." As he said this, he slipped in the sand, and he began sliding down the hill toward her. On instinct, she put out her arm to keep him from falling.

He grabbed her hand. "Thanks."

"Of course." Her eyes landed on him as he let go of her. Admittedly, Wyatt didn't have Luke's golden aura. He was more like titanium, and anything but easy. Yet as much as he drove her insane, she couldn't imagine that the people who loved him would want him to be anyone other than the sharp, sure-footed, and yes, cocky man that he was. "Who on earth would want you to be someone else?" she asked once she'd caught her breath.

He lifted his sunglasses to look at her, and something strange and unknown shot through her. Why did he do that? She didn't need to make eye contact with him to have a conversation. And yet she couldn't deny that it shifted the mood . . . even if she couldn't say what, exactly, the mood was now. "My parents," he said plainly. "Other people, too. Women I've dated, friends, my old boss, his boss. Whatever, none of that matters. The parental wounds are always deepest, right?"

So she hadn't been wrong about Wyatt's mother's role in his problems. "Yes," she agreed. "But didn't you get your MBA from, like, Harvard or something? How could your parents be upset about that?"

"Penn," he said, grimacing.

"Oh, yeah, that's definitely slumming it," she said, and they both began to laugh. His laugh was deep and enveloping, and almost felt like a gift he'd picked out just for her.

She stopped laughing when she realized what she was thinking. It was *not* just for her, and clearly her brain was still on the fritz.

"That's not what I meant," he said, smiling.

"Maybe not, but I still don't get it," she said seriously. "Who cares if you quit your job? It's not like you're a societal dropout or something. You'll find something else to do. Something good, I'm sure."

Wyatt looked away. "Yeah, tell that to my dad."

"What does he care?" said Aly, who knew enough not to add what she was thinking—which was *At least his father cares.* Because her own father hadn't reached out to her in two decades, not even after Luke died. In his will, Luke had requested they skip a memorial service—a fact she only knew because Wyatt had told her as much the previous September. She shook her head, as though she was trying to shake the memory right out of it. She didn't want to go back to hating Wyatt. Not today, at least.

"My dad wanted me to take over his brokerage firm," said Wyatt. "His father started it and created our family fortune. I was supposed to carry the torch."

"You didn't, though." She knew he'd worked for a large chain bank before he left.

"Nope. No interest whatsoever. But as long as I'd worked in finance in some capacity, he'd been able to maintain the fantasy that I was on the verge of changing my mind, not to mention getting married and having a gaggle of kids to inherit ye olde family business. Now that I've officially dropped out, it's over. My parents are devastated, and I'm tired of hearing about it."

"That's not fair of them." They'd started to hike again, and sand flew behind them as their feet sank into the hill. "What *do* you want to do, anyway?"

"I'm not sure, but I'll figure it out. What I do know is that I'm sick of living the way I'm supposed to."

"I get it," she said, though as someone who'd always wanted nothing more than to simply fit in, a small part of her didn't fully understand him. Then again, though Cindy had plenty of opinions about Aly's career path, she'd never pushed her to do anything else. When Aly had told her she'd received a partial scholarship to college, Cindy had simply said, "I hope that means you'll be able to help take care of me when I'm old."

"Almost there," said Wyatt. His breath sounded as shallow as hers felt. "Just a little further."

Aly wiped her brow on the back of her arm; all of the moisture in her body seemed to be escaping through her skin, and her throat was dry and scratchy. "I need water," she told him.

"Got it," he said, stopping in his tracks. He twisted to pull his backpack from his back, but as he did, his feet began to slip. "Crap," he said, but it was too late—he'd already collided into Aly, knocking her over. The next thing she knew, his legs were around her waist, and they were sliding down the dune.

"Ahhhh!" she yelped as sand sprayed into their faces.

"Hold on," he said, digging his heels into the hill to stop them. But it was too sudden, and before she knew it, he'd rolled right on top of her.

"Are you okay?" he said, looking down at her. He didn't pry himself off of her, though, and she didn't try to wiggle out from under him. He was heavy, but it was a good kind of heavy, like a weighted blanket. Aly could feel his heart beating staccato against her chest; his pupils were enormous. She didn't respond. How could she when she wasn't sure she was still breathing?

Then he abruptly pulled back and stood. "Sorry," he muttered.

Aly felt more naked than the day she'd walked in on him in the bathroom. What was he sorry for? Looking at her like that? Not kissing her when she knew—she just *knew*—he'd wanted to?

No, she realized at once. He was sorry because he saw her as someone who was too broken to be with. Why, oh *why* had she told him about the Incident, about her grief? Why had she shown her vulnerable side to him, when he so obviously could only handle steely resolve?

But obviously he'd been right about her. Because how else had she ended up here, exactly where she didn't want to be, with the person she least needed to get tangled up with?

She *was* broken.

And now it was time to glue herself back together and get on with her life.

"I'm just . . . confused," he said, looking up without meeting her eyes. "You're Luke's sister. He wanted us to be *friends.* Not . . . you know. That would ruin everything."

"I get it," she said, turning away so he couldn't see her face. Because she would not shed a single tear in front of Wyatt Goldstein. Not today. Not ever. "We should go."

"Aly," he said, and the confusion in his voice nearly broke her all over again.

"Let's go," she said. "I need to get home and pack."

She rose, brushed the sand from her clothing, and began down the hill.

"Aly," he called. "Wait!"

But she didn't wait, and she didn't look back. Because Aly had vowed years ago that she was done being hurt. She'd forgotten that promise to herself somewhere along the way, but she wouldn't make that mistake twice.

No—she would sooner attempt to swim across Lake Michigan than give Wyatt Goldstein the opportunity to hurt her again.

EIGHTEEN

The silence on the car ride back was not the comfortable kind.

The minute they pulled into the driveway, Aly uttered a terse *thank you* to Wyatt, who looked like he was ready for the earth to swallow him whole, then got into her rental car and drove downtown. She didn't have anywhere to be, and she was far too wired to get coffee or eat. So she headed to the boardwalk that spanned the river and called Harry. He'd been about to step into a meeting but said he'd call in half an hour.

Seven minutes later, he was back on the phone.

"That was fast," said Aly, feeling at once elated to talk with him and guilty for taking up time in his workday.

"Ninety percent of meetings are completely unnecessary, and this one was no exception. I told my team to email me the details and stop wasting my time."

"You did not."

"As least half of that is true," he said. "Now, I sense a disturbance in the Force. What's going on?"

"Oh, Harry," she said miserably, watching a seagull swoop down and steal a fry someone had dropped on the boardwalk. "You won't even believe it. How could you, when I barely do?" And then she told him everything.

"*Oooh*, now you've gone and done it," he hooted when she'd finished. "And for the record, not only do I believe it, I called it ages ago."

"I'm aware, Harry. But *nothing* happened." She was glad he couldn't see the whole-body flush that came over her as she recalled Wyatt rejecting her. How could you simultaneously want something with every fiber of your being, yet know you should avoid it at all costs?

"I know, sweetheart. But maybe it should have, no?"

"Harry, did you get a lobotomy? You're acting like this is a good thing. It's the *exact opposite*. It's a massive mess that I don't know how to clean up. I have to get out of here!"

"Or maybe not?" he said, and she could just picture him smiling devilishly.

"No," she said firmly as she stepped aside to make space for an elderly couple and their Labrador. "Not even an option. I'm leaving Friday, but honestly, I have half a mind to take off tonight."

"Aly, said with love . . ."

"That's like starting a sentence with *I don't mean to offend you* and then saying something super offensive," she said, shooting a tight smile at a young woman sitting on a bench, who'd presumably overheard and had shot her a thumbs-up.

"This is different. For the record, I do love you. I also wonder if you should stay put for a few more weeks."

"And why would I do *that*?"

"Well, I haven't come to see you yet." Harry had gotten placed on a major case the week before and had been working around the clock since then.

"So? There will be other chances," said Aly. Then she clapped her hand over her mouth, realizing that she'd just implied she was going to return to the house at some point. "Or not."

"*See?* Admit it. Part of you likes it there."

"I don't hate it," she confessed.

"High praise from a city slicker," he teased.

"It doesn't matter, Harry," she said with exasperation. "As long as Wyatt's living here, I can't be."

"Well, correct me if I'm wrong, but you don't have a place to return to in New York."

"Staying in Michigan is decidedly *not* going to help me find an apartment in New York."

"Have you put feelers out with friends and colleagues?"

"I'm going to," she said, thinking of Seth. She was going to have to message him and see if he was amenable to a houseguest for a few days. "I do have a broker in mind, though." Now that she had thousands of dollars sitting in her bank account, she could enlist the help of the rental agent who'd helped Jada find her place.

If only the thought of using that money didn't make her stomach twist into knots.

"Or you could just hold tight," said Harry.

"I don't know if I can change my plane ticket," she said weakly. "Also, I'm pretty sure Wyatt's ready for me to leave as soon as humanly possible." She'd done her best not to look at him on the ride back. But every time her eyes accidentally flitted to him, she could see the muscles in his jaw twitching and the vein in his temple throbbing so hard she could've taken his pulse with it.

"Oh, I suspect your little sand tumble had the opposite effect," said Harry, and Aly snorted in protest. "As to your plane ticket, I will personally pay for your change fee."

"You will not."

"Try me. Listen, love. How about I come out there? Just for like a night or two?"

"You said work was crazy."

"It is—and so is your pal Harry. I plan to get this motion filed before next Thursday. I can come Friday."

That was more than a week away. "I don't know, Har. I should really probably stick to my plans."

"I'll bring Beckett and Tim to sweeten the deal. Unless you don't want to snuggle a ridiculously chubby little six-month-old?"

She couldn't suppress her smile. "You're bribing me."

"I've done worse in my time. I've gotta run—the minions are about to storm my office. But text me and tell me how things go when you get home, 'kay? Love you."

"I will. Love you, too," she said. It was only after she'd slipped her phone back in her pocket that it occurred to her that she was going to have to tell Harry to stop calling Luke's place home.

~

Aly was not surprised to find Wyatt's car missing when she pulled up. Really, she didn't expect to see much of him before she left for the airport in two days. But as she entered the kitchen, only to discover that no mess had been made for her to clean, she felt oddly deflated.

Where did he disappear to, anyway? She knew he wasn't working, and he didn't seem to have friends in town. So how was he filling the hours? *Did* he have a girlfriend? She almost hoped so. At least then he would've rejected her for a reason other than . . . well, her being herself.

As she surveyed the first floor, which was disturbingly tidy, it occurred to her that the question she should ask was why she was worried about how Wyatt Goldstein spent his time. A few years earlier, she'd interviewed a psychologist for an article on healthy habits who'd said that an untended mind was akin to a toddler let loose in an antique store. "You have to give your brain something to do or it's going to break everything in sight," said the psychologist.

So *naturally* she was focusing on Wyatt; she hadn't been focusing on work. Fortunately, that was a fixable problem. And now it was time to get down to business.

There was still coffee in the pot, and though it was cold, she poured herself a mug anyway. Then she went up to her bedroom, took her notepad and pen from the nightstand drawer, and sat on her bed. After a minute or two, she scribbled *Multimillion-Dollar Brand* at the top of the page and *Constantly Declining Revenue* at the bottom. Then, without censoring herself, she began to write in the gap between them.

Nearly an hour later, her mug was empty, and she'd filled twelve pages with ways to turn the magazine's fortunes around. Some of her ideas were ridiculous, as they required resources that she and the company didn't have. But more than a few ideas had real promise. *This is why I'm perfect for this job,* she thought, rereading her proposal to pair with a streaming service to create original content. *And this is how I'm going to convince them not to fire me.* Innovate was worried about her video circulating on the internet? Fine—they'd squeeze those lemons into dozens of curated *All Good* videos, which would quickly bury the footage of her unfortunate meltdown. And in doing so, the magazine would become something greater. Because as much as it pained her, Innovate needed to recognize that the time for print magazines was nearly over. In order to survive, they would have to—well, innovate. It was the only way.

She couldn't exactly send her barely legible pages to James. It was a shame she'd relied on Innovate for a laptop all these years, but maybe she could use a computer at the local library to type up her plans.

For now, though, she simply needed to do one thing.

She pulled out her phone. *James,* she wrote in an email from her personal email account, *I've come up with a plan for making* All Good *stronger than ever. Can we talk soon? —Aly*

NINETEEN

The next morning, Aly tapped on the email icon on her phone with trembling hands. The sun was still hiding beneath the horizon, but the adrenaline high from the previous day's brainstorming session had yet to wear off, and she'd awoken without an alarm.

And there it was: a new message from James, sitting at the top of her inbox.

Glad to see you're feeling like yourself, he'd written at four that morning. *Let's hop on a call. Can you do one o'clock tomorrow?* He must have assumed that she could, as one of his assistants, who'd been cc'd on the email, had immediately followed up with a calendar invite with dial-in information.

Aly's elation evaporated when she saw he'd scheduled a conference call. James hated conference calls. And on a Friday afternoon? That had *termination* written all over it. Worse, Linda—who James relied on to deliver bad news—had been invited to said call, too.

Was James going to *fire* her?

He was, she realized with a sinking sensation. That's why he hadn't reached out sooner, and why Jada had called to tell her about a job opportunity. Complicating matters, the call was scheduled just an hour before her flight to New York. Given that Aly had not yet figured out how to breach the space-time continuum, she obviously would not be taking that flight. Not when there was a possibility—an impossibly slim one, but still—that she could somehow save her job.

Yes, she decided. That was exactly what she'd do. Because her other option—admitting defeat—was too unbearable to consider.

Wyatt was in the kitchen when she came downstairs. "I'm just leaving," he said as he put a lid on his travel mug. He did not look at her as he spoke.

That terrible confused feeling came over her again—the one that made her want to cry but also scream at him, or at least run the other direction. "Okay," she said carefully. "But you don't have to."

She saw dark circles under his eyes when he glanced at her, and he'd grown a five o'clock shadow. Aly hated that he still looked attractive to her—maybe even more so than he had before. "I know that," he said. "I just wanted to give you some space."

"I didn't *ask* for space. What I'm asking for is for you to not be weird to me."

"If I'm being weird, it's not because of you," he said, looking away from her again. "And I'm sorry I, uh, crashed into you and made things . . . tricky."

"It's fine," she said.

"Well, I'm sorry."

I wish you weren't, she thought, but she couldn't make her mouth open.

He fiddled with the lid on his mug. "I know you're leaving soon, so I'll try to stay out of your hair until then. And if you want me to move out before the fall, just say so, and I'll take off."

"Um." She swallowed the lump in her throat. "I'm actually going to need to stay a little bit longer. I have a meeting tomorrow that conflicts with my flight, so I have to postpone it. And, uh, my best friend and his family want to come visit next weekend."

Wyatt's eyes widened in surprise. "Oh."

"If that's a problem, I can tell them to wait."

"No, that's not it," he said quickly. "I just—well, when I suggested you stay the month, you didn't seem into it."

"I wasn't," she admitted. "But things have changed." She didn't volunteer that if the meeting went poorly, it was possible she'd have no reason to return to New York.

Wyatt cleared his throat. "Got it. Um. Do you think we can try to keep things between us—you know. Normal?"

Normal? She didn't even know what that meant for the two of them. Was normal when they lobbed barbed comments at each other? Or when they talked about Luke and their pasts? Or was normal her sensing heat between them, and knowing she'd get burned if she got any closer?

"We can try," she said.

"Thanks," he said. He looked as tentative as she'd ever seen him, and she almost wanted to reassure him. Then she remembered the Dunes, the way he'd backed away from her as though she had a raging case of smallpox.

"Yeah," she said. "Don't mention it."

"See you later," he said, meeting her eye briefly before heading for the door.

After he left, Aly decided to go walk on the beach. She needed to clear her head and figure out how to handle her meeting with James. But as she strolled along the water's edge in her bare feet, she couldn't seem to focus on *All Good*. Not when Wyatt's words loomed over her like a storm cloud.

Normal.

Confused.

Luke wanted us to be friends.

Was that last part true? She thought back to the first time she met Wyatt, nearly a decade earlier. He and Luke had worked together their first year out of business school and had become fast friends, but at that point Wyatt had already moved back to Chicago, and he'd flown in for a quick weekend visit. They'd agreed to meet at a restaurant near Luke's apartment; the place had a long mahogany bar and tables with red checkered tablecloths, and as usual, it was full of bright young things dressed in business casual, each with a drink in one hand and a cell phone in the other. It was not Aly's scene, but they sold four-dollar glasses of red wine, and Luke seemed to know everyone there.

"You'll love Wyatt," he'd hollered to Aly over the din. "He's on the quiet side, but he's sharp as a tack and as loyal as they come. A lot like someone else I know," he'd said, raising his glass to Aly.

Aly actually *had* been excited to meet him. While Luke liked every-one, he let few people get close, and she figured that this Wyatt must really be something to have stayed tight with her brother even after he'd moved eight hundred miles away.

But the stone-faced man in a starched button-down and pressed jeans who sat down across from her in their booth had the magnetism of a wet sock, and barely looked at her. Aly tried addressing him by name—repeatedly, in fact—to try to engage him. But even when he did acknowledge her presence, he looked at the space above her head rather than directly at her.

"Don't leave me with him," Aly had said under her breath when Luke stood to use the bathroom.

"He's just nervous," Luke had whispered back. "You have that effect on people sometimes, Al. Come on. Try to be friendly."

So Aly did, because when had Luke steered her wrong before?

Questions—people liked it when you asked them questions. She'd read this in one of those self-help books.

"So, Wyatt, what do you do?" she asked after Luke was gone.

Wyatt looked down at his pint glass. "I'm in banking."

"Right. What kind?" she said.

"Investment banking."

The questions were supposed to be open-ended—that gave the other person an opportunity to talk longer. "What do you like about it?"

"Not much," he said, and although he'd been nursing the same beer for more than an hour, he suddenly drained the remainder.

Fine. If he wasn't going to talk, she'd have to.

"Well, I'm an editor at *All Good*," she said.

Wyatt raised an eyebrow. "Good for you."

She stared at him, aghast. What was *wrong* with this guy? And honestly, what was wrong with Luke, that he'd chosen such a dud for a friend?

Aly had excused herself for the night soon after Luke returned to their table. She remembered walking from the restaurant to the subway and feeling deeply relieved that she wouldn't have to see Wyatt again anytime soon. And each time he came to New York to visit, she reminded Luke about their disastrous attempt at conversation and told him that under no circumstances would she be joining them for dinner or drinks or—well, anything.

Then Luke broke Aly's heart and moved to Michigan, and she no longer needed to worry about avoiding Wyatt.

Aly had made it perfectly clear to Luke that she couldn't stand Wyatt. Forget buying a place entirely too close to their hometown. What on earth had he been thinking, leaving his house to both of them?

Forget you, Wyatt, she thought, kicking at the sand. Even at ten in the morning, it was already blazing hot. *I'll take Manhattan and you can have Michigan.* With her bank account no longer barren, she didn't have to sell the house as soon as possible. For all she cared, Wyatt could have the whole thing and Cindy could move in with him. What did it matter?

It didn't. Now that Luke was gone, the only thing Aly needed to care about was getting back to her job and getting on with what was left of her life.

"James, I want to come back more than anything," said Aly, blinking back tears. Oh, this was such incredible news! "You know the only thing I've ever wanted is to be *All Good*'s editor in chief." She took a deep breath and wiped her eyes—thank goodness this wasn't a video call! "In fact, I've had some time to brainstorm and think through next steps for *All Good*, and I've come up with what I think is a foolproof way for the magazine to not just survive this new media landscape, but actually thrive. I'm eager to share my insights with you whenever you're ready."

"So that's the thing. Aly, we all know you've been through a great deal lately—"

Who was this "we all" he was referring to? Did *everyone* know about her brother now?

"James," cautioned Leticia.

He cleared his throat. "However, we're still working on getting that video taken down. You represent the *All Good* brand and Innovate as a company. Until the dust settles, we'd like you to fill the role of editorial director for *All Good*."

"Then who will be the EIC?" she asked. The room was starting to spin again, ever so slightly.

"Meagan is the interim editor in chief," said James. "We'll announce it on Monday."

Aly shook her head, the relief she'd been feeling already long gone. "You're putting *Meagan* in charge?" *Meagan, whose name you couldn't even remember?* "James, when you offered me the job, you said I was exactly the right person to take the magazine to the next level. I don't mean any disrespect to Meagan, but she . . . doesn't have the same skill set."

"I'm sure she doesn't, which is why you'll be her direct supervisor."

Translation: Aly would be doing the same job, but Meagan would get credit for it. "This is temporary, right?" said Aly feebly as she tried to reassure herself. "You said until the dust settles. When will that be, exactly?"

"I don't have a crystal ball, kiddo."

By which he meant: not anytime soon, and possibly never.

"But I want to be editor in chief." Aly clapped her hand over her mouth—she hadn't meant to blurt that out, however truthful it was.

"Change is never easy, but it's how we grow."

He sounded like he was reciting a line from a motivational poster. "James—"

"Aly, this is how it needs to be for now. We've already spoken to Meagan, and we'd like to have the two of you speak soon and work things out before you come back to the office."

"Okay," she said, and maybe it would be. "I can be back in the office first thing next week." She'd have to cancel on Harry, but he'd understand. After all, this wasn't just her career; it was her *life*.

James coughed. "Aly, it'll be good for you to take the whole month off as planned. Get some rest, clear your head. You'll probably never have an opportunity like this again."

No, and she never wanted to. She knew James was trying to be kind. But he had no idea what was good for her! Well, she'd show him. She was going to work on the magazine—with or without his help.

"I need my laptop," she said. "Is there any way you can mail it to me?"

"We can send a courier," said Linda.

"Um . . . I'm in Michigan right now, dealing with a family issue," said Aly.

"All the more reason to come back next month," said James.

"We can definitely FedEx it to you," said Linda.

"Thank you," said Aly. "I need my email turned back on, too."

"We'll have it reactivated," said Leticia. "It's my understanding that every message sent to you during your leave of absence will still be there for you to read."

Aly wasn't sure that a zillion unread emails was a victory, but it was better than the alternative.

"I'll put your new contract in the FedEx package with your laptop," said Linda. "You'll have it in twenty-four hours. I'll need you to sign the contract and send it back prior to your return to the office."

"Looking forward to having you back on board, Aly," said James. "I've got a one-thirty, but let's get a meeting on the books to discuss your ideas."

"Thank you. Thanks, all of you. I . . . I'm grateful that I'll be returning."

"We are, too," said James. "And this new position will be even better for you. You'll see."

Would it, though? Aly numbly clicked the "End Call" button. Then she slid out of the chair and onto the floor.

As she'd told Wyatt, *All Good* was the only thing that had gotten her out of bed after Luke had died. It was all she'd had.

And she still had it! Her job had changed, but this was a promotion—not a demotion. Once she stopped training Meagan, though, it wouldn't feel that way. Editorial directors had a hands-off role; although *All Good* had never had one, she knew that the position mostly served as a liaison between Editorial and Advertising. She wouldn't be editing pages anymore or holding meetings with her team. Correction: *the* team.

But she would still be at *All Good*. And she might even be able to ask for a raise.

So why wasn't she happy?

She was still lying on the ground when she heard Wyatt come in.

"You okay?" he said, walking over to her.

Aly looked up at him. "Yes."

He raised an eyebrow.

"No," she admitted. "I don't know."

"Want to tell me what happened?"

She shook her head. "Alcohol," she said. "I need alcohol."

"You're a teetotaler," he said, not unkindly. He'd laughed when she'd had three whole sips of her margarita at the Mermaid before pushing it aside, and he told her that next time, he'd order her lemonade. (She'd agreed that was probably the right call.)

"Not anymore," she said, pressing her lids together as James' voice echoed in her thoughts. *Meagan is the interim editor in chief. You'll be her direct supervisor.* "Please bring me something strong."

"It's going to be alright, Aly," he said. She wondered how he knew that her angst had nothing to do with him, but then it occurred to her that she wouldn't have asked him to bring her a drink if it had. So maybe he wasn't a complete Neanderthal.

He put a hand on her shoulder, but she didn't care if he'd regret touching her later or would soon tell her he hadn't meant to. A human hand, albeit one the size of a bear's paw, was nearly as soothing as a sedative, or so she assumed. (Meagan had offered Aly a Xanax that time she'd found her crying in the bathroom stall, but Aly had declined.) She wondered if she could ask him to lie beside her, to keep his hand on her until tomorrow, maybe even wrap his whole giant body around her until she lost consciousness.

"Booze," she commanded.

"You sure?" he said, peering at her.

She nodded, even though she knew he'd have to move his mitt to fetch her something.

"Okay. Wine?" he suggested. "Beer?"

"Stronger."

He grimaced. "As you wish. But I'm going to keep an eye on you."

She closed her eyes and listened to him tinkering at the bar cart on the other side of the living room. Their unfortunate collision at the Dunes already felt like it had happened years earlier. Maybe they could forget all that, and he could simply . . . take care of her.

Just for today.

"Try this," he said, sitting down beside her. The amber liquid inside the tumbler he handed her practically radiated fumes, but it was his scent that she inhaled. He smelled a little different—clean, like he had the other day, but woody, too. And he had sawdust on his shoulders. Had he been chopping down trees? Rolling around in a lumber mill? She was tempted to make a crack about him being a long way from Chicago's Gold Coast, but she couldn't find the energy.

She took a sip, then sputtered.

"You said strong," said Wyatt. "But I can still open a bottle of wine if you want."

"No, I like it," she said, because even though it tasted like lighter fluid, she knew that in very short order she was *going* to like it.

"It's bourbon. Your brother's favorite label." Luke hadn't shared Aly's alcohol aversion. Not only had he not worried about turning into their mother, he'd set standards for himself. Never more than two drinks; never two days in a row; and any time he felt like he had to have a drink was precisely when he opted not to.

"Journeyman," she said, remembering the bottle from the nearby distillery. "You should pour one for yourself."

Wyatt nodded. "Maybe just a splash," he said, rising from the sofa. "Is this . . . about him?" he asked when he returned. She could tell he didn't want to upset her.

"No," she said, and then had another sip. Whooo. Her chest felt like it was on fire. Was that a good thing or a bad thing? Good, she decided. Quite good.

She took one more drink, then glanced up at Wyatt and saw that he looked concerned. But not in the scared, *maybe-I-should-get-away-from-her* way that her childhood friend Jennifer Beddles had looked at her when she saw the purple bruise running down the side of Aly's face. Nor did he appear to have the rubbernecking fascination of her college boyfriend, Nick, who'd pushed for details even when she'd made it clear she didn't want to rehash the particulars of her past. Aside from Harry, Nick was the first, and last, man she'd discussed her childhood with.

No, Wyatt was looking at her . . . differently. Once again, she had the uncanny sensation that he already understood. But how?

"I got a promotion," she told him. "I thought I was going to get fired. But now I'm in a position I never asked for."

His lips curled. "Sounds terrible."

"I'm serious, Wyatt. I know I should be excited about it, but . . ."

"But you want your old job back."

She scrunched her nose. "Yes."

He nodded. "Luke said you're incredible at what you do."

"Did," she said, tossing back another swig. The bourbon was going down easier. She didn't intend to make a habit of drowning her feelings, but right now, it was just what she needed. "Now I supervise the woman who said terrible things about me behind my back and pretended to be my friend. We're a *team*!" she said, making air quotes around the word.

"Well, that's crap," said Wyatt. "Why don't you leave?"

The anger in his voice surprised her—and the certainty. "I don't want to. I have no idea what I would do if I wasn't at the magazine." Where would she work? Not in her office. Oooh, Meagan was probably sitting in Aly's refurbished Aeron chair right now, grinning like the Cheshire cat. Had this been her strategy all along?

"I know Luke would've already hired a lawyer to help you figure out your options." Wyatt was swirling his drink the way some people jiggled their legs when they couldn't figure out what to do with their energy. "Maybe you should do that. You could see if Roger knows someone."

"One more? Please?" she said, holding her glass out to him. "I could get it myself, but whatever you did was perfect."

"I literally just poured it," he said, the corner of his mouth rising. But then he narrowed his eyes. "I feel like I'm going to regret this later."

"I won't lure you into doing something you don't want to, if that's what you're worried about," she remarked. Then she blushed—or maybe it was just the booze warming her skin.

"I'm not," he said, raising an eyebrow, and even though she'd just alluded to what had happened between them the other day, she suddenly found herself working hard not to think about it. "I just don't want you to get too sloshed."

"I'm a grown woman, Wyatt."

He sighed, then stood and put his hand out for her tumbler. "Fine, hand it over. But I think we should go outside, maybe move a little, so the booze doesn't hit you too fast."

"Nope," she said. She knew that she was only delaying the inevitable and that disappointment and sadness were waiting just up ahead. But right now, she was feeling saucy. "Better if you and I steer clear of sand," she added before she could stop herself.

"Fair," he said, smiling slightly. "But I'm cutting you off after this one."

"Go ahead." Given that the room was already beginning to tilt on its axis, she probably wouldn't even be able to finish her second drink.

Wyatt returned with drinks and a bowl of potato chips.

"Eat," he said.

"Bossy," she said, sitting up. "I don't eat potato chips."

He pushed the bowl toward her. "You should. And you'll thank me later."

"Maybe," she said, reaching into the bowl. The chips were so greasy and salty that she had to wonder if she was already halfway to a coronary, but now was hardly the time to worry about her heart. "Theseareamazing," she said, her mouth still full.

"What was that?" said Wyatt, smiling down at her. "Did you just say, 'Thank you'?"

She nearly laughed, but then her face fell. That was the kind of joke that her brother would've made.

"What?" he said. "Did I say something wrong?"

"No." Wyatt was so hot and cold that she had no idea how he'd react if she told him the truth. She decided to anyway. "I . . . just wish Luke was here right now."

"I know," he said, sitting down beside her. "I do, too. Have you seen a therapist or anything?"

"No. Impossible to find one. Have you?" she said, certain he'd say no.

"Yeah. A couple times," he said.

"*You* went to therapy?" she said, incredulous. "Why?"

"You're not the only one who's lost someone."

It was terrible to lose a good friend. She didn't need to live through it to know that. Still, it wasn't the same as losing your sibling, especially when that sibling was literally the only person who understood you—like, *really* understood, because they'd lived through it, too. But buzzed or not, she knew better than to say that.

Wyatt gazed into his glass, and Aly took this as a cue to empty her own. She had a sneaking suspicion that *she* would regret it—and probably sooner rather than later—but she still rose to pour more bourbon. When she got back to the sofa, Wyatt was staring at her curiously.

"What?" she said, looking at her tumbler. Admittedly, it was about twice as full as when he'd served her. But now she wouldn't have to get up again to refill it.

"Nothing. Why don't we go walk?" he said, already on his feet.

"Don't plan to take no for an answer, huh?"

"I will, but not about this," he said, taking her hand to help her up.

"Fine," she said as she rose. "But I'm bringing my drink."

His eyebrows shot up again. "You do that."

"Stop judging me, Wyatt."

"Oh, I'm not. Think of me as your friendly roommate, who just wants to make sure you don't drink so much that you end your day hunched over a toilet bowl."

"Friendly, huh?" she scoffed, but she couldn't deny that she liked that he was still looking after her. It was a weakness on her part, wanting to be cared for. Once she got to the other side of this whole job debacle, she'd have to address that. Because she was now facing the rest of her life alone, and it was time to adjust accordingly.

Aly wobbled as they headed toward the lake. Wyatt must have noticed, because he looped his arm through hers to steady her as they descended the stairs. Arm in arm, they walked to the water's edge, and once they'd reached the beach, they wordlessly sat down in the sand.

"Luke didn't want it to be like this, you know," said Wyatt after a moment. Their shoulders were touching—something that was only possible because he slouched over his long legs, which he'd folded like a pretzel. He was obviously intent on destroying every disk in his spine, but she wasn't about to complain. It felt good, to feel someone else beside her.

"Like what?"

"He didn't want you to suffer after he was gone."

"How would you know?" Everything was a little blurry now, and the midafternoon day sun was blindingly bright, but she swore his cheeks pinkened when she said this.

"We talked about stuff like that," said Wyatt. "Worst-case scenarios. That kind of thing."

That was strange; Luke was a sunny-side-up kind of person. It must have been Wyatt's gloomy influence that made him talk about such things.

"Well, I *am* suffering. He never should have gotten in that stupid sailboat, let alone gone out on his own."

"I know. I think about that every single day. I never should have let it happen."

Hearing him admit this—that it had been a terrible mistake—did not make it any better, nor did his wrecked expression. In fact, she felt even worse. She drained the rest of her drink.

"It wasn't up to me, Aly," he said after a moment. "I begged him not to go. I still don't understand why he chose to go anyway."

"You asked him not to sail? Why didn't you tell me that?" She was slurring a bit. "I spent months hating you for not stopping him."

"I know. You're allowed to."

"You were there. Why did he go when he knew better? Did he have some kind of death wish or something?" Aly never would've asked this if she were sober, but now the words came tumbling out.

Wyatt glanced out at the horizon. "I . . . I'm not sure."

She didn't believe him, but she'd have to press for details later. For now, she was in serious need of several bags of potato chips and maybe a liter or two of water. Why would her mother willingly choose to put herself in this state? Being drunk felt *awful*.

"I think I need to go back," she said. "I'm tired."

Now he eyed her skeptically. "You're sloshed, huh?"

"Little bit."

She stumbled slightly as she rose, and Wyatt quickly put his arm around her waist. "Let me help you."

"And what if I say no?" she said. He was strong, and surprisingly solid for someone so lanky.

"Then I pretend I didn't hear you and help you anyway," he said.

Why was he being like this? "You don't need to be nice to me just because I'm Luke's sister," she blurted.

"I'm not."

"You are."

"Am *not*."

"I know you are, but what am I?" said Aly, and Wyatt laughed.

"You're something else, Aly Jackson," he said.

She hoped he couldn't feel the goose bumps on her skin. "Yeah, I get that a lot."

When they reached the house, she slid out of his grip and sat down on the stairs. Wow—she was really quite intoxicated. Maybe she could just stay here a while, until this icky feeling wore off.

"Come on. You're going to get sunburned if you sit out here. Alcohol makes it even easier to fry," said Wyatt.

"I can't," she mumbled. Her legs felt wooden, and her head was an anvil on her shoulders.

"Then I can," he said, and scooped her up into his arms like she was no heavier than a rag doll. "I think it's time for you to have some ibuprofen and take a nice, long nap."

"I don't nap, Wyatt," she said as he carried her through the door back inside. He didn't stop at the sofa, though; he started right up the stairs toward her room. "It's not possible for me."

"I think this might be an exception," he said, striding down the hallway with her.

Oh, she thought as he stopped in front of her bedroom. Was he going to make a move? Under normal circumstances, she'd give him hell, especially after his whole Jekyll-and-Hyde routine the other day. But now? Aly didn't hate this idea. Not at all.

"I like your face like that," she murmured, barely resisting the urge to run her hand along his stubble.

"I like your face like that, too," he said, somehow managing to turn her doorknob without letting go of her.

Did he? This was promising.

"But I like it even better when you're fully cognizant," he added as he set her down on the bed.

Cognizant? She knew that word. Didn't she? Oh, well. "Wyatt, lie down with me," she said as she sank into the downy pillow top. "I've already seen half of you naked." She was tired, so very tired, but she wasn't ready to abandon her quest yet. "Or just . . . you know. Touch me."

"I wish I could," he said so quietly that she could barely hear him. "I can't, Aly. Not if we're going to be sharing a home."

But it was one more conversation Aly wouldn't remember. Nor would she recall Wyatt tenderly tucking her in, drawing the curtains, and waiting until she was snoring softly to close the door behind him.

TWENTY-ONE

"Argh," groaned Aly. Her head was pounding. Where was she? And what time was it?

Oh. Fragments of the day before came back to her as she sat up and squinted in the bright morning light. She'd slept right through the afternoon and all the way through the night, which was probably the only reason she was semifunctional.

What *had* happened before she'd fallen asleep? As she peered at her puffy eyes and tangled hair in the bathroom mirror, she was forced to admit that she could only remember so much. There was the call with James; then Wyatt, being so nice to her; and their little jaunt to the beach; then him carrying her into the house . . .

Everything after that had vanished.

Her pulse quickened as she splashed water on her skin. Even if nothing were wrong with her—and obviously, there was—she'd made it worse by pumping toxins directly into her system. Maybe it was time to see a neurologist or a psychologist. Probably both.

She changed out of yesterday's clothes, which smelled of booze and just a hint of beach, and pulled on a clean shirt and pair of shorts. When she got downstairs, she found Wyatt sitting cross-legged on the counter.

"Morning," he said, lifting his mug to greet her. This was an unusual turn of events—him, practically perky, while she felt like a human rainstorm. "How are you feeling? Back on the wagon today, I assume?"

She blushed. "If by 'on the wagon' you mean never drinking again, then yes. Um . . . I don't remember going to bed last night." It was so mortifying to admit it, but she had to, in case she'd done something she needed to know about.

"You mean yesterday afternoon," he said with a wry smile.

"Uh, yeah. Did I do anything . . . you know. Stupid?"

Wyatt looked away, just for a moment, and her stomach sank. What had she done? "You honestly don't remember? I should've cut you off sooner."

"I think something might be wrong with me," she mumbled. "I'm sorry if I embarrassed myself."

He met her eyes. "You didn't embarrass anyone. And nothing's wrong with you."

She shook her head. "Obviously that's not true. First, I completely block out an argument with my coworkers. Now this?" She did not volunteer that this had happened to her when she was younger because—well, this was different.

He set his mug down and folded his arms over his chest. "Let's be clear—these are two separate things. You drank enough to black out, which is a pretty common phenomenon, however unpleasant. The situation with your coworkers is completely unrelated."

"How so?"

"I did a little research after you told me what happened."

He was hesitating; his shifting gaze told her so. "What is it? You don't have to tiptoe around me."

"You're right—I'm sorry. It's just that . . . I read that memory loss after an argument or a super stressful situation is usually a sign of post-traumatic stress disorder."

"PTSD?" she said, incredulous. "That's ridiculous. I haven't been through a war or something."

"No?" he said gently. "Luke said you guys had a really rough childhood."

"Millions of people have rough childhoods. And you didn't see Luke suddenly forgetting every stressful situation," said Aly, recalling the stories he'd told her about unreasonably demanding bosses and the toxic work culture he'd had to operate in.

"You're not Luke, Aly."

He could say that again. Luke never would've lost his temper in the first place.

"Different people respond differently to trauma," Wyatt continued. "And you just went through another trauma on top of that."

"I did," she conceded, "but I still don't get it. If that's the case, why aren't I forgetting everything right now?"

"I don't know, but I'm guessing some things are more stressful than others."

"Sure—but that doesn't explain what's wrong with *my brain*."

"From what I read, PTSD can shrink your hippocampus. That's where memories are stored."

"Great. So I'm going to get early-onset dementia," she said flatly.

"I didn't read anything like that. It sounds like it's more of a defense mechanism that kicks in when your brain really thinks you need to be protected. Aly . . ." His smile, which was disarmingly kind, almost made her forget how upsetting this was. Except she was only warming to Wyatt because they'd spent so much time together. Forget PTSD—she had textbook Stockholm syndrome. "You've been through a ton lately," he said. "Doesn't it make you feel better to at least know why you might have forgotten the incident?"

Well, yes . . . but also no. Because erasing anything unpalatable from her memory was not how she wanted to operate.

Then again, it was a shame she hadn't forgotten that Meagan now had her dream job.

"Listen, I'm no expert," said Wyatt. "I'm just telling you what I found on some university health websites. The point is you shouldn't feel bad. There's nothing wrong with you."

"Tell that to my shrunken hippocampus," she muttered.

"There are ways to treat it if you think it's more than a one-off. Neurofeedback, stress reduction, that kind of stuff. It's probably worth talking to someone."

A deep dive into her miserable past? She'd take memory loss over that. "Maybe later," she said.

"Okay," he said evenly. He glanced at the microwave. "Uh-oh— gotta go. I have an appointment."

This was more information about his whereabouts than he'd ever willingly volunteered. And yet it wasn't remotely satisfactory.

He slid off the counter, then glanced at her before grabbing his backpack from the hook beside the door. "I'll be back tonight. Call me if you need anything, okay?"

Oh, she needed something, alright. But what she needed most was to rid herself of the urge to ask this grumpy, too-tall, entirely unsuitable roommate to fill that need.

TWENTY-TWO

Mari Perez was a hugger. And not just any kind of hugger; she pulled you in and held you tight, only to release you seconds before you started to wonder if she'd stolen her moves from a python.

"I'm so glad you called me!" she said to Aly. They stood outside of the small coffee shop in downtown Douglas where they'd agreed to meet. "I wasn't sure if you would."

Aly hadn't been sure, either, but now that she knew she'd be in town the rest of the month, she needed to find someone other than Wyatt to talk to. "I just thought since I was here, we should try to catch up," she said, holding open the door to the coffee shop.

"Well, I like that thought! Now, tell me everything," said Mari.

"I will—but first, coffee's on me," said Aly.

"Only if you let me get the next one."

"Deal," she said with a smile. It felt a little odd to speak so casually with someone who she'd once addressed as Ms. Perez. Then again, Mari had the same sort of effortless grace that Luke had and had always acted as though she was simply an older, wiser friend to her students. After they'd retrieved their coffees from the bar and had begun walking toward the water, Aly said, "Well, a lot's already changed since I saw you last week."

"Really? How so?" Mari was an ambler, but for once, Aly didn't mind slowing down. Douglas was every bit as charming as Saugatuck, but smaller and rarely as crowded. Aly could feel the knot between her shoulders beginning to loosen as they walked along, pausing to admire the sidewalk displays outside of art studios and shops.

"To start, I'm not the editor in chief of *All Good* anymore," said Aly.

"Oof," said Mari, putting her hand on Aly's arm. "You okay?"

"I should be," said Aly, smiling tightly. "They promoted me to editorial director. That's a big position."

"Judging by the look on your face, you're not excited about that."

"I mean . . . I thought they were going to fire me, so this is an improvement. And I *am* itching to get back to New York and get to work." Even she could tell that her voice lacked conviction. "It's just that I was hoping I'd be going back to my regular job."

"You thought they'd fire you? That's hard to picture. What happened?" asked Mari.

"You sure you want to know?" said Aly.

"Only if you want to tell me."

Aly knew Mari wouldn't judge her, so she told her about the Incident. When she finished, Mari pretended to be horrified. "Oh no— sounds like you acted like a human in public. I'm so sorry that you let down anyone who mistook you for a robot."

"That's funny, but I guess you're right," said Aly, who did feel a little better. "The fact is, though, it had to be really bad for them to remove me from my job when I was doing it so well. For all I know, I said something extremely offensive."

"No," said Mari bluntly. "If it had been anything like that, they would have just fired you. And they sure as heck wouldn't have waited almost two weeks to do it. I may not know about your industry, but I know how the world works."

"Maybe," allowed Aly. She trusted Mari's instincts—if only because during high school, she'd innately understood that Aly's home situation left something to be desired and that she needed her help.

Mari took a sip of her coffee, then regarded Aly. "So if you don't really want the job, have you thought anymore about what you *do* want to do?"

"What else is there?" said Aly honestly. "If I really don't like the gig, I'll put feelers out for another editor in chief position." Another magazine would never matter to her as much as *All Good*. But if the past year had taught her anything, it was that life was filled with disappointments. Best if she at least *tried* to get used to that.

They'd reached a small, grassy park that ran along the river. "What about writing?" asked Mari as they sat down at a bench in front of the water. "That was always a strength of yours."

Aly chewed on her lip, considering this. The days when a writer could make a decent living contributing to magazines were long gone. Anyway, she wasn't sure that would be the best use of her time. "I like writing," she said, "but I'm better at helping other people improve their writing. You know, coming up with ideas and editing and whatnot."

"I bet there's a good market for that sort of thing. Maybe you could start your own company."

"Probably, yeah," said Aly. It wasn't a bad idea, but she was hardly jazzed about the idea of going corporate or becoming a consultant. And yet her lack of enthusiasm annoyed her. What was wrong with her, that she couldn't just accept that so-so was far better than bad? "Thanks for brainstorming for me."

"Of course. And if you're looking for something to do over the next few weeks," said Mari with a sly smile, "the kids in the area always need help with reading and writing. I'm sure you remember that from high school."

Aly nodded—she did. She'd breezed through her assignments and often spent the extra time helping other high schoolers craft their papers or get a handle on their homework. She'd never really fit in, let alone been popular, but the other students had accepted her more when they realized she had something to offer them.

"Yeah, things haven't really gotten much better. They're worse, if I'm honest. Teachers are stretched thin, and there aren't a lot of outside resources to help. I'll never understand why this country doesn't want to spend more money on education," said Mari, a shadow falling across her face.

"I wish I could help, but I'm not really good with kids," said Aly. Carefree children—the ones who ran around and laughed and misbehaved, knowing their parents would perhaps scold them but that would be the end of it—made her anxious, and kind of sad, too. The production manager, Helena, had brought her seven-year-old, Octavia, to *All Good* in April for Take Your Child to Work Day. Octavia was polite, if not eerily well-spoken, and Helena had proudly trotted her over to Aly's office. But Octavia had taken one look at Aly, who was going over page proofs, and announced, "I'd like to see the break room, please." To be honest, Aly felt more relieved than insulted when the girl left.

Perhaps Harry would help her learn how to be normal with Beckett, but as this had yet to be seen, she was in no position to mingle with children. High schoolers? Maybe. But certainly not those young enough to still be learning to read.

"I understand, but you might also be surprised," said Mari. "If you're up for volunteering, I know of an amazing children's center right in Saugatuck. You can lend a hand for a day or become a long-term volunteer. It just requires a quick background check and a willingness to show up."

"Okay," said Aly, knowing full well she wasn't going to take Mari up on this offer. With just two weeks left in town, it wouldn't really be worth it to volunteer.

"So, want to tell me more about the gentleman you were eating with?" said Mari.

"Wyatt? He's no gentleman," retorted Aly, but then she thought of the way he'd carried her up the stairs and put her to bed. "He's not that bad, though," she admitted. "Sometimes we talk about my brother. I've

138

been having a rough time since he's been gone." It felt good to say this out loud—to stop pretending that there wasn't a Luke-shaped hole in the center of her life.

"I'll bet." Mari gave Aly a quick sideways hug. "I said this before, but I really am sorry."

"Me, too," said Aly softly. "I don't know if I'm ever going to get over this. I don't really know how to feel good anymore, and it seems like that's never going to change."

"Probably. But maybe we're not supposed to get over things like this. I should know—I lost my husband, José, last year."

"Oh, Mari, I'm so sorry. I had no idea."

Mari smiled sadly. "No wonder—we haven't seen each other in ages. Point is, I get it. Everyone else acknowledges how bad it is at first, but then over time, they move on, and you're still carrying around that heavy loss. I don't know." She looked out at the water, which was covered with tiny, green duckweed leaves. "Call me crazy, but I don't really mind the weight. It reminds me of how much I love José."

Love. Not *loved.* He was still real for her, just as Luke was for Aly. Her eyes welled with tears. This was the first comforting thing anyone had said to her since Luke had died.

They sat in silence for a few minutes, staring out at the river. Then Mari said, "So, anything happening between you and Wyatt?"

Aly laughed. "No way. We're roommates for the time being—Luke left us both his house." She sighed deeply. "I don't know what my brother was thinking. He knew we didn't get along."

The corners of Mari's lips turned up. "Maybe he was thinking you two would be good for each other."

"He's a cranky slob who wants to go wherever the wind blows him. He's the *opposite* of good for me."

"Is that so."

Aly eyed Mari, who was still smiling to herself. "What do you mean?"

"Oh, nothing. Just, you know. Could've fooled me."

"Even if he wanted to, and he doesn't," said Aly as Mari snorted in dissent, "we *can't* be involved. I have plans to leave, and as Wyatt himself pointed out, it would ruin everything."

"So you've discussed this."

Aly blushed in response. "Maybe."

"Aly, I know we haven't seen each other in a while, but I remember how much you relied on your goals and plans. Sometimes what got you here won't take you there, though. You know?"

Aly did not, in fact, know. But she didn't want to disappoint Mari, so she nodded like she understood.

"Just leave a little space for spontaneity," added Mari. "You might be pleasantly surprised by what happens when you let life happen to you."

TWENTY-THREE

Spontaneity was for surprise parties and skinny-dipping—not living arrangements, and certainly not love. Mari was nuts, Aly decided as she drove home. It didn't matter if she'd never steered Aly wrong in the past. Aly wasn't the same person she was nearly two decades ago. Besides, Mari didn't even know Wyatt!

As lovely as it had been to see her old counselor, Aly filed Mari's advice in her mental wastebasket . . . right beside whatever she'd said to Meagan and Ashleigh. Because Aly knew one thing, and that was that she needed to focus on the big picture and not inconsequential distractions like Wyatt.

He was vacuuming the living room when she got home, but he quickly turned off the machine when he saw her. His shorts hung low on his hips, and he was wearing another one of the rags he called T-shirts.

"Vacuuming?" she asked as she approached. "What's gotten into you?"

"Nothing," he said, wiping his brow on the back of his arm. "I'm just trying to chip in more."

She eyed him suspiciously. "Thank you?"

"You're welcome." He tilted his head and regarded her for a moment, then reached toward her face. Aly flinched, then stepped back, but it wasn't until she saw Wyatt's stunned expression that she realized what she'd done.

"There's a leaf in your hair," he said quietly. "I was just going to pull it out."

Aly turned away, mortified. "Sorry," she mumbled. "I should've figured."

"Aly." His voice had dropped an octave. "Please look at me."

"No, thanks," she said, but after a moment she turned back toward him. When she did, his eyes were blazing.

"Don't ever apologize for that."

"For what?" she said flatly.

"You know, and so do I." He put his hand to his forehead and took a deep breath. "I know your father was terrible to you, and I hate him for that," he said after a moment. "If he ever dared to show up again, I'd run him out of town so fast he wouldn't remember having been here. And don't get me started on your mother."

"My dad wasn't that bad," Aly said softly. She began mentally cataloguing his virtues, as she'd done many times over the years—because who wanted to hate their own father? Dan was always cracking jokes to make strangers laugh, and some of them seemed to think he was funny enough. And he'd liked to brag about how well she did in school. He'd sent her mother money after he took off, which had helped keep a roof over their heads.

Most importantly, he'd finally left. His rage had only intensified as Aly and Luke had gotten older, and by the time she was in her teens, Aly sometimes worried that he'd accidentally, or even not so accidentally, kill her. He'd come terrifyingly close to striking her temple and had on occasion hit her so hard, he'd given her whiplash that took weeks to recover from.

Really, it was no wonder her brain malfunctioned these days.

"He was worse than bad. Luke told me how horrible he was to you two. My parents are pretty awful, but him . . ." Aly couldn't read

Wyatt's expression. He looked furious, but . . . protective, too. Just like Luke had always been.

But as Aly regarded him, she recognized that Wyatt wasn't trying to be her brother. And although he was angry, she wasn't afraid of him—not even a little. She knew somehow that he would never hurt her, and not just because Luke must have trusted Wyatt immensely in order to leave him the house, too. Why *had* Luke chosen to do that? Was Mari right? Or had something been wrong with Luke at the end? Plenty of people quit their jobs with no plan in mind. But to also buy a home where none of his friends lived—and then go on a sailing trip that was so clearly destined for disaster? Maybe she wasn't the only one whose brain wasn't working quite right. Luke had always been Teflon tough, but Aly had to admit that trauma might have affected her brother more than she'd realized.

"Your father was a monster," growled Wyatt. "Look at you, Aly. How could anyone hurt you?"

She frowned, remembering how she'd vowed to stop thinking she needed his care. "I don't need anyone to take care of me."

"*Everyone* needs someone to take care of them."

"Oh yeah?" She eyed him. "Who do you have taking care of you?"

"No one. So ask me how I know," he said bluntly. "And for the record, I told Luke I'd take care of you. Even if you don't like it, I'm trying to do right by the person we both loved."

He looked so raw, so vulnerable, that it broke something open in her.

"When did you agree to that, exactly?" she asked, but her voice had lost its sharp edge.

"A long time ago, Aly. Way before he . . . before his death," said Wyatt, who seemed to have lost his train of thought. Then, with more certainty, he said, "He knew he was the only family you could count on. That if anything happened, you wouldn't have a safety net." Aly's father's family was scattered around the West Coast and had never tried to have a relationship with her and Luke. Her mother had been an only child, and her parents had died when she was in her early twenties.

"Fine," she said. "But you realize that this means you *are* only being nice to me because you have to."

"No, Aly." He stepped closer to her, so close that she could feel heat radiating from him. "I'm being nice to you because I don't know how not to."

Aly willed herself not to look away from him. He was right—this would ruin everything, probably immediately.

And yet she wanted it. Badly.

"Then why are you just standing there?" she whispered.

"Because I am definitely not part of your plan. And this," he said, gesturing between them, "is *not* what your brother had in mind."

His pupils were enormous as he gazed down at her, and Aly thought her legs might buckle. *So that whole weak-knees thing is literal,* she thought. And yet she felt emboldened—impulsive, even, and for once she didn't hate that label.

"You're the one who wants to ditch the plans," she said, inching even closer to him. "Don't you want to be spontaneous, Wyatt? That's what you like, right?"

"You want spontaneity, Aly?"

At once, his mouth was on hers—insistent, searching, starving.

This, she thought as Wyatt's hands cupped her face like he wanted to protect her even as he devoured her. *This is what it feels like to be alive.* They were roommates; he'd already told her he could not, and would not, do this with her. And yet the rational part of her brain was shutting down fast, and she wanted him to carry her straight to her bed. Because she had not felt like this in—well, ever.

And now that she had, she had zero interest in returning to reality.

"How is this?" He pressed her against the living room wall and kissed her again. "For spontaneity?"

"Good," she gasped between kisses. "But I think you can do better."

"You have no idea," he said, picking her up so that her legs wrapped around his waist, as he put his mouth to her neck. "You honestly have no idea how much better I want to do."

Every inch of her hummed with desire as his mouth trailed from her throat to her collarbone. "Show me," she said.

"This could mess everything up," he warned, making no attempt to stop touching her everywhere his hands could reach.

"Wyatt, everything is already messed up," she said, running her fingers along his jaw just as she'd thought about doing dozens of times over the past few days. They would regret this. That much was certain. But when was the last time she did something for the sheer pleasure of it? Heck, when was the last time she'd been *capable* of experiencing pleasure? She honestly couldn't recall. She saw now how very perfunctory intimacy with Seth had been. And even before Luke's death, she'd spent so much of her life jumping from one accomplishment to the next, never truly experiencing the happiness each was supposed to bring.

"Are you sure?" he said.

"Please," she said, pressing her mouth against his neck. "Now."

Yet again, Wyatt carried her upstairs—but this time, Aly remembered everything.

The way he pulled her shirt over her head, then tore off his own. How her skin felt electric as their limbs tangled together. How he bent over her on the bed in reverence and kissed every inch of her until she couldn't take it another second. The way they both cried out when he entered her, and immediately found a rhythm so good, so satisfying that Aly marveled as she moved beneath him. *Now* she understood the difference between having sex and having someone make love to you. When she came, she didn't think about how her face looked, and she didn't squeeze her eyes closed. Instead, she stared up at Wyatt, who was staring back in wonder, and she held his gaze until he had finished, too.

Afterward, they lay side by side on the bed, breathing hard and staring at the ceiling. Only then did Aly's fear begin to resurface. Was he going to tell her he shouldn't have? That he'd somehow betrayed Luke or made a terrible mistake?

But instead of saying anything like that, Wyatt leaned onto one elbow and kissed her tenderly. Then he whispered, "No matter what happens next, I want you to know that I'll never hurt you, Aly. I promise."

TWENTY-FOUR

"Aly?"

"Yeah?" she said.

It was early the following morning, and Wyatt had just stirred beside Aly in bed. She hadn't expected to literally spend the night with him, but after they'd scarfed down sandwiches he'd thrown together for dinner, they'd immediately gone back up to her bedroom. Once they'd finally exhausted each other, they had fallen asleep side by side. If she'd dreamt, she couldn't remember it, and she'd awoken feeling downright refreshed.

"I need to tell you something," said Wyatt, who was still lying beneath the covers.

Her stomach sank—so much for refreshed! How foolish she'd been, to spend the evening convincing herself that the other shoe wouldn't drop. It *always* dropped.

"Are you going to tell me why you were so rude to me when we met in New York all those years ago?" she said, raising her eyebrows. "Because that was *so* weird. I hated you after that."

He grimaced. "You want the truth?"

"You know I do."

"I thought you were beautiful, and if you hadn't been Luke's sister, I would've asked you out immediately. But you were, and I didn't want to creep on my best friend's sister."

She laughed. "Yet here you are. Creeping."

"Little bit," he said. His expression shifted. "That's not what I was going to say, though."

"Is this about Luke?" she said, because she'd just recalled what Wyatt had said about her brother the other day: *I never should have let it happen. I still don't understand why he chose to go anyway.* She'd been too inebriated to dwell on it then. Now it struck her as curious, maybe even ominous. Did Wyatt know something he wasn't telling her?

Now he looked upset. "Sort of," he said.

"Wyatt," she said, rubbing the sleep from her eyes, "just tell me. The longer you make me wait, the more my imagination is going to spin out of control."

He glanced across the room, away from her, and her stomach lurched again. Then he said, "My sister died when I was thirteen."

Aly startled. "I . . . don't even know what to say. I'm sorry. I had no idea." Her chest flooded with guilt. *Of course* he'd understood her pain. He'd lived through it.

"It's okay," he said, meeting her eyes. "I don't really talk about it."

"I'm so sorry. Thank you for telling me."

He closed his eyes for a moment. "I am, too. I just thought you should know why I've been moping around. Obviously, losing Luke was awful all by itself. But it also brought up some old issues for me. Then when you got here, and I saw how you were struggling . . . It's just been a lot to handle. I'm sorry, Aly. I know I've been weird. I'm trying not to be, but it's hard sometimes. And now we're doing this," he said, smiling softly at her. "I might get even weirder."

"It's okay," she said, throwing her arms around him. She wanted to kiss him until he forgot; she wanted to weep. What was wrong with this world, that the best people were taken too soon? "What was your sister's name?" she asked.

"Ruby. She was eight. She had pediatric glioblastoma—it's a type of brain cancer. They have better treatments for it now, but back then . . . nothing worked."

She hugged him. "Oh, Wyatt."

"I know," he said, kissing her forehead. "I know you get it."

"Do you have any other siblings?"

He shook his head. "My parents weren't control freaks until after everything happened with Ruby. At first, they just wanted to keep me . . . alive, I guess. But it wasn't long before they started wanting to orchestrate every last detail—who I dated, where I went to school, what I did for a living, even which apartment I chose and what kind of clothes I wore. My mother called me twice a day, no matter what, just to check in."

"Called? Doesn't she still?" Aly had seen his phone light up with her name several times since she'd bumped into him at the café. Each time, he had declined the call.

"Yes, but we're not talking right now. I needed . . . some space," he said with a pained smile. "It was ugly when I left banking and left Chicago—my father basically told me I was a disappointment, so I decided to stop being around to disappoint him. I hate cutting them off, but it was the only way to get them to stop attempting to micromanage me; they literally wouldn't stop telling me what to do with my life. Anyway, it's not the same as you and Luke, but . . . I thought you should know that about me."

"Except it *is* the same." Worse, maybe. Aly had been lucky enough to live thirty-three years with Luke, and Wyatt had only had eight with Ruby. She suddenly felt like an ungrateful jerk. "Thank you for telling me," she repeated.

"I should've sooner."

"You did when you were ready."

Now he smiled broadly. "You surprise me sometimes, Aly Jackson."

"Oh yeah?" she said, raising her eyebrows. "How do I do that, exactly?"

"I have no idea, but feel free to keep doing whatever you did last night."

"Which time?" she said saucily.

"All of them," he said, leaning toward her.

He was really good at kissing. And . . . a lot of other things, too. Was that why she'd had such a strong aversion to him—because deep down, she knew that the moment she gave in to his magnetic pull, she wouldn't want to do anything else?

But as he pressed his body against hers, she decided that just for this one time, she was going to focus on the present, rather than the past or the future. Because although he'd opened up about Ruby, she couldn't help but think that there was something else Wyatt wasn't telling her—and that if she tried to find out what it was, this little fling they were having would end long before she hightailed it back to New York.

TWENTY-FIVE

"Do you want to go out this evening?" Wyatt said to Aly. They'd just finished lunch and were stretched out on lounge chairs on the porch.

"Out?" said Aly blankly. Wait—was he talking about a *date*?

"You. Me. An activity that requires being fully clothed," he said, winking at her. "I can't promise the evening will end that way, but we could at least start with conversation and good company."

Aly liked spending time with him; she couldn't pretend she didn't. But going on a date was something else entirely. "What do you have in mind?" she ventured.

"Well, we could rent a boat and go up and down the river, then go out to dinner somewhere."

Her spine stiffened. "No boats."

"Right," he said, cringing. "That was stupid of me."

"No, it's okay. I'm just . . ."

"Not crazy about being on the water." He reached over to squeeze her hand lightly. "I get it. I should have thought it through more before I suggested it."

"Really—it's fine," she said, and she meant it. "But what about a hike? There's a state park nearby that's supposed to be nice and leads right to the lake."

"I'd love to do that, but for tonight, I was thinking maybe something where we could sit and talk?"

So there it was. But one date wasn't exactly a proposal. She could do this. "Okay—that sounds good," she said, and it was at least half-true.

Wyatt must have detected the other half because he leaned forward and lifted his sunglasses to examine her. "You feeling alright about this?"

She wasn't sure if his definition of *this* was the same as hers—and she wasn't about to ask. He'd just barely gotten away from people who wanted to control everything about him, right down to the most inconsequential details. Whereas for Aly, opening a new planner would forever feel like Christmas; deciding on the particulars of a trip excited her as much as the experience itself. She was who she was. But when it came to Wyatt, there was no need to define their affair, let alone discuss it at length. Especially since it would be so short-lived.

"What about it?" she said nonchalantly.

"Well, we've now slept together four times."

"Four, huh? Didn't know you were counting," she said. Her stomach dipped as he grinned playfully at her. Just being around him made her entire body buzz, and it was hard to focus on much of anything other than him. Aly had heard about this kind of passion—but now she understood why people composed sonnets and songs and entire symphonies about it. Though she'd never gone skydiving or surfing, she was still willing to bet the rush of really, *really* good sex was the most alive a person could feel. It was such a revelation that she wasn't even upset that it had taken her thirty-four years to experience it. (Poor Seth! Maybe he would eventually discover it for himself one day.)

Still, passion had the shelf life of a basket of berries. It could not, and would not, last.

"That's right," he said.

"That's a lot, given you thought we shouldn't be doing this," she teased, already grateful for the turn their conversation had taken.

"Do I look like I'm *not* okay with it?" he said, leaning toward her to run a finger up and down her arm.

She shivered with pleasure. "No."

"Good." He leaned in and kissed her slowly, then said, "Because I'm not ready to stop."

"Me, neither," she murmured. "Why don't we finish this conversation in the shower?" Going at it in the shower had always sounded complicated to Aly, and even dangerous—how, exactly, did one not break a hip while thrashing about like a single-celled amoeba on a slippery surface? But danger was no longer a deterrent.

"Now?" he questioned.

"Yes. You look . . . filthy," she said, pretending to be disgusted, and the next thing she knew he was chasing her into the bathroom as she squealed with laughter.

Later, after Aly had toweled off and wandered downstairs to get a snack—all of this physical exertion made her ravenous—she opened her laptop, which Innovate had overnighted to her along with her new contract. They'd offered her an extra ten thousand dollars, which was still less than her old salary, as well as a far more generous bonus structure for any increased revenue and circulation while she served as editorial director. She was still struggling to feel excited about her new role, even though Jada and Helena had both texted their congratulations. Because it *was* cause for celebration . . . wasn't it?

As she'd predicted, her inbox contained hundreds of unread emails. Most were pitches from publicists and invitations for editorial meetings that she'd already missed. Seth still hadn't contacted her, but Aly was tired of wondering if he was going to ask Goodwill to come pick up her things; it was time to be proactive. She sent him a quick text asking him to FedEx her the few pieces of jewelry she hadn't packed, as well as the two small albums that contained photos of her and Luke as children, and to put the rest in storage until she returned to the city and found a place.

He texted back immediately. *Not a problem. You okay?*

No doubt James had told him about her so-called promotion. *I'm good,* she said, because it was at least somewhat true. *You?*

Same. Maybe we can get coffee or a drink when you're back in town.

She wondered if he was just saying that to be nice, or if he truly missed her.

Sure, she wrote back. *I'll reach out.*

Great. Take care of yourself, Aly.

It was like texting with a virtual stranger, she thought, shaking her head in wonder. It wasn't Seth's fault that she'd barely thought about him since she'd arrived in Michigan. Yet it was unsettling to think that she'd spent three years—three whole years of her life!—with someone she could move on from so easily. Luke had asked her if she was sure about Seth. "Really sure?" he'd said when Aly had called him to tell him they were moving in together.

"As sure as a person can be. Seth's perfect for me," she'd responded.

Luke had grunted his disbelief. "I don't want you to be alone, Al, but there's nothing lonelier than being with someone who isn't right for you."

He should know; he hadn't had a serious girlfriend since college. "You're an odd duck, Luke," she'd responded.

But now she couldn't help but think that he'd been onto something.

She was deleting pointless pitches when she spotted Meagan's name in the middle of her inbox. So she *had* reached out. Was Aly shocked? Unsurprised? Both, she decided. She didn't really feel like reading the email but made herself do it anyway, since they would soon be working side by side again—and Meagan *would* need her help, after all. Really, *All Good* needed her help, and that mattered most. No matter what, it would never be "just a magazine" to Aly. It was her life manual; it was a printed catalogue of her childhood hopes and dreams. And reminding herself of that stirred up the excitement she'd been missing since her last conversation with James.

She scanned Meagan's message.

Hi Aly,

I just wanted to let you know how sorry I am about what I said at the salad bar. I was just letting off some steam. You know how stressful this business can be and I was reeling a bit from the news that we were in trouble (you remember I turned down that job at Shape last year? I was feeling like maybe I shouldn't have). I never meant to hurt you or imagined that someone would tape you.

I have so many ideas I want to share with you. Can we catch up before you get back in the office? Call me anytime.

xo,

Meagan

Even Meagan's signature made Aly squirm with discomfort. Her barbed comments at the salad place shouldn't have come as a surprise—hadn't Aly listened to her say crappy things about Ellen, as well as many other people they'd worked with? Even though Aly hadn't participated in the gossip, she'd condoned it with her silence . . . which had helped perpetuate it; she realized that now.

Still. Aly might be able to eventually forgive Meagan—but she'd rather just forget her. She had no desire to speak with her before she returned to Innovate. Or after, for that matter. And she sure as heck didn't want to work with her on *All Good.*

And yet she was going to have to.

As a child, whenever Aly accidentally hurt herself—slamming her fingers in a drawer or tumbling after missing a stair—Luke would make sure she was okay. Then, once her tears had dried, he'd say with mock sternness, "Don't do that!" It made her laugh every time. But now she saw the brilliance lurking behind his playful advice.

She'd need to make sure she never made the same mistakes with Meagan ever again.

Aly hit the "Delete" button, then listened to her computer make the satisfying crumpled-paper sound that confirmed Meagan's email had gone to the trash (where it belonged, she thought to herself).

She heard Wyatt's footsteps behind her before she even saw him. "Hey. You ready to head out?"

"Hey yourself," she said, smiling back at him. He'd changed into a fresh but worn T-shirt and had trimmed his beard so that it was close cropped, which turned out to be just how she liked it. "I was just going through some work emails."

Wyatt leaned against the counter. "Oh yeah? You tell them to shove off?"

"I did nothing of the sort," she said, laughing. "And this time, I'm pretty sure I would've remembered if I had."

"Progress." He ran a hand through his hair, and her stomach flipped. "Want to head out?"

"Let's go," she said. Aly wasn't sure why she suddenly felt nervous. They were already sleeping together and had dined out before, the time when they'd run into Mari. This didn't have to be any different.

It felt like it was, though.

It was just Wyatt, she reminded herself, and then without thinking, she put her hand out. He took it and laced his fingers with hers like it was the most natural thing in the world.

I am holding hands with Wyatt Goldstein, she thought as they walked to his car. *That doesn't mean that we're in a relationship. It's just two friends-with-benefits having a meal together in a public place.*

But when he opened her car door for her, it struck her that it was as significant as the first time they slept together.

And Aly wasn't sure what to think about that.

~

Half an hour later, her nerves had barely settled.

Wyatt must have noticed, because he took her hand from across the table and said, "You sure this is okay?"

"Of course," she said with a terse smile.

"We could ask to be seated inside if you want," he said.

She shook her head. They were at another riverside restaurant and had snagged a table at the end of the long patio overlooking the water. "I don't mind that at all," she said. "I just have a lot on my mind. You know, with the situation with Meagan and everything." She'd rambled about the email in the car ride over.

"Got it," he said, smiling at her. It was almost hard to believe he was the same grunting caveman who'd scared the living daylights out of her the day she'd arrived. He looked . . . really happy. "Well, try not to think about it too much."

This was easier said than done. As Aly regarded him, she realized she knew only the big-picture details of his life. But the finer points, and the memories that he wanted to remember—those remained a mystery.

"Tell me about Ruby. If you want," she added quickly.

"No, I do." His face lit up again. "She was really funny, even when she was tiny—my mom says she was born with a huge smile on her face. She used to play practical jokes on me all the time, and even though I almost always figured it out in advance, I would go along with it anyway because I loved to see her laugh."

Aly couldn't help but grin back at him. "Did she ever fool you?"

He nodded. "This one time she put frosting all over an old kitchen sponge and said she'd made me a tiny cake. I never saw it coming and bit right into it. It was absolutely disgusting, but Ruby was cracking up so hard I couldn't even be mad at her." He sighed deeply and met Aly's gaze. "Man. I haven't thought about that in ages. Thank you."

"For what?" she asked.

"Asking," he said. "Most people don't. They think it'll be too sad or strange or whatever, so they just act like I never had a sister. Do you ever get that?"

"Sort of?" She bit her lip. "I guess it's kind of my fault that they don't—I barely told anyone after Luke died. I didn't want everyone bringing it up all the time." She hesitated, then admitted, "I didn't want anyone to think I couldn't do my job, either. I know that sounds terrible, but it's true."

"Oh, Aly," said Wyatt. "I'm sorry."

"Thanks," she said quietly. "I probably should be more open about it."

"Maybe, or maybe not. It's still pretty new for you."

"Yeah."

They sat wordlessly for a few minutes, staring at the water as boats drifted by.

After their server brought them drinks and bread, Wyatt cleared his throat. "Hey. I was thinking . . ."

On instinct, she steadied herself. What good ever followed that phrase?

For once, he looked like the nervous one. "Why don't you stay for the summer, Aly?"

Her eyes bulged. What was he even *saying*? "You know I can't."

"Says who?" he asked, cocking his head.

Why not suggest she tour Antarctica on an ice floe while he was at it, or start applying Rogaine to her chin so she could join the circus? She'd never heard of anything so impractical in her entire life. "Says my employer," she said firmly.

Wyatt frowned. "You haven't actually asked if you could extend your leave. And you don't really want the job they just offered you."

"That's not what I said. I won't know if I like it until I go do it," she said, hoping she sounded more certain than she felt.

"I've been trying to figure out how to tell you this." He shoved his hands in his pockets and looked away. "Luke's life insurance . . ."

"What about it?" she demanded.

He looked at her again. "It's . . . a lot," he said sheepishly.

"Define *a lot*."

"More than a million." He must've known that this news would be staggering—not just the amount itself, but the fact that he'd waited until now to share it with her—because the tone he used was one that Aly would've used to inform someone she'd accidentally run over their cat.

She was so stunned that it took her nearly a minute to speak. "And you didn't tell me this earlier because . . . ?"

"Well . . . I . . . uh, kind of didn't follow up with the paperwork until you arrived." He had the grace to look mortified. "And I was waiting to find out the details before I said too much, because I knew it was going to change things for you."

"Uh, you think?" she said.. "Trust me—I've been an ostrich about Luke's death, too. But you're the executor of his estate. Didn't you think you should have checked?" Even as she said this, though, she realized that it wouldn't have changed much of anything before she arrived in Saugatuck. She wouldn't have moved out of Seth's apartment—because she didn't think anything was wrong with their relationship. If anything, she probably would have volunteered to reduce her salary even more than she already had.

He leaned in toward her. "I'm sorry. I guess I was doing worse than I even realized."

"It's okay," she said. "I get it."

"Thank you," he said. "The real point is, Aly, you're about to have enough money to take a *decade* or two off if you want, and that's even without selling the house. Or many more if you play your cards right. I know a thing or two about investing. I could help you."

"You hate investing," she said, though mostly she was thinking that she didn't want the money. In fact, she'd happily throw it into the ocean or burn it in a bonfire if it would bring Luke back.

But nothing would bring Luke back. And although she was loath to admit it, he would've wanted her to use the money.

"He wanted you to have it," said Wyatt, echoing her thoughts.

Aly blinked back tears as the truth sank in: this was the last way Luke was ever going to be able to take care of her.

"Are you okay?" asked Wyatt. He picked up his chair and moved it right next to hers, then took her hand again. "I really am sorry that I surprised you, and that I didn't tell you earlier. I just wanted you to know that you have options other than going back to *All Good*."

"I'm . . . overwhelmed," she admitted. "It's going to take me a while to wrap my mind around this. And yeah, I do wish you'd told me sooner." Had he only told her now because he didn't want her to leave Michigan? Was he really serious about making this thing between them last—if only for the rest of the summer?

She hoped not, because it was going to be awful to disappoint him.

"I know, and I'm sorry. For the record, I'd be happy to help you—if you want me to, that is. I don't hate the numbers or the game, or even money. It just makes you more of who you are, and in your case, that's a good thing. I just hate the industry and the kind of people I was working with."

His smile began to thaw her. "Here I was thinking that being more of who I am was guaranteed to make you nuts," she said.

He put his lips to the top of her head, but instead of kissing her, he inhaled deeply. "I like the way you smell."

If Seth had done this in a restaurant, Aly probably would've been mortified. But with Wyatt she didn't mind. "Thank you. Is that you trying not to confess that I drive you crazy?"

"You do, but in the best possible way."

She was about to say something flirty but instead brought up his comment about Luke. "Hey—since we're talking big things, I need to ask you something about what you said a few days ago."

"I actually do love the way you look when you're on top of me, if that's what you want to know," he said in a low voice.

She could feel her body growing warm, but she wouldn't be so easily diverted. "For the record, I believe you. But this is about Luke."

His expression clouded over. "Right."

She broke free from his embrace and regarded him. "What did you mean when you said, 'I never should have let it happen'?"

"Just that I wish I'd told him not to go," said Wyatt, but it seemed to Aly he'd answered too quickly.

"Anything else?"

"No. And I don't think it's a great idea to rehash that day—not when it's going to make us both feel lousy. We can't change what happened."

"I *know* that." She was having to work hard not to get irritated. This was her brother they were talking about. Didn't she have a right to hash it out if she felt like it? "I just don't like to be left in the dark. For me, more information is better."

Wyatt's frown deepened. "I said I was sorry about the life insurance."

"That's not what I was talking about. I honestly don't care about that." Why was this starting to feel like an argument?

"I don't know how you couldn't care a little. And for the record, I'm sorry I didn't let you know sooner." He reached out and touched her elbow. "Are we okay?"

"Of course," she said.

But she couldn't shake the unsettled feeling that had come over her—not during dinner, and not even when he took her in his arms that night and carried her to bed.

Wyatt was definitely keeping something from her. And although she was leaving soon—she *was*—Aly couldn't help but worry that her reluctance to press him for details meant she was already in too deep.

TWENTY-SIX

Aly tossed and turned that night, but sleep wouldn't come. She kept thinking about Luke and his final moments.

She'd already gone over his last day dozens, maybe even hundreds, of times in her mind. A few days before he went to Florida, he tried to talk her into going to the Keys with him and Wyatt. After she'd regretfully but firmly refused, he'd flown out to New York and surprised her, even though his Florida trip was just days away. She'd been flustered at first—*All Good* had made a last-minute decision to combine the December and January issues to adjust for the low advertising revenue, and she'd been working around the clock to get the magazine shipped on time. But her brother was the one thing Aly was willing to set work aside for. Besides, Meagan owed her for the many occasions Aly had covered for her while she was traveling or not feeling well or out of the office for reasons she chose not to elaborate on. Though Meagan had made it obvious that she wasn't thrilled about the last-minute request, Aly made it equally obvious that she wouldn't take no for an answer. It was arguably the only time that she'd deserved Meagan's ire—and yet Meagan had bitten her tongue and done what Aly had asked. At the time, Aly had foolishly assumed it was because she was her friend.

"I just wanted to see you," Luke had explained when she'd asked about his unannounced visit. They were out to eat at an elegant yet homey Italian restaurant she'd never heard of, even though it was just five blocks from her office. In typical Luke fashion, he'd texted an old friend for a recommendation, then somehow managed to snag the last reservation available. "Can't your brother surprise you from time to time?"

"It's not like you, is all," she said before taking a bite of the buttery burrata and tomato appetizer he'd ordered. He'd encouraged her to eat up, but she remembered thinking that he was the one who looked like he needed a steak and a big bowl of pasta. He claimed he'd never been happier. But if that was true, why did he seem so worn out?

"Maybe stepping out of the rat race has changed me," he said. "By the way, I splurged on a suite at The Plaza. Why don't you stay over?" he said. "It's honestly too swanky for me to deal with on my own."

"Are you sure?"

"Have you ever known me to say what I don't mean?"

She hadn't, and so she'd agreed, even though Seth made a snide comment about how it was kind of weird that she was staying over with her brother when their apartment was barely a mile away. "You're weird to say that," she'd shot back at him—not because she believed it, but because she hated the idea that Seth thought something was wrong with her. "He's only here for twenty-four hours, and I want to take advantage of it."

The Plaza was the kind of hotel she'd imagined as a child, one where a fun-loving nanny would chase her around and where parents were always blessedly off somewhere else, unconcerned whether their free-spirited child might, say, flood the bathroom or even the whole hotel while taking a bath. It wasn't really Luke's style, but couldn't a person try new things? And even if he had chosen it because he thought she'd like it (as she suspected he had), she was still going to appreciate the crap out of it.

As she and Luke sat side by side in the cushy king-sized bed, eating the ridiculously overpriced ice cream sundaes that room service had delivered and watching *It's a Wonderful Life* (even though Christmas was still several months away, it had always been their favorite), Aly had thought to herself: *It doesn't get better than this.*

Looking back, she was glad she hadn't known how true that would turn out to be.

Before Luke had left town the next day, he'd given her the keys to his beach house, as well as his word that everything would be taken care of. At the time, she'd thought he was just being himself—conscientious, generous, forward-thinking.

Now she wondered if there had been more to it. Had her brother intuited—the way she'd heard that some people just did—that he would die the very next week?

Was *that* what Wyatt was trying to hide from her?

She shivered, even though Wyatt, asleep beside her in bed, was practically a space heater.

No. Luke would never have willingly gotten in that sailboat if he'd known it would mean leaving her behind.

She had to believe that.

Because the alternative was that her brother had not loved her enough to stay.

TWENTY-SEVEN

A few hours later, Aly took a sip of coffee and gazed out the double doors at the beach. Upstairs, Wyatt was still asleep, and the sun had just appeared in the sky; the beach was empty. Maybe she'd go for a walk before lunch. After all, there were less than two weeks until she headed back to New York.

Focus on now, Aly reminded herself. *Not tomorrow. Not next month or next year. Just right now.* She'd literally rolled her eyes when she read this advice in a mindfulness column the magazine had run a few months earlier. Even though she was already the editor in chief at that point, she didn't feel secure in the position—and she had the bank balance to prove it. Not thinking about the future was out of the question.

She wasn't rolling her eyes anymore. Apparently, money had this impact. When you weren't always worrying about how to pay for your life, you could actually take a beat to enjoy it.

But it occurred to her that part of what she enjoyed most about life was being an editor—creating beautiful, meaningful content and sharing it with the world. Maybe Wyatt didn't understand this, and that was why he wanted her to stay.

In the kitchen, Aly's phone began ringing. She'd left it on the counter the evening before, and she was surprised the battery hadn't died. When she saw Meagan's name on the screen, she wished it had.

"This is Aly," she answered curtly.

"I know, Aly. It's Meagan. Did you get my email?"

"Yes."

"Oh. I wasn't sure if you were still using that address."

"I am." She could practically hear Meagan squirming on the other end of the line. Good—let her.

"I really am sorry, Aly."

"Thanks. I accept your apology." That wasn't true; she hadn't fully forgiven her yet. But there was no need to get into that right now. "Why are you calling me?"

"Well, because I wanted to apologize for what happened. I have to say—I was really impressed by what you said."

"Pardon?" sputtered Aly. What *had* she said, anyway?

"I know you seemed a little . . . uh. You know. Upset. But honestly, I was relieved."

"About?" said Aly, since she was not about to confess that she couldn't remember their argument.

"Just—you've been holding your feelings in for months now. It was a relief to see you be . . . well, normal."

Normal? Whatever happened, it was the opposite of normal. "I have not been holding my feelings in."

"Hmm," said Meagan. "My point is, I was glad to see you say what you were thinking. I have a lot of respect for that, and I'm sorry that someone thought it was a good idea to tape it and put it online."

So it hadn't been Meagan who uploaded the footage to YouTube. Aly was surprised to realize how much better she felt, knowing that.

"What you said about work . . . It really got me thinking," Meagan continued. "Which brings me to the real reason I'm calling. So . . . are you ready?" Aly half expected her to add a drumroll for dramatic effect. "I left *All Good!*"

What? It took Aly a moment to process what Meagan had said. Once she had, the relief she'd felt instantly disappeared. Here she was, fighting to get her job back at the magazine, and Meagan was casually walking away from it? What did she want—congratulations? A certificate of completion? Perhaps a lifetime membership to the Lemming Society?

"Don't you want to know why?" said Meagan.

"Not really," said Aly. Did this mean perhaps James would rethink his decision to make her editorial director? There were no other viable contenders on the staff, and training someone who had no prior knowledge of the magazine would be a beast.

"Okay, I deserve that. But the whole situation with the video opened my eyes to the truth."

"Which is?" asked Aly, still thinking about who would fill the vacancy Meagan had created.

"Consumer magazines are getting it backward, and they're completely wasting top talent, too. Like, obviously, you."

"Okay . . ."

Meagan cleared her throat. "I'm starting a custom publishing company. It's going to be entirely staffed with former editors, and we'll help major brands create magazines for their consumers and employees. I want you to be the first to join me."

The sip of coffee Aly had just taken shot down the wrong pipe, causing her to choke.

"Are you okay?" said Meagan.

"Fine," she managed. "But why would you want to work with a . . ." Even now, she heard Luke, reminding her to use the dictionary and not the thesaurus, and she couldn't bring herself to repeat the word Meagan had used to describe her at the salad place. "You know."

"I never should've called you that," said Meagan quickly. "I was so jealous of you for getting the top job, even though I knew you deserved it. And obviously I know you weren't behind the pay cuts. I've been seeing my therapist twice a week, and she's helped me recognize that. I want to make things right between us, Aly."

"So you're offering me a job."

"Yes! I'm not going to make the same mistake James did. I've hired a business coach and confirmed that this is a sustainable model. I have start-up capital, too." Meagan didn't say from who, but Aly already knew it was from her parents, who owned a shipping business and had homes scattered across the country. "The companies who hire us will cover all production costs, so we never have to worry about advertising again. We can be more inventive, and the profit margins are so, so good. I already have a client signed up and everything," she said, then named a major outdoor adventure retailer; Aly was willing to bet the company's CEO was friends with Meagan's parents. "They've given us a budget of one million, just for one year!"

"You did all that in two weeks?" said Aly, whose mind was spinning at the thought of it. "No," she said before Meagan could answer. "You've had this in the works for a while now." It made her wonder why Meagan had even bothered running her mouth about Aly's job performance. What did she care?

"Of course! I've known for at least two years that I wanted to build something bigger than *All Good*. But I need staff to get started, Aly. And I can't think of a better person to be editor in chief."

"Of which magazine?" said Aly.

"*All* of them," said Meagan. "Every single magazine we work on. I'll make sure you have all the support you need. And Aly, I promise I'll have your back."

This was the most demonstrative apology Aly had ever received. And being the editor in chief of not one, but multiple magazines: really, it was the perfect job for Aly.

And yet she couldn't bring herself to say yes, or even that she'd consider it. Because hadn't she just decided that she no longer wanted Meagan in her life?

"Aly?" said Wyatt. He'd wandered down the stairs in his boxers, and his sleepy expression told her he'd just awoken.

"Is that Seth?" said Meagan.

"Actually, we broke up."

"What? I hope it wasn't because—"

"Meagan, I've got to run," said Aly, waving a hand at Wyatt, whose eyebrows had just shot up.

"Just tell me you'll think about it, Aly. Please? You'd have complete autonomy and the freedom to hire your own team. I could start you at two hundred."

"A day?" That was a pretty decent rate.

"Thousand, Aly. Plus benefits, though I'm still trying to hammer those out," said Meagan. "Let's talk soon, okay? Call me when you've had a chance to think it through."

"I . . . will," said Aly and hung up the phone.

Wyatt frowned. "Judging by the look on your face, that was the same Meagan who upended your life."

"That was her," said Aly. She felt oddly guilty, even though she had no reason to. "She's starting a new company, and she . . . wants to hire me."

"Isn't that rich. I hope you told her you weren't interested."

"Don't you want to know the job she's offering? And the salary is nearly three times what I make at Innovate." It wasn't that Aly was convinced it was the best opportunity. Really, she'd barely had a second to digest the offer. But Wyatt could at least ask for the details before he passed judgment.

He crossed his arms over his chest. "She could make you the queen of Spain and I'd still think it was a terrible idea. When people show you who they are, believe them."

"You got that from Luke," said Aly. She attempted to take a sip from her mug, only to discover she'd already finished her coffee.

"Who got it from Maya Angelou, but yeah—that's where I first heard it. And for the record, they're both right. Meagan's a snake in the grass. She's asking you to join her because she knows she can't do it without you. She's a hack, Aly."

That was taking it a bit far, thought Aly, though she didn't hate that Wyatt was defending her so adamantly. "You've never even met her," she said.

He looked away, and at once Aly knew.

"You watched the video," she said quietly.

"Yes," he said, slowly turning to meet her eye. "I wanted to see what had happened. You didn't do anything wrong, Aly. You really didn't. And I think you should leave anyone associated with that soulless company in the dust. *Especially* Meagan."

"I told you, I don't want to hear anything about my meltdown."

"I understand that, which is why I never brought it up. I just don't want you to feel bad, because there's no reason to. Hey," he said, walking over to her. He put his arms around her and pulled her close. Damned pheromones—she felt herself soften as she leaned against his chest. "You can't blame me for not wanting to see you get hurt again."

"No," she said quietly. "I'm not blaming you for anything. But I have to make this decision for myself."

"I know that. Watch the video sometime, Aly," he said, kissing the top of her head. "I think you'll understand where I'm coming from."

"Maybe later," she told him.

And by *later*, Aly meant *never*. Because seeing herself act that way might lead her to channel her mother again the next time she was stressed out.

Yes, if she decided to work for Meagan, she would approach it with the strategy of a hardened warrior—right down to the contract she'd have Harry draw up for her, which would specify all sorts of things, but especially the type of language Meagan could use around her.

And if she kept letting Wyatt Goldstein into her heart, she would have to come up with a similar defense. Because as she looked into his eyes, which were big and brimming with something unfamiliar to her, she knew that if she wasn't careful, she'd forget all about her future.

TWENTY-EIGHT

While her elementary and middle school friends were developing crushes on their peers, Aly was busy being obsessed with their mothers. Her pining wasn't romantic, but the intensity was no different; she spent hours imagining how her life would be if she could walk home from school, open the door to another home, and have an entirely different person from Cindy waiting for her inside.

Aly's friend Jennifer's mother, Lisa, was the object of her longest-running infatuation. There was nothing particularly notable about Lisa; she was most often found in a faded sweat suit, nose in a bodice-ripper. She served snacks of the prepackaged variety, and unlike many of the other girls, Jennifer got the hot lunch every day because Lisa couldn't be bothered to make a sandwich. Lisa seemed to like Jennifer, but she didn't fawn over her or act like she was anything special.

And maybe that was the draw—how utterly unremarkable Lisa was. Aly would've given almost anything to have a parent who didn't vacillate between forgetting she had a child and screaming bloody murder at her in front of an entire parking lot full of students. Aly longed for a mother who blended in, whose flaws were garden-variety and whose love and affection were no more notable than the clouds in the sky.

Perhaps that was why, even all these years later, Aly had the same sinking feeling when she spotted her mother's car pulling into the driveway at the beach house. No one was around to witness Cindy's humiliating behavior, and of course, as an adult, Aly had agency. But her early programming went deep. And unlike the last time Cindy had appeared, Aly couldn't hide behind Wyatt, who'd gone out for the afternoon. She considered waiting inside the bathroom until Cindy stopped knocking and went away, but she knew it would only delay the inevitable . . . whatever that was.

"I *did* call," said Cindy by way of a greeting. "If you'd picked up for a change, this wouldn't be a surprise."

"And you could've waited for me to call back," retorted Aly. It occurred to her that she and Wyatt had this, too, in common—always hitting the red button on their phones when the word *Mom* appeared on the screen.

"Right—from New York?" said Cindy. Aly could tell by the sharpness of her tone that she was definitely sober today.

"I'm not leaving just yet," Aly volleyed back.

Cindy glanced around. "Where's that boyfriend of yours?"

"He's not my boyfriend." Aly realized what she'd said too late.

"Oh no?" said Cindy, eyeing her. "Last time I was here, you two were singing a different song. Did he move out?"

"No. And it's complicated."

"Only if you make it so."

Aly shook her head. A minute and a half in her mother's presence and her blood pressure had already shot up to unhealthy levels. "Why are you here, Mom? And if it's about the house, we're—I'm—not selling," she said, correcting herself.

"I figured that. You and Wyatt look too cozy here. Is he staying?"

"Through the summer."

"And you're leaving?"

Aly crossed her arms over her chest. "Yes."

"And here you criticized me for letting Billy crash at my place," said Cindy, sitting on an arm of the sofa.

Aly wasn't about to tell Cindy that the house belonged to Wyatt as much as her. "Would you like to try a chair, Mom?"

"No. I'm not staying." Cindy sighed deeply. "I was just thinking about Luke this morning. And when I think about Luke, I think about this house."

"He wasn't even here two whole years," pointed out Aly.

Cindy glanced around. "Doesn't feel that way, does it? I never could make a place cozy like this."

Aly wasn't going to argue with her on this count.

"So . . . you were thinking about Luke."

Cindy gnawed on a cuticle, seeming reticent to discuss it. "I'd love a glass of water if you don't mind."

"You know where the cupboards are, Mom. And the faucet." Aly never talked to her mother this sharply, but today felt different. She felt . . . not unhinged, exactly, but not inhibited, either. And she was tired of pretending, tired of tiptoeing around the reality of her past to make her mother more comfortable. "While we're making demands, I'd love an apology."

"For *what*."

"For letting Dad hurt me."

"You're not the only one who had a bad childhood, Allegra. Your father's was way worse. You're lucky he didn't treat you the way his father treated him."

"Lucky?" spat Aly. "You've got to be kidding me. I don't call getting smacked upside the head whenever I looked at him the wrong way 'lucky.'"

Cindy slid off her perch. At least now she had the decency to look guilty. "Your father did the best he could."

"Let me guess: and so did you." Aly shook her head with disgust, but mostly she felt sad. Normally she'd call Luke after having a heated conversation with Cindy, because he was the one person on the whole earth who understood. And before she knew it, he'd have talked her down, and they'd both laugh about how screwed up the whole situation was. "You should have protected me, Mom. I was just a child."

"It's obvious you don't want me here, so I'm going to go, Allegra," said Cindy, starting for the door.

Aly didn't respond.

Cindy spun around. "I only came over to ask you if we're going to do anything about your brother."

"What do you mean?" asked Aly suspiciously. Was this her mother's way of asking for money?

"I want to do a memorial. Or something."

Now Aly felt twice as irritated, which was no small feat. "Luke didn't want anything. He made that very clear." Her brother had been cremated, and his remains were in a box in the credenza in the living room, where Aly intended to leave them until she came up with a better idea.

"A memorial isn't for the dead. It's for the people the dead leave behind. I know you wish I wasn't the one still here with you. But I am. So, Allegra." Cindy met Aly's eyes. "Let me know if you decide you want to join me in saying goodbye."

"Oh, I do," hissed Aly. She pointed at the door. "Goodbye, Mom."

TWENTY-NINE

"Ho, ho, ho," said Harry. He had a diaper bag slung over his shoulder and wheeled a large suitcase behind him, which he dropped when Aly opened the door for him.

Even several days later, Aly still felt raw from her conversation with her mother, and her career remained a question mark. But Harry had arrived; everything was going to be okay. "Is that you, Harry Claus?" She folded him into her arms. "I can't believe you made it," she said, holding him back to examine him. Her old friend was still as lean as the day they met, but now he had the budget to accommodate his sartorial sense, and he wore a tailored shirt, shorts adorned with a designer belt, and polished leather loafers. "Where's that delicious baby of yours?"

"No eating the baby," said Tim, walking in behind Harry. Harry's husband was built like a lumberjack, and he had the rosy cheeks and suspenders to match. He set the car seat on the ground and unlatched Beckett, who'd just started to squirm. "Let's go see Auntie Aly. Okay, muffin?" When he caught himself, he looked up and grinned at Aly. "Okay, so maybe you're not the only one who's thinking food when it comes to this little guy."

She laughed. "It's so amazing to see you all."

"It's been too long," agreed Tim. He passed Beckett to her like she knew how to hold a baby—which she definitely didn't, or at least not one who no longer lay there like a sack of potatoes, as he had as a newborn.

"Oh," she said as Beckett put his hand on her nose and squealed with delight, revealing two tiny teeth emerging from his bottom gums. He really *was* an entirely different baby from the last time she'd seen him. "I'm almost expecting him to start speaking complete sentences to me," she said to Tim.

He smiled. "That makes two of us. It's crazy, the way it's flying by so fast."

"Except at night," remarked Harry, kicking off his shoes. "Then time's like molasses. So . . ." He sidled up to Aly. "Where's the Wild Thing at?"

Aly had told Harry everything—including the fact that their roommate-with-benefits arrangement was approaching its end. "Harry," she hissed. "I don't know, and don't call him that."

"Correction: the Wild *Man*," said Harry, pretending to be exasperated. Then he eyed Aly gravely and said, "He does know we're visiting, right?"

"Obviously. Not that I need permission from him."

Harry smiled drolly. "I wasn't implying you did. I just wanted to know if he was on board."

"Yes," said Aly. The truth was, she'd been dreading the two of them meeting. No matter how short-lived or hedonistic her fling with Wyatt was, introducing him to Harry would make it . . .

Real.

Then again, Harry had deemed nearly every man she'd ever dated a dud, and she had no doubt that he'd file Wyatt into his folder of unsuitables. She almost looked forward to that part—it would be one more reminder that this was merely a fling.

"Where should I put our stuff?" asked Tim.

"I'll show you," she said, handing Beckett to Harry. "Let's head upstairs."

Although she'd barely been able to step inside Luke's room since her arrival, having Harry and Tim sleep there didn't bother her; she knew Luke wouldn't have minded. Anyway, with only three bedrooms, there was no other place in the house for them to sleep. Tim whistled as he opened the door. "Look at the lake—doesn't look quite as good from the Chicago side," he said, immediately walking over to the window. After a moment, he turned to Aly. "Why are *we* getting the best view in the house? You should be putting us on the sofa or something."

"There are three of you and only one of me," she said. "And there's room here for the Pack 'n Play, too."

"Well, thank you. We haven't been anywhere since Beckett's birth," said Tim. "Even if he keeps us up half the night, this will be a delight."

"I hope so," said Aly, her eyes landing on the dusty mantel. She'd tried her best to tidy up for their visit, but she hadn't been able to stay in the room more than a few minutes, and she saw that she'd missed a few spots. "I apologize if it's a little musty."

"Don't even worry about it." Tim grimaced. "Harry may or may not have brought an air filter from home, not to mention three different baby monitors. He's off the deep end when it comes to Beckett."

"I would be, too," said Aly. "He's the cutest."

"We won the family lottery," said Tim, looking a little misty-eyed. "I wish I could go back in time and tell fifteen-year-old me that one day I was going to have a happy family."

Aly tried to keep the sadness out of her smile. She wouldn't mind going back to her teens, if only to see Luke again. But she'd never be able to reassure her teenage self that one day the hole in her heart would finally be filled.

Instead, she'd have to inform her that it would soon come to resemble a canyon.

As Aly and Tim descended the stairs, she heard Wyatt before she saw him. He and Harry stood in the living room, both laughing like two people who already knew each other. And Wyatt—

Well, he was jiggling Beckett on his hip in the manner of a man who actually *did* know what to do with a baby.

"We were just talking about you," said Harry.

"Greaaaat," she deadpanned. She eyed Wyatt. "When did you turn into the baby whisperer?"

"I love babies," said Wyatt. He stuck his tongue out at Beckett, who giggled. "And babies love me."

"Now you're just bragging," said Harry, and Wyatt laughed so openly that he seemed like an entirely different version of the man she'd mistaken for a squatter a few weeks ago.

They liked each other, she realized. Instead of Harry's disapproval, Wyatt had already won him over.

This was *definitely* not the plan.

"Who even are you right now?" she said to Wyatt, not really joking.

"I have lots of cousins," he said, still bouncing Beckett. "Kids are so much easier than adults."

"Yes and no," said Harry, and Wyatt laughed again. "We're less messy but more complicated."

"*Wyatt* isn't less messy," Aly said, looking pointedly at him.

"Hey, I've been trying a lot harder lately," said Wyatt, pretending to pout.

She had to agree that he had been, but she couldn't get over the change in his demeanor. Where was the storm cloud of a man she'd grown accustomed to? Granted, he had been more cheerful since they'd started sleeping together. But this sunny, jovial persona was next level. She didn't dislike it, necessarily. It was just that she preferred knowing what to expect from a person.

Especially one she was spending time undressed with.

"You know, we could watch Beckett if you two wanted a little break," Wyatt said to Harry. "Maybe brunch tomorrow or something?"

And now he was suggesting they *babysit*?

"Whoa—that's quite an offer. Are we ready, honey?" Harry asked Tim.

Tim laughed. "I think we might be."

"By the way, I made reservations for us at the Mermaid at six," Wyatt added. "But if that's not a good time for you all, I can change them."

He did *what*? "You did?" said Aly, not even bothering to hide her amazement. What was next—he was going to tell her he was a member of a strange religious cult or had once performed on Broadway?

Then again, he'd already surprised her in bed a few times. The man knew every button and exactly when to press them. *If only this month could stretch forever.*

She shook her head hard, almost violently, to clear her mind. This was worse than Stockholm syndrome. It was like teenage infatuation on steroids.

"You okay, babe? You have a look on your face," said Harry.

"I'm fine," she murmured. "Sorry—I was just lost in thought."

"You sure?" said Wyatt, peering at her with concern.

Aly flushed. She wasn't used to having so many people worried about her at one time. "I swear I'm okay. Just . . . I probably need more sleep."

Harry waited until Wyatt had walked over to the infant carrier to get some toys for Beckett. Then he whispered to Aly. "From where I stand, what you need is right here in this room."

"Harry!" she hissed. "What are you saying?"

"I'm saying I like him. And I can tell you do, too. I haven't seen you look so . . ." He held her at arm's length, taking her in. "Well, you look like yourself."

She frowned. "I wasn't aware I was beginning to resemble a stranger."

"The light's back in your eyes, babe. It was out the last time I saw you, and I'm relieved to see it again."

Was it? She wished there were a mirror nearby.

Harry slung his arm around her. "So I guess what I'm saying is, if you're not going back to being editor in chief, why not extend your sabbatical and stay the summer?"

Her eyes widened; she hadn't even told Harry that Wyatt had asked her to do that very thing.

"Give Wyatt a chance," Harry added. Then he glanced around the house before pulling her in for a hug. "Or at least give this *place* a chance—a real one. I think Luke left it to both of you for a reason."

THIRTY

"You're sure you've got this?" asked Harry as he handed Beckett to Wyatt.

"We do," Aly assured him, even though it was obvious that the person who had things under control was Wyatt.

Harry ran his hand over Beckett's head. "Be good, okay, love bug?"

"Forgive him—we haven't left Beckett with a sitter yet," Tim said to Aly and Wyatt. A tech journalist, Tim had only taken the occasional assignment since Beckett's birth, so he could stay home to watch him.

"Then you haven't been by yourselves for six months? You definitely have to get out of here," said Wyatt. He pretended to shoo them away, then took Beckett's hand and made a waving motion, which Beckett immediately began mimicking. "Bye-bye, daddies!" Wyatt said in a playful voice. "Enjoy your grown-up time!"

As someone who didn't even like children, Aly never would've guessed that watching Wyatt with an infant could be such a turn-on. But something about a large man with a tiny baby pressed some primal button in her. Or maybe it was just seeing him look so happy that made her feel all tingly.

"Okay, okay," said Harry as Tim pushed him toward the door. "Do *not* hesitate to let us know if you need anything."

"We will. Enjoy your brunch!" Aly called after them. She turned back to Wyatt. "*Now* what do we do?"

"We hang out with this cute little fella," said Wyatt. "Easy as can be."

Aly shook her head. "I'm sorry—who are you, and where is the giant grump I call a roommate?"

Wyatt grinned at her. "He's been in a better mood since *his* roommate started sharing a bed with him."

Aly had to laugh. "You are so ridiculous."

"But I'm right," he said and kissed the top of her head.

"Hmph." Beckett reached for her, and the next thing she knew, he was in her arms. "He *is* pretty charming," she admitted as his chubby little hand explored her face.

"Sure is. Makes me excited to have a little one of my own."

Aly did a double take. "Really."

"Yeah," said Wyatt with a lopsided smile. "Don't you want to have kids one day?"

Aly glanced at Beckett. Even if she had a child like him, she wasn't sure she wanted to be a mother. "No." But this sounded more certain than she truly felt. "Well, I don't know. I'm afraid . . ."

"Of what?" he asked lightly.

"That I won't know how to do it," she admitted. After a moment, she added, "That I'll end up being like my parents."

"No way," he scoffed. "I don't need to have met both of them to know that the apple fell far from the tree."

"I'm sure my father didn't think he'd turn out like his dad," said Aly, thinking about what her mother had said about Dan.

"Didn't he, though?" asked Wyatt, arching an eyebrow. "He could have at least put some thought into how to be a halfway decent human being. Meanwhile, look at you. Practically maternal."

Without thinking, Aly had begun swaying with Beckett. She'd never babysat as a teen, but this seemed natural. Of course, Beckett was Harry's child; it stood to reason that she felt a bond with him.

"Hardly," said Aly. "And watch—the minute he starts walking and talking I'm going to freeze up. I'm horrible with kids."

"If you say so," said Wyatt.

"I do. That's exactly what I say. Isn't that right, shmoopy?" she said to Beckett. "Uncle Wyatt is so weird."

"Uncle!" he said, laughing.

She flushed when she realized what she'd said. Why were they even talking about this? "Don't get any ideas. It's just a term of endearment. Speaking of parents . . ."

Wyatt sank into the sofa. "I haven't spoken to my mother, if that's what you're going to ask."

"I wasn't. But maybe I should," she hedged. "Why don't you ever pick up when she calls?"

"I told you. I'm taking a break from them."

Aly handed Beckett a rubber giraffe, which he immediately began gnawing on.

"Seems like she hasn't gotten the memo. And from what you've told me, she's not *that* bad."

"We could make that argument about Cindy, no?" said Wyatt, raising his eyebrows.

"Actually, that's what I was going to tell you. She came over again on Tuesday and wanted to talk about Luke."

He frowned. "Why didn't you tell me earlier?"

This was a good question. "I don't know," she admitted. "I guess I was trying not to think about it. She . . . she wants to have a memorial."

"But Luke didn't want that," said Wyatt, whose expression had clouded over.

"I told her that, but she said that they're for the living. Not the . . . you know."

"I do." Wyatt rose from the sofa and walked over to Aly and Beckett. He leaned in toward the baby and said, "What do you think, big guy?"

Beckett banged his hands on Wyatt's chest, and he laughed. Then he looked at Aly. "I don't know—it's not the worst idea."

"Who would even go?" asked Aly. Luke hadn't dated anyone seriously in years, and although she knew his friends missed him, most were in New York or Los Angeles and weren't likely to fly to Michigan for a brief event.

"You. Me. Your mom. Not your dad," Wyatt said pointedly.

"Even *I* can't plan something like that *that* fast," said Aly.

"Not this month," said Wyatt, touching her cheek lightly. "It would be in September."

In September, thought Aly, *I'll be nowhere near here.* But she couldn't say it; not with the way Wyatt was looking at her.

Tim and Harry had said Beckett would need a nap soon after they left, and sure enough, his lids were already beginning to sag. Wyatt warmed up his bottle, and after Beckett drained it, they took him upstairs to his crib.

Wyatt lay Beckett down and rubbed his belly, and within moments, he was asleep. He turned to Aly and drew her into his arms. "This isn't that bad, is it?" he murmured.

She didn't know if he was talking about taking care of Beckett, or them being together, or the house. Probably all of it. "No," she whispered.

It wasn't bad at all. In fact, she would miss it terribly after she returned to New York. But the fact was, she had places to be and things to do—a life to live. And now that Luke was gone, Aly understood the privilege she had in a way she had not before. She would not—could not—waste it by playing house and pretending that this thing between her and Wyatt would last.

THIRTY-ONE

They set out for Oval Beach later that afternoon, hoping to swim and sun themselves. After they were settled, Wyatt and Tim wandered off while Harry and Aly stayed behind to keep an eye on Beckett, who dozed peacefully on a blanket in the corner of the tent they'd set up for shade.

"Harry," said Aly in a low tone.

"Uh-oh," said Harry, fanning himself with the copy of *All Good* that Aly had packed, hoping it would help get her in a work state of mind. "I know that voice. What's up?"

Aly shot him a tight smile. "I have to tell you something, but you have to promise not to say a word to anyone."

"Not even Tim?" said Harry.

"You can tell Tim," she said. "But no one else. And you *can't* bring it up when we're around other people."

"What about the Wild Thing?" said Harry. After even just a short while in the sun, his freckles were starting to stand out from his olive skin.

"He already knows what I'm about to say—and for the record, you absolutely *have* to stop calling him that."

"He does look rather tame with his facial hair all neat and tidy," said Harry, taking a sip from his can of sparkling water. "Have you two used the L-word yet?"

"*No,*" she said, more defensively than she'd intended to. In a softer tone, she added, "This is a fling."

Harry arched an eyebrow. "That's what I said about Tim. Eight years later, here we are, drowning in diapers and domestic bliss."

"Sure, but this is different." Aly's eyes scanned the beach. Wyatt had decided to jump in the water to cool off, but she couldn't see him anywhere. She had to remind herself not to panic. There was no lifeguard on duty, but there were dozens of people, maybe even a hundred, around. Someone would spot him if he'd been pulled under.

Wouldn't they?

"I like being with him," said Aly. "That's not the same thing as loving him. Also . . ."

"What is it?" pressed Harry.

"I think he knows something about Luke's death. Something he isn't telling me."

"Hmm."

"I hear disapproval in your *hmm,*" said Aly, leaning back on her elbows.

"I just wonder if anything good can come of starting down that path," said Harry.

Good? Good wasn't the goal. The goal was to get the truth, so she could . . . well, if not feel better, then begin to get over Luke's death. "Anyway, that's not what I was going to tell you. The big news is, Wyatt just informed me that the thirty thousand he handed me was chump change compared to the life insurance I'm about to inherit. It's like a million. *Dollars,* Harry. A million dollars!" she said, then clamped her hand over her mouth when Beckett shifted. "Sorry," she whispered.

"Whaaaaat?" Harry's eyes were bulging. "That's . . . I don't even know. Awful? Amazing?"

"Both," said Aly glumly. "Bad enough that Luke left the house to me and Wyatt. But now a pile of cash? It's just all so . . ." She couldn't find the words to express how she felt. "I just don't want any of it. I want my brother back."

"I know you do, love," said Harry, squeezing her arm lightly. "I do, too. But this gives you choices. Choices that you never had before—ones that most people will never have. There was a little magical thinking on my part when I told you to stay longer, but Al—" He widened his eyes. "Now you can *actually do that*. Isn't that crazy?"

"Yeah. Maybe a little too crazy," said Aly, looking out at the beach. She still saw no sign of Wyatt, unless he was the swimmer breast-stroking through the waves out beyond the designated swimming area—and she hoped he wasn't, as that didn't seem particularly safe. She wasn't especially risk-averse, but she didn't trust the water. Really, she needed to stop coming to the beach. It might be beautiful, but it was nothing if not a death trap. "Anyway, Meagan called me the other day."

"And I trust you hung up on her."

"I did not. She wants to hire me."

Harry's eyes widened with surprise. "At *All Good*? How is that even possible?"

"It's not—she left the magazine."

"After being named editor in chief? Is she *insane*?"

"Probably," concluded Aly. It was unlikely Meagan's departure meant Aly could have her job back—Innovate clearly wanted her elsewhere—but she might ask for it anyway. That was, if she said no to Meagan. "She's starting a company that will create custom magazines for major companies. No ads, just big budgets and freedom. Or so she says. She wants to make me editor in chief of the whole operation."

"Is that some backward sort of apology? Because you *do* know she's only asking you to do this because she doesn't know how to do her job without you, right?"

Aly laughed. "You sound like Wyatt."

"I knew I liked him," said Harry with a dazzling smile. Then his face grew serious. "What do *you* want to do, Al?"

The easy thing would be to take the gig at *All Good* as editorial director—or even the one that Meagan had offered. But *want?* The only thing Aly really wanted to do right now was . . . nothing.

Which was a bit alarming—it was almost as though her affair with Wyatt had sapped her of her ambition. And who was she without that?

Harry picked up on the confusion in her silence. "Listen, babe, you don't have to figure out anything now. But aren't you glad that you have funds? You've been worried about your next career move. Now you can take your time and find something—or maybe even invent something—that's even better," he said with a wink.

Aly tried to smile back. The truth was, she didn't *want* to go searching for some glittering new endeavor. Hadn't the past year brought about enough change? And from where she stood, *change* was just a more palatable word for *loss*.

"Speaking of work!" said Harry, whose phone had begun buzzing in the diaper bag. "Ugh," he said, scanning the screen. "This partner is trying to murder me. If I weren't so intent on taking his place, I'd tell him exactly where to stuff his brief." He frowned. "Looks like I'll be glued to my laptop on the car ride back tomorrow. Are you sure you want to go back to work?"

"I guess," said Aly. She had enjoyed not having to check her work email as soon as she woke up, and again before bed, not to mention all weekend long. Having the time to do normal-people things like read and watch TV—and yes, make love to Wyatt—wasn't so bad, either. But living that way year-round, or even for the rest of the summer, would make her . . . rudderless. Everyone was put on this planet to do something only they could do, whether it was curing cancer or brightening strangers' days with a megawatt smile; Aly truly believed that. And she was supposed to be a magazine editor.

Good for You

Now she just needed to get on board with being a magazine editor's boss.

"You're sure you can't stay longer?" she said to Harry after he'd put his phone back. They were leaving first thing on Sunday, so he could head into the office for a few hours that afternoon. But Aly wasn't ready for him to go so soon. Or, as she remarked to him, ever.

"I wish I could." Harry squeezed her arm lightly. "But what if we meet back here at the end of the summer?"

"I don't hate that idea," Aly admitted.

"I knew you wouldn't. And once I make partner, maybe I can buy a cute little place down the road from you." He'd been on the verge of adding *two*—the twinkle in his eyes told her as much.

She snorted. "You wish! I'm not sure if I'll sell or just give it to Wyatt, but I still plan to get out of here as soon as possible."

Suddenly Wyatt's endlessly long legs appeared in front of her. He squatted down, but he looked at Harry instead of her. "Am I interrupting something?"

"Course not. Want something cold?" asked Harry, nodding toward the cooler that Tim had packed with sandwiches and drinks.

"Sure," said Wyatt, but she could sense the carefree attitude he'd had over the past few days was gone. "You want one, Aly?"

The lump in Aly's throat felt like a large rock. She swallowed hard and forced her lips into a smile. "Yes, thanks," she said.

He met her eye briefly as he handed her a seltzer, then looked away. He'd obviously overheard her—but why was he being weird about it? She'd never agreed to stay the summer, let alone return regularly. And not once—not even after one of their marathon lovemaking sessions, after oxytocin had snuck in and made her feel all cuddly and couple-y— had she suggested that this thing between them could last. They were just . . . two people who had found a creative way to pass a little bit of time together as they tried to move past an insurmountable loss.

But as he shielded his brow and looked out at the beach, rather than at her, she couldn't shake the feeling that she'd made a terrible mistake.

The uneasy sensation only intensified when they got back to the house. Wyatt mumbled about needing to go "take care of something," then got into his SUV and drove off. Aly pretended that this was business as usual—it was, in a way, even if it did bother her that he still hadn't told her where he disappeared to. She would have to talk to him about that.

If Harry noticed anything was amiss, he didn't say. When Wyatt resurfaced a few hours later, he seemed normal again, and even put his hand on Aly's knee during dinner.

He'd just needed to blow off steam, she decided. After months of being by himself, he wasn't used to having a house full of people. There was nothing to worry about. She was doubly heartened when he tiptoed to her room that night. But his mind seemed to be elsewhere as he made love to her, which made it hard for her to enjoy herself (though a so-so night with Wyatt still beat her best night with anyone else she'd slept with).

"Where did you go earlier?" she whispered to him afterward. "And where are you always disappearing to?"

"I just need to be alone sometimes," he said vaguely.

This was not an actual answer, she thought with frustration, though she didn't push him on it. And to her dismay, he'd slunk back to his room when it was over.

As she fell asleep with one arm extended to the side of the bed where Wyatt had slept the past several nights, she made a note to clear the air between them as soon as Harry left. She was willing to apologize, even if she'd done nothing wrong. And if that wasn't enough to appease Wyatt, then so be it. She wasn't ready to end this thing they had going—not just yet. But the fact was, it had to come to an end.

Everything did.

THIRTY-TWO

For once, Aly got up before Wyatt, and she brewed the coffee. It wasn't very good, but at least she was proving her self-sufficiency. After all, she would be alone again as soon as she returned to New York. Best to get used to that sooner rather than later.

Before long, Tim and Harry, with Beckett in tow, came clambering down the stairs; Wyatt, rumpled and sleepy eyed, followed. After rushing through toast and dark roast, Tim declared it was time to set out, so they could make the majority of the drive during Beckett's morning nap.

"That went way too fast," Harry said to Aly as Tim loaded Beckett into the car.

"Oh, Harry," she said, embracing him. "I miss you already."

"Me, too, babe. Me, too." He looked over Aly's shoulder at Wyatt, who'd just finished filling the dishwasher with their plates and mugs. "Why don't you two come visit us in Chicago? This summer is lighter than usual for me, and Beckett is finally starting to sleep through the night."

Wyatt smiled. "I'm kind of trying to steer clear of Chi-town for now, but I'd love to see you three again soon."

Aly wished she hadn't heard him say *I* rather than *we*. He was obviously still upset about overhearing her tell Harry she intended to sell and skedaddle. She hadn't promised him anything other than the house for the summer. Why was he being like this?

"Wyatt!" said Tim, who'd just come back inside. "Before I forget, I found this in the drawer of the bedside table." He handed Wyatt a plain white envelope.

Wyatt shoved the envelope in his back pocket, though not before Aly recognized the handwriting scrawled across it. But . . . why would Luke leave a letter for Wyatt here?

"Thanks," he said. He glanced at Aly, but he quickly turned away when he saw she was looking at him. "Knowing Luke, it's probably cash he thought he owed me for drinks or something," he mumbled.

Aly nodded, but she wouldn't be thrown off course so easily. After she and Wyatt hugged Tim and Harry one more time and waved from the end of the driveway as they headed down the road, she turned to him. "What's in the letter?"

He cleared his throat, then said, "Well, since I haven't opened it yet, I have no idea."

"When are you going to?" She knew she was being pushy, but this was her brother they were taking about.

"Would you like me to read it to you before I have a chance to see for myself?"

"Yes," she said.

"That was sarcasm," he said, starting for the house.

He was walking fast—fast enough that she couldn't catch up. "Wyatt," she called from behind. "What are you trying to hide?"

"Again, how can I be hiding something I haven't read yet?" he said over his shoulder.

"You at least owe it to me to tell me why you're being cagey."

He spun around. "Owe it to you? Is that how you think of our relationship?"

"Actually, it's how *you* do." She was beginning to feel lightheaded, and her limbs felt kind of tingly, too. "You're the one who said you owed me for letting you stay this summer—remember? And I guess on this one count, yes. I do feel like you owe me."

But as she saw his face twist with confusion, and then watched his lips purse as he remembered what he'd said to her, she realized she didn't want to fight with him. Not when they already had so little time left together. Not ever, but especially not now, right before she was leaving. "I hate this," she said. "Can we please stop?"

"'This'? You mean being here with me? Because given what I heard you say at the beach yesterday, you're eager to get out of here as fast as you can," he said.

And there it was. "I knew it," she muttered. "I *knew* you overheard me and Harry. You didn't even get the whole conversation—you're upset based on one tiny part you overheard."

"Can you blame me? I don't need to hear the whole thing to get the gist of what you were saying."

"And what's that?"

"That you're making plans that don't include me. Which means you don't intend on continuing this," he said, gesturing between them.

"You always knew I was leaving, Wyatt. I never said otherwise. And sure, you asked me to stay once, but that wasn't a serious conversation."

"Because you wouldn't let it be, Aly," he growled. "I know I told you we couldn't be together. But damn it, we *are*. And it feels good. It feels right. So why are you so insistent on pushing me away?"

"I'm not. Come on, Wyatt. Let's stop fighting. Come inside," she said, putting her arms around him. But instead of reciprocating, his torso stiffened. She immediately let him go and stepped back. "Who's pushing away who?"

"That's not what this is about."

"Then what? Because your body just responded like I was a porcupine."

He shook his head. "I just don't want to move straight to sex when we're in the middle of an important conversation."

No? Because she did. Except, hearing him point this out made her feel ashamed—like she'd just broken some sort of code of conduct. She wondered if this was what happened when no one had ever modeled healthy relationships to you: you just kept making a fool of yourself while everyone else was busy being a well-adjusted human.

"Aly, I need a breather," said Wyatt, opening the back door. Instead of going inside, though, he reached in and grabbed his keys from the hook on the wall.

"You're always doing that!" she said angrily. The dizzy sensation was getting worse. Well, good. She'd be lucky if this entire episode—the whole year, really—was wiped from her memory.

"Doing what?" said Wyatt, who'd yet to move in the direction of his SUV.

Her eyes bulged as she pointed at his keys. "Running away!"

"That's rich, coming from you." He shook his head with disappointment, and Aly couldn't help but feel that in disappointing Wyatt, she'd somehow let Luke down, too. Which made everything even worse. "I just need a little space. Let me go read this letter and think for a minute, okay?"

"Fine," she said, because she desperately wanted to believe that it was fine. But as she watched Wyatt climb into his vehicle, she couldn't avoid the truth: he was leaving.

Just like everyone did when they found out who she really was.

THIRTY-THREE

Aly couldn't bring herself to go inside after Wyatt drove away. They'd made love in nearly every corner of the house, save Luke's bedroom, and so each room held a cache of memories that she'd prefer not to recall, lest she be reminded of how her lust surfaced at the most inappropriate times—and worse, how she'd pushed the object of her affection away by . . . well, by being herself.

Instead, she walked to the water and threw herself down in a heap in the sand, miserable if grateful that with the exception of a few beach-combers, she was alone.

And then Aly cried, and then she cried a little more. She was going to have a wicked headache the next day; she could already feel it. But she'd lost control of her emotions, and she was entirely too close to los-ing control of her career, too. What had she expected—that somehow her harebrained whim to have a fling with her dead brother's best friend would magically work out? Whims were not how she'd accomplished a single thing in the past. Yet her subconscious had played the worst trick on her of all, making her think that giving in to impulse this one time might—just might—be okay.

This was the problem with . . .

No. She wasn't going to call it love. With *infatuation*. Pheromones. Trying to trade emotional grief for physical relief.

And oh, what a relief it had been. When Aly finally reluctantly dragged herself back to the house, she realized that she had yet one more reason to sell the place: now every time she set foot in it, she would think of Wyatt, and how she'd unceremoniously put an end to the most fun she'd ever had with someone other than her brother.

She had nothing to do, so she decided to make herself a sandwich for lunch but ended up cleaning the fridge instead. Then she scoured the inside of the cupboards, even though they didn't contain a single crumb or speck of dirt. She finally threw together the sandwich that she'd intended to make earlier and ate it joylessly.

When she was done with that, she picked up a book, but the words refused to register as sentences. Instead, her thoughts formed a truly unfortunate trail of bread crumbs. There was the envelope; and how she and Wyatt had fought; and the strange comment he'd made about Luke having a plan; and getting drunk after James and Linda and the stupid conference call; and the incident with Meagan and Ashleigh; and Meagan finding Aly sobbing in the bathroom; and the call from Wyatt that sent her there.

Of course, all of it led directly back to Luke's death.

How could it only be five o'clock? She wanted the day to be over, so she took a Benadryl because it usually made her drowsy. When that did nothing to slow her mind, she took another and topped it off with a splash of the bourbon she'd had the night she had gotten drunk. Soon her head felt hazy, but strangely, the horrible heaviness in her chest only intensified, so she had a bit more bourbon and that finally seemed to do the trick. Before she crawled beneath the covers, she took some of the blue tape Wyatt had used to divide the house and fastened a note to her door. On it, she'd written, *Need to be by myself.*

Moments before she fell asleep, a fleeting thought came to her. *You're a liar, Aly Jackson.*

~

Aly awoke a new woman. Now, she was willing to bet that nearly every person who'd just slept twelve whole hours felt this way. But there was more to it than that. In the clear, bright light of morning, she saw how she'd overreacted. If Wyatt needed clarity, she would give it to him. If he didn't want to tell her what was inside that envelope, she would have to live with that, too. As soon as she saw him, she would apologize so he'd know that she was willing to dial it back, and to make sure he knew he was in control of his choices.

And hopefully then, she would continue being one of those choices until she returned to New York.

Aly hummed to herself as she brushed her teeth and fixed her face. The smell of coffee wafted through the air, and it struck her as a good omen. Surely Wyatt was ready to put all this behind him, too.

But when she got to the kitchen, he wasn't there. Instead, she found boxes scattered across the living room floor—at least eight or ten of them, by the look of it. Aly vaguely recalled some bumping and thumping in the night, but the second allergy pill had done a number on her, and she hadn't gotten up to find out what the racket was.

Never in her wildest dreams had she imagined that the noise could have been Wyatt, boxing up all his things.

Aly's stomach sank. It was too late for apologies—she'd already scared him off.

"Good morning," said Wyatt, who'd just walked through the door with a large box in his arms. He frowned when he saw her expression. "I'm sorry it's a mess, but I'll take care of it."

"I don't know how you can say that," said Aly tearfully, because it hadn't registered that he was hauling the box inside, rather than outside.

He set the box on the dining room table. "Say what?"

"'Good morning.' It's not a good morning at all," she said miserably, throwing herself down in a chair. "I say one wrong thing—okay, maybe more than one—and you decide to just up and leave!"

"What are you talking about, Aly?" he said. He looked tired, and no wonder: apparently, he'd been up half the night packing.

"You said you were staying through the summer," she said, blinking back tears.

"I still am. *You're* the one who's leaving."

"Well, sure," she said, sniffling. "You know I need to."

"No, you don't," he said firmly. "We've discussed this. But this isn't about your career, is it?"

"What do you mean?"

He sighed. "I mean, your need to know what's going to happen. If you don't know, you head for the nearest exit in order to regain control."

"That's the meanest thing you've ever said to me." As she wiped the stupid tear that had just escaped the corner of her eye, though, Aly realized it was also true. Here she'd been thinking everyone left, but that was backward; she didn't give them the chance. After all, Seth wasn't the only man she'd beaten to the punch. Really, the only person who'd ever preempted her was . . . Luke.

"Maybe I do like control. But apparently, so do you," she said, looking pointedly at the boxes.

Wyatt crossed his arms over his chest. "Those are Luke's. *Not* mine. I was getting some of them out of the shed. I don't know what's in them, but I thought you'd want to sort through them before you left."

"I . . ." She didn't even know what to say. "I'm sorry."

"It's okay," said Wyatt. He walked over to her and reached his arms out. She hesitated, then stood and let him pull her into his embrace. Was there any better feeling? If so, she couldn't think of one.

Aly stared up at him, as relieved as she was grateful. "I could come back in August. Just to visit, but maybe we don't have to end this so soon," she said. "And for the record, you don't have to leave when fall comes. Stay as long as you want. After all, it *is* yours, too. I'm not selling." She would need to tell Luis, who'd left her a few messages to see if she was interested in moving forward.

Wyatt's eyes widened. "You're not?"

She shook her head. "I think we should keep sharing it, even if I'm not here all the time. That's what Luke wanted, after all."

In fact, she'd decided this mere seconds before she announced it to him, but she knew it was the right choice. She would take some of the vacation she'd put off over the last decade at *All Good* and spend it right here in Saugatuck. And if James wasn't okay with that, well . . . she guessed she'd just go work for Meagan.

"I won't complain about that," he said, hugging her even tighter. "And I really am sorry I overreacted yesterday. I felt like you were trying to use what we have between us to get me to tell you about Luke, but I realize that idea had nothing to do with you."

"I would never do that. Not intentionally, at least." She had wanted to know about the letter, but her affection had been an attempt to end their fight and feel better.

"I know, and I'm sorry," he said. "Like I said, that was about me, not you. You know I have issues with people controlling me. Especially people who want something from me. My mother used to be nice to me when she wanted to get information about my dad."

"How so?" asked Aly.

"He cheated on her. Cheats on her," clarified Wyatt, shaking his head with disgust. "I think it started after Ruby died, although I can't really be sure. My mother would always be really nice to me right before she talked me into spying on him or getting me to tell her what I knew, because she knew my dad would slip up and mention things to me that he shouldn't have. Point is, it isn't fair of me to compare you to her. I'm sorry."

"You don't have to keep apologizing," said Aly. "But . . . you should talk to your mom, Wyatt. She's not a monster, and she needs you.

Imagine having a husband who wasn't loyal *and* being cut off from your only child."

"I don't know. I'm not sure I can trust her not to try to run my life."

"You can," said Aly. "And for the record, I forgive you—and you don't have to tell me about that letter. I just . . . want us to be okay. Are we?"

Wyatt's smile disappeared. "Aly, there's something I need to tell you." He closed his eyes and took a deep breath before looking at her again. "And you're going to want to sit down for it."

THIRTY-FOUR

Aly knew what Wyatt was going to say before it came out of his mouth. Not the details; never in a million years would she have guessed that her brother, who hadn't put a single cigarette to his lips, had been diagnosed with small cell lung cancer six months before his death. But one look at Wyatt's stricken expression, and suddenly all of it—Luke's wan appearance when she'd last seen him, the perpetual back pain he'd tried not to complain about, the cough that he'd chalked up to the asthma he'd suffered from since he was a child—came together like the pieces of a horrifying puzzle.

Luke had been sick.

And Aly had been too self-absorbed to see it.

Even the beach house made sense now. Luke hadn't known about his cancer when he'd quit his job and moved back to Michigan. But intuition is a powerful thing; he'd told Aly that countless times. Something deep within him must have known that he wasn't long for this world, and that he had to do the things he wanted to do while he still had the chance.

"That's why he decided to take that sailing trip, even though he knew the weather was going to be bad," explained Wyatt, whose eyes were wet. He'd tried to hold Aly's hands as he talked to her, but she couldn't bear his touch. Everything—the sun streaming through the windows, the sound of the gulls circling overhead, the blood whooshing in her ears, and yes, Wyatt himself, yet again delivering the worst news of Aly's life—was much too much.

"Luke would never take his own life. *Ever.*" She sounded shrill, maybe even hysterical, but for once she didn't care. "He loved being alive too much for that."

"Trust me—do you think this hasn't slowly been destroying me?" said Wyatt, pulling at his hair. "All I can think about is whether I helped my best friend die by suicide. And you, Aly . . ." he choked. "Every time I look at you, I can't help but wonder if I'm the reason you're grieving. For all we know, he might still be alive right now."

Her chair toppled as she stood suddenly, but she didn't bother picking it up. "Then *why* did you let him go? You said yourself he knew there was a storm brewing."

"I don't know," said Wyatt miserably. "He'd always wanted to sail far enough to see Cuba. He was losing strength and wasn't willing to wait any longer."

"Not even another week? Or even a day or two, after the storm had passed?"

He shook his head, and Aly turned away from him. Logically, she understood that the choice hadn't been his to make.

Emotionally, she felt like he'd personally thrown Luke into the ocean.

"Why didn't you at least go with him? You're an expert sailor!" That's what Luke had told her when he called Aly to tell her about their trip. "Wasn't that the entire point of you going to Florida with him?" The two men had driven down from Michigan so that Luke could haul his sailboat with him.

"I was there to support Luke, Aly. I was never there to take the boat out with him. I think he wanted me to . . ." To deal with what happened after Luke never made it back to shore—they both knew what he left unsaid. Wyatt was crying, and although she was furious with him, Aly had started to weep.

"I don't understand. Why wouldn't he tell me he had cancer? I could have helped him. I could've looked for clinical trials and gotten him through treatment!"

"That's exactly why he didn't," said Wyatt, who made no attempt to wipe his face. "The five-year survival rate is less than three percent, Aly, and the treatments can be as bad as the cancer itself. Luke said he didn't want to spend the time he had suffering. I wouldn't have made that choice, but it wasn't mine to make."

"That doesn't explain why he wouldn't tell me," she said, pulling on her face. She wanted out of her skin; she wanted out of her mind. Just when she thought nothing could be worse than losing Luke, then . . .

This.

"You were on the verge of accomplishing your biggest dream," said Wyatt. "He knew you'd drop everything to be with him. That you'd spend all your time worrying about him. He didn't want that for you."

"No," she cried. Her career dream was nothing—nothing—compared to her brother.

"That's what I meant when I said Luke had thought about it, that we'd discussed it. He never came out and said it, but all the plans were in place—the house, the papers, the inheritance. He had to have known he might not make it back."

"He *had* to have known he wouldn't," said Aly. "That's why he wanted me to be there. He wanted one more chance to say goodbye." And she had not given it to him because she was working.

The gears were clicking into place at an alarming pace. Whether intentionally or not, her brother had decided to take a risk that cost him his own life. And her ambition—her stupid, pointless ambition—had prevented her from making one final goodbye.

"You lied to me," she said to Wyatt. "You've been lying to me for nearly a month. Ten months, if I really want to get specific about it.

You could've told me back in September what really happened. Instead, you've been nodding along while I talk about 'accidents' and 'fate' like an idiot, and then constantly disappearing without telling me where you're going, which probably has everything to do with this whole mess, too."

"It doesn't," said Wyatt firmly, shaking his head. "Aly, I've been careful never to lie to you. I kept my mouth closed until I had enough information—that's why I didn't tell you about the life insurance. I was waiting for them to rule out suicide and agree to make the payout."

"Did they?" Aly asked shrilly.

"Yes," he said. "And I pray to God that's the truth, even though we'll probably never know for sure. Aly, Luke didn't want you to know—he didn't want you to go through what you're going through right now. As his friend, I wanted to honor his request. When I agreed, I never thought you and I would get involved, but now we are, and . . ." His voice caught. "I couldn't keep you in the dark anymore. I told you the minute it began to feel like a lie."

Aly stared at him. Even with his red eyes and tearstained cheeks, he was the best thing she'd ever seen.

She was going to miss him terribly.

"Even if that's all true, you still lied to me," she said in a low voice. "Because you said you'd never hurt me. But you did, Wyatt, and I am *done* having other people hurt me. Now, please leave."

THIRTY-FIVE

Wyatt left immediately, and Aly was glad. She wanted to be what she already was: alone.

This time, she couldn't even manage to cry. Crying seemed to her an act of hope, in that letting out the sadness would make way for something better.

But there was no better, and there never would be. Luke had not behaved impulsively. *He'd had a plan.* The fatal flaw in the logic Aly'd been using to navigate her life had become glaringly apparent: having a plan didn't save you from disaster.

No—sometimes it led you directly to it.

Without registering what she was doing, Aly walked outside and down the path, and suddenly the lake was right in front of her. The water felt cold on her feet, and colder still on her legs, but by the time she'd submerged her lower body, she didn't feel anything. There was a steep drop-off not far from the shoreline; that, along with the rip current and thick seaweed, was why this stretch of water wasn't designated for swimming. Which was fine. Aly had no intention of swimming.

And then her entire body was in the lake. The drop-off was so surprising that she accidentally inhaled a mouthful of water, but she didn't try to push back up to the surface. It wasn't that she was actively trying to stay under. It was just that she wanted to know what it was like to drown. Had Luke changed his mind in the end when it was already too late? Had he struggled when he realized there was no winning against the water, the storm? Or had he been at peace when he gave himself to the ocean? His body hadn't been recovered; only his battered sailboat, which a yacht had found drifting miles from the southernmost point of the continental US.

She would never know if he'd seen Cuba.

At once she felt something pulling on her hair, hard.

Not something—some*one*. And whoever it was had grabbed her shirt, and her waist, and dragged Aly's head above water.

"Allegra Jackson," gasped her mother. "What has gotten into you?"

Aly sputtered, then vomited up the lake water she'd swallowed. "Nothing," she finally managed to say. "I was just going for a swim."

"I may not be smart, young lady, but I'm no dummy," said Cindy, pulling her toward the shore. She was surprisingly strong, and as she hauled Aly onto the sand things began to come back into focus, and Aly realized that her mother had swum out to save her. Cindy had grown up on the lake, just like she and Luke had, but Aly had no idea her mother could swim so well.

She stood in front of Aly, soaked, her mascara leaving long black trails down her cheeks. "You don't just go wandering into the lake in all your clothes," she said, practically shouting. "Especially not walking in like that—you weren't even pretending to swim. Now don't you do that! Don't you ever do that again. Don't *you* leave me, too." Cindy had started to cry. Aly had never seen her mother cry before—not sober, at least. It didn't look anything like it did when she was blubbering after a binge. This was different. Not just the lucidity in Cindy's eyes, but the fear.

And the love.

A fissure had already formed in the wall around Aly's pain, but now it split wide open, and she began to wail like a child. She curled into a ball and rocked back and forth, and Cindy knelt and folded her thin body around Aly and rocked with her, stroking her hair and making soothing sounds, just like Aly had always wished she'd done when she was younger. "Shhh," said Cindy. "I know. I know. You're going to get through this. You are."

"I don't want to," cried Aly.

"I know that, too," said Cindy, holding her tight. "Trust me, I do. But I'm here. You're here. It's going to be okay."

~

"Why were you on the beach?" asked Aly an hour later. Cindy had made her take a shower while she put on tea, and then she'd tucked a blanket around Aly and had been pretending to clean up while circling the couch to keep an eye on her. It would've been nice had it not been so unnerving. Had someone secretly sent Cindy to a finishing school for wayward mothers? "I figured after our fight, you wouldn't come back," Aly added.

"I don't know," said Cindy with a shrug. "I know you like me to call first. I was just missing Luke, and since you didn't want me at the house, I walked out to the beach. And then I saw you bobbing up and down and . . ."

Even after the tea and the shower, Aly was still shivering, but a new chill came over her. What if Cindy hadn't come by? Aly really hadn't been trying to end her life, but she hadn't been trying to save it, either. "Thank you," she said softly. "It wasn't what it looked like."

"I never said what it looked like," said Cindy, sitting on the edge of the coffee table across from her. "But you scared me real good. You want to tell me what happened? Was it Wyatt?"

Just hearing his name made Aly's heart hurt—literally hurt, as though someone had stomped on it. "No. Well, not really. I'm just . . ." Maybe she would tell her mother about Luke's illness one day. Probably not, though. Cindy would blame herself for smoking around him all those years. Even if that had contributed to his cancer in some way, Aly realized that she didn't actually want her mother to be in even more pain than she already was.

"I did have a fight with Wyatt," she confessed. "But mostly I've been upset about Luke." Upset—no, that was how you felt when your fridge broke, or you didn't get a promotion you were up for. "Devastated," she clarified. "And I guess kind of hopeless. At least today."

"I'm glad to hear you say it."

Aly eyed her mother. "What do you mean?"

Cindy rubbed her eyes before looking at Aly. She'd washed her face, and without her makeup she looked younger, or at least less weathered. "Just, you'd been acting like everything was normal every time I called you. I know you're strong, Allegra, but no one's that strong. Not about the important stuff. And Luke was your most important person in this world."

"That's the thing, Mom," she said quietly. "I don't think I *am* strong." In fact, she knew she wasn't. If she were, she never would have lost her temper with Meagan and Ashleigh or wandered out into the lake and scared her mother half to death.

And she definitely wouldn't have told Wyatt to leave. He wouldn't come back now—not when she'd tried to control him. She hung her head as she realized just how badly she'd bungled their relationship.

"You're one of the strongest people I've ever met," said Cindy with a new fierceness. "I know you didn't like how it went when you were at home with your dad and me. But you came out of it with a spine like a steel rod."

Aly pulled her head back in horror. "I seriously hope you're not implying that the way that Dad treated us was good for us."

"I'm not," said Cindy, whose gaze had shifted to her feet. "I *am* sorry I didn't step in sooner. And I should've said that the other day, so I'm sorry about that, too."

"*Sooner?*" Aly was grateful to her mother, but she wasn't about to let this go. "You *didn't* step in. That's the whole problem. Not only did you not step in, you acted like we deserved it!" How many times had Cindy said, "Wait until your dad gets home," knowing full well that the minute she so much as insinuated that Aly or Luke had misbehaved, Dan would unleash his fury on them? Aly stared at her mother in disbelief. "Mom, do you know what happens when someone tries to touch my face or hair?"

Cindy didn't say anything, but she looked up at Aly.

"I flinch," said Aly bluntly, recalling Wyatt's reaction. "And when someone slams a cupboard or shuts the door too loud, I squeeze my eyes closed. Every time, Mom. I can't hear children crying without feeling sad—or worse, terrified for them—and then I get even more upset because I know there's nothing I can do if they're really being hurt. I can spend an entire day worrying about some random kid I saw at the grocery store. That's not strong, Mom. That's *damaged.*"

"I'm sorry, Allegra," said Cindy woefully.

"Yeah," said Aly, shaking her head. "Me, too."

"I know I didn't do right by you. And I know that I turned to the bottle to try to forget about that. But I'm trying to now, the best I can."

It took Aly several moments to respond. As she contemplated what her mother had said and what she wanted to say back to her, Cindy sat motionless on the edge of the coffee table, looking not unlike a defendant awaiting a verdict.

"Thank you," Aly finally said.

"No, thank *you*," Cindy said softly. She wiped her eyes, then stood. "How about I fix you some food?"

"Okay," said Aly, not because she was hungry—she had a strong suspicion everything would taste like sawdust—but because Cindy was trying.

And if there was one thing Aly could appreciate, it was effort.

"I know you don't want me to be here too long," called Cindy from the kitchen, "but I don't want you to be by yourself after I go. Can you call Wyatt, maybe patch things up?"

Aly had decided she'd been on the sofa long enough and moved over to the island. As she sat on one of the stools, she spotted a tiny sliver of blue tape at the edge of the granite countertop, which she must have missed when she'd peeled the rest off. "I'll be okay, Mom," she said, pulling the tape up with the edge of her nail.

"No, Allegra. Sorry—Aly," Cindy corrected herself. She stood at the stove, stirring the eggs she'd just cracked in the pan. "That's what I told myself all those years, that I was okay with it being just me against the world. But as my sponsor keeps reminding me, you always have a choice. We all have someone who will be there for us if we'd only ask them. So, my girl," she said, her steely gray eyes trained on Aly, "don't choose to be alone, okay?"

THIRTY-SIX

Cindy had made it sound like Aly had a choice. But as Aly stared at the ceiling later that night, listening for the sound of Wyatt even though she knew she wouldn't hear the jangle of his keys or his footsteps on the stairs, she sure didn't feel that way.

She supposed she could call him, or even text, but what would she say? *I'm still so upset that you didn't tell me the truth about my brother—but also, I accidentally fell for you, and now I see that I've ruined everything and understand if you won't forgive me, because I certainly wouldn't if I were in your shoes because I told you I was leaving anyway?*

Yeah, no. She wasn't doing that.

She tossed and turned throughout the night, and by five the next morning she was wide awake, even though it was still dark out. She got up and made coffee and puttered around the house, forcing herself to wait until seven—which was still only six in Chicago—to call Harry.

"I just had the weirdest dream about you," he answered.

She smiled at the sound of his voice. "Was I submerged in a lake and Cindy was rescuing me from a semiaccidental drowning?"

"Um, *no*. You were a television news anchor, and you were sending me coded messages through the screen. But please tell me you're joking about the whole semiaccidental drowning thing, because I haven't had nearly enough espresso to deal with you being serious."

"I'm joking? Except also I'm not." And then she told him what had occurred—but only after she made him promise not to drive straight to Saugatuck the second she'd finished her story. "Well?" said Aly after she'd finished, because Harry had been too quiet for far too long.

"Oh, babe," he said in a voice that immediately made her tear up. "I'm so sorry to hear that about Luke—and about Wyatt. And I am *so* proud of you for confronting your mother, although I may have to send Cindy a whole florist's shop full of flowers for saving your life. Point being, I'm giving you the biggest telepathic hug that ever was right now. Can you feel it?"

She could. "I love you, Har."

"I love you more. So forgive me when I say: *Wake up!*"

Aly jumped. "What?" Where was soft, sweet Harry, who loved her unconditionally and would never judge her?

"I'm not judging you," he retorted.

She had to laugh. "I hate it when you read my mind."

"Oh, I know you do. But as the person who loves you almost as much as the Wild Thing does—"

"Harry!" she interjected. "He doesn't love me."

"Let me finish, babe."

"Fine."

"You do know you're still interrupting, right?"

She laughed again, and he continued. "I adore your brother, but I think it's important to recognize that he put Wyatt in an impossible situation with this. On top of the whole leaving-the-house-to-you-both thing, he obviously must have known about his sister dying and could have at least guessed that this would be really, really hard for Wyatt— first he loses his sister, then his best friend?"

"I know," said Aly. It had been a rare misstep for Luke. Then again, she didn't have terminal cancer, and she was *still* making one screwup after another. And really, didn't it come back to intent? She wished Luke had made different decisions, starting with telling her that he was sick.

But the fact remained that he had not, and still she knew he'd taken every one of his actions with love.

"I'm not saying Luke needed to predict the future," said Harry, "but he must have known that this would be hard for Wyatt, and he still asked him to keep his trap shut. I think you should cut Wyatt some slack here."

Aly had to admit that her friend had a point.

Harry continued. "Now, maybe he would have done things differently if he had another chance, but we have to assume that he was doing the best he could at the time."

Bless him. With one simple word—*we*—he'd already reminded her that she wasn't alone.

"All that said," he added, "you do need to fix this while there's still a chance."

"How?" she moaned. "I don't think I'm fixable, Harry. I'm pretty much broken beyond repair."

"Aly, I said fix *it*—not yourself. *You're* not broken. I understand that you truly believe that story about yourself—and I also know there's nothing I can say that's going to get you to let go of it and start telling another one. But may I give you one small piece of advice?"

"Always."

"Go watch the video."

"You watched it, too?" A rush of shame-induced nausea came over her. Of course, Harry would love her regardless. But also . . . she didn't want him to see her like that.

"I went to look for it the second you mentioned it existed."

"Wait—it's been up this entire time?" said Aly.

"Not sure, but when you told me that James had seen it, I knew it would be up sooner or later—that's just the nature of these things. So I kept searching for it, and eventually spotted it the day before your coworker told you someone had posted it. How the hell else was I going to protect you if I didn't know what we were dealing with?"

So that was why he hadn't sounded surprised when she told him it was live.

"Thank you," she said, and she *was* starting to feel a little less mortified. "But . . . I still don't get why I have to watch it."

"Just do it, okay? I feel like it might give you some insight on . . . Well, you'll see."

"You're an odd one, Horatio Medellin."

"And you wouldn't have it any other way. I'm going to text and call about four hundred times over the next week, so be expecting it."

"You're also the best."

"Best friend? Yes, yes, I am. Love you."

He really was the best, Aly thought to herself. And she was incredibly grateful to have him in her life.

But as she looked toward the driveway, only to confirm that Wyatt's SUV was still missing, she couldn't help but wish that someone else was making her feel less alone.

~

Aly had clicked the "Play" button no fewer than ten times. Yet each time the video began, and she saw herself jabbing a finger in the air at Meagan and Ashleigh, the latter of whom appeared to be off camera, she immediately pressed "Stop."

Because although Aly and Cindy bore little physical resemblance to each other, damned if she wasn't the spitting image of her mother hollering at her and Luke.

How could this possibly be helpful? To see herself traumatized and losing her job—even if Innovate wasn't framing it that way. Harry must have read an article about aversion therapy on one of those health websites that never cited their sources. There really was no other explanation for him insisting she watch the video.

The sun was setting when she finally summoned the courage to watch the whole thing. This time, she hadn't poured herself any bourbon, nor had she taken an allergy pill or even tried deep breathing. Instead, she sat on the back porch, phone in hand, and stared at the woman having a tantrum on the screen . . . who happened to be her.

"You're the beach!" she yelled at Meagan.

"Me?" said Meagan, shooting her a look that could have melted glass. "Give me a break."

"You give *me* a ducking break!" cried Aly.

But of course, she didn't say *ducking*, and her face seemed . . . wrecked.

Except Aly didn't remind herself of her mother anymore. She looked like someone else, even if she couldn't put her finger on who, exactly.

On camera, she continued yelling. "You know my brother just died. And you know you're the only person I told. You could have backed me up in there, Meagan. Or even here!" she said, waving her hands around.

"What? Your brother died?" said Ashleigh, but Aly had cut her off to yell at Meagan.

"Instead, you accuse *me* of letting *All Good* fall to pieces? Well, news flash!" Aly was shouting now. "That has zippity-do-da-day to do with me and everything to do with a management team who continues to chip away at our lousy little salaries and cut back on resources while they keep their expense accounts and assistants and ignore the fact that the media landscape is changing and we—and by *we*, I mean every single person at Innovate—*have* to change with it if we're going to survive. *That* is why the magazine is failing. And by sitting here and gossiping about me, knowing full well I'm living through the worst possible time in my entire life—which, by the way, is saying a whole lot for a girl whose father used to beat the crap out of her—instead of lending me a hand or at least keeping your mouth shut, you're making it even worse." At this point in the video, Meagan was silent and regarding her with . . . No, it wasn't disbelief. It almost looked like relief.

As she sat on the porch, ignoring the mosquitos feasting on her limbs, Aly suddenly realized who she reminded herself of. A few years back, she'd seen a video on social media in which a coyote accidentally wandered into a sandwich shop in downtown Chicago. As she watched her own eyes dart around the salad place, seeming to look for an exit, she realized she looked exactly like that coyote had.

Wild.

Trapped.

Yet determined to get out of there and keep living.

The video had stopped. Grimacing, Aly scrolled down and braced herself for horrible comments.

But there weren't any.

Instead, she scanned through a long string of remarks that, with few exceptions, seemed to agree that Innovate—not Aly—was the problem.

Whoever posted this is going to get flattened by a tree or struck by lightning. Sleep w/ one eye open, creep!

Seriously bad karma on the part of the person who put this up.

Just cancelled my subscription to All Good. *I'll renew when they start treating their staff right.*

This poor girl. I lost my brother, too. It's rough.

Take this s&*t down and let her grieve.

Gross. Why would you crap on someone in crisis?! Take this down.

This is a REALLY bad look for Innovate. They're already paying freelancers less than a dollar a word, and they've been taking six months to pay photographers, too. They'd better not fire this chick.

No lies detected from this editor. Magazines are dead. Kudos to her for being brave enough to say why.

Aly's jaw hung open. The reason she'd been removed from the masthead had nothing to do with her losing control. It was because she'd revealed the magazine's biggest problem—which was James and his management team. And because she hadn't said a single thing that wasn't true, they'd probably had to triple-check with Legal to make sure she couldn't sue them, hence her month-long break. She'd listened to Harry talk shop long enough to know that as a private employer, Innovate had every right to can her—but they knew doing so would probably lead to even more negative publicity. Which was why they'd quietly shuffled her offstage with a promise of autonomy and a little more money.

More importantly, she understood why Harry had encouraged her to watch it, and why Meagan had commended her for finally—*finally*— speaking the truth instead of continuing to act like . . . well, a robot, to be honest.

It turned out that Aly *wasn't* broken. She was . . . normal.

She had been all along.

Because grief? That was normal.

So was trauma, even—or maybe especially—if it had been lingering for decades.

And anger? As normal as a clear blue sky in June, especially when it involved telling the truth about a career and an industry that you loved, but that didn't love you back.

Maybe normal was even forgetting all the things you'd yelled at your coworkers, then having to watch yourself on video—right along with anyone else with internet access and the will to Google you—in order to remember.

Wyatt had nailed it: it was almost certain that Aly had PTSD. And that was a relief, too. Now that she could put a name to it, she could get help.

As Aly turned off her phone that night, she felt at peace for the first time in a very long while. Because although she wasn't clear on what she needed to do next, she knew one thing: finally facing what was wrong with her was the first step to making whatever came next right.

THIRTY-SEVEN

"I cannot thank you enough for doing this," said Mari as they pulled up in front of the children's center. She'd called Aly that morning to see if there was any chance she'd fill in for her volunteering shift; her supervisor at the restaurant had fallen ill, and she needed to cover for him.

Aly'd been tempted to say no; deliberately spending time with children who weren't Beckett sounded ill advised. But with Wyatt still gone—he had yet to come back for his belongings, and she had a feeling he'd wait until she'd left the state to get them—she had nothing but free time on her hands. And although she doubted her ability to actually make a difference, a small part of her thought that maybe this would be another thing that helped her heal.

"You nervous?" asked Mari.

"Not too nervous," said Aly, but she smiled when she met Mari's eye. "Okay, I am a little. I'm not sure if I mentioned this, but I'm not great with kids."

"You might have mentioned it seven or eight times," said Mari, smiling warmly at her. "But I have a feeling you're going to do just fine. Anyway, it's just for today. Remember—the main thing is to try. It doesn't have to be perfect."

Aly nodded, thinking of her mother. "I'm happy to at least do that."

The center was located down a long dirt road near the river, right next to an arts colony. Three separate barns housed the children's center, each with a metal corrugated roof; the sides of one were painted red, another navy, and the last one was white. "This used to be a farm," said Mari, answering Aly's unspoken question. "The family who owned it couldn't have children, but they'd always wanted to, so they started setting up after-school activities for kids who needed something to do. Before they died, they created the children's center and donated their entire estate toward its funding."

"Incredible," said Aly, thinking of the money Luke had left her. She'd been feeling so guilty about it that it hadn't occurred to her that she didn't have to keep all of it for herself. She could use some, or even most, of it to do . . . well, she wasn't sure what, but something of service that would honor her brother. Luke had rented space at the marina to operate his sailing school, and it had already been closed for the season at the time of his death. But where had he stored the extra sailboats? Maybe she could find a new purpose for those. She made a note to ask Wyatt when she saw him again.

If she saw him again.

"Oh, just wait until you check out the literacy building," said Mari, guiding her toward the entrance of the blue barn. "I have a few minutes—I'll go in with you."

Aly murmured her appreciation as Mari pulled back one of the sliding doors to reveal the barn's interior. Floor-to-ceiling bookshelves lined the walls, packed with books of all sizes and reading levels, each with a tall library ladder to access the higher shelves. A seating area had several comfy couches and at least a dozen beanbags, and some round tables surrounded by chairs. Kids sat everywhere, their heads bent over books instead of tablets or phones.

Aly would've loved this place as a child—before she found magazines, she'd lost herself in books. Honestly, the center was the sort of place she loved as an adult. She took a deep breath: it even *smelled* like books. Did a better scent exist?

Only one, but she quickly inhaled again to rid her mind of it.

"This is pretty great," admitted Aly as she and Mari walked over to a far corner of the building, to an administrative desk.

"I'm so glad you think so," said the man seated behind the desk, who stood to greet them. Both of his arms were covered with tattoos, and he wore a bow tie with his short-sleeve button-down. Aly liked him on sight. "Mari, thanks for finding someone to take your spot today."

"Glad to help," said Mari. "Aly, this is Jon Nguyen. He's the center director. Jon, this is Aly."

"A pleasure to meet you," said Aly, shaking his hand.

"Likewise. Mari has told me a lot about you, and we're delighted to have you. Of course, we'd love to have you sign on as a long-term volunteer if you find that you enjoy the work."

"I wish I could," said Aly honestly. "But I'm heading out of town soon."

"Well, if that changes, you know where to find us," said Jon with a smile. "Now, before you get started, I'll give you a quick tour of the other buildings. Sound good?"

"Sounds terrific," said Aly.

"I've got to get over to the Mermaid. You okay to take it from here?" asked Mari. She'd driven them there, and Aly had already told her she'd walk the two miles home; a walk would be just the thing to help keep her head clear.

"I am," said Aly, hoping this would turn out to be true.

"Thank you. I owe you coffee before you leave. Call me to collect," said Mari, and Aly smiled and promised her she would.

As Jon walked Aly around, he explained that volunteering had nothing to do with workbooks or writing drills. Instead, volunteers mostly listened to the children read, and helped them with words and phrases they stumbled over. They passed a volunteer perched on a sofa, reading storybooks aloud to a group of young children. "Our goal is really to get kids to love reading," explained Jon. "We let them pick the books they want, and we don't talk about phonics or levels or anything like that. We do have staff who specialize in disabilities and help children with dyslexia and other issues. But what you'll be doing is encouraging kids to keep turning those pages and being there when they need a hand."

"I love it," said Aly. But just then, she caught a boy who was maybe six or seven at most, staring at her from the other side of the room. She looked away quickly, thinking of the disdain her coworker's daughter had shown toward her at Take Your Child to Work Day. What if her very presence was a deterrent to some kids?

She dared herself to look back at the boy again. When she did, he flashed a crooked grin at her.

Aly nearly tripped over a beanbag. With the exception of his sandy cowlicked hair, the boy looked nothing like Luke. But that lopsided smile—it was almost identical to her brother's.

She didn't believe in reincarnation or omens. She wasn't even particularly superstitious. But after her mother's unexpected appearance at the lake the other day, and now this—well, she had to wonder if Luke was still watching over her.

She wanted to believe he was.

"How about we check out the other buildings before you start?" said Jon, whose cheerful demeanor eclipsed even Aly's chipper management style. "I want you to have a complete picture of what goes on here."

"Definitely," agreed Aly, stealing one last glance at her brother's smile doppelgänger.

With different stations for clay, pastels, paint, and drawing, the fine arts building was every bit as impressive and magical as the first building. Then Jon walked her over to the red barn at the end of the property. "Our third building is dedicated to woodworking and crafts," he explained, pulling back the heavy barn door. "We try to work with local artisans and give kids as much of a Michigan-based experience as possible."

"That's—" Aly stopped midsentence.

Because there, in the center of the barn, was a large sailboat. And amid several children, ranging from maybe eight to eighteen, was a man with his back to her, sanding the boat's hull.

Aly immediately stepped out of the building before she could draw attention to herself. "Would you mind if we didn't go in right now?" she said quietly to Jon.

"Of course not. Can I ask why?" he said.

Aly exhaled as Jon pulled the door closed. "Um, sure. It's just that . . ." What would Luke do in this situation?

He'd be honest, she realized.

And so would she.

"The guy in there?" she said to Jon. "The one who's working on the boat with the kids?"

"Wyatt Goldstein?" said Jon, looking at her quizzically. "We just promoted him to assistant director. He's here all the time—he even runs evening workshops with some of the teens, since they tend to be night owls. We're big fans of Wyatt. Do you know him?"

Know him? She knew that corny jokes made his eyes crinkle at the corners, and that he squirmed whenever she touched his wrists. She knew that he'd lived through the loss of a sibling, too, and that he was perhaps the only person in her life who understood what she was going through.

And she knew that her brother—who had nothing if not exquisite taste in human beings—had chosen Wyatt to be his best friend . . . and to share the beach house with her.

I'm in love with him.

The thought sent an electric current through her core. She had been in love with him all along, even if she had fought tooth and nail to deny it and push him away.

And oh, how she'd pushed him away.

"Yes, I . . . I live with him," said Aly softly, well aware that this would probably confuse Jon; after all, why would she hide from the person she lived with? And wouldn't she already know he worked there?

But there was a relatively simple way to explain it. "And the sailboat he's working on with those kids?" she said. "It belonged to my brother, Luke. He was sailing it when he died last September."

THIRTY-EIGHT

Simply asking Wyatt to forgive her wouldn't be enough. Aly needed to do something bigger, something to demonstrate how sorry she was.

And yes, show him that she loved him.

Even if he didn't change his mind and come home—and she wouldn't blame him if he didn't—she wanted him to see that her heart was finally in the right place.

The entire time Aly was volunteering, she wondered if Wyatt would walk by and see her, but he never did. Afterward, Aly walked back to the beach house slowly, waiting for the right idea to surface. She could write him a letter, or maybe etch an oversized apology in the sand. She could hire a plane to fly a banner over the lake, but that was just more words, not to mention a waste of money.

For once, carefully crafted sentences wouldn't be the answer to her problems.

What, then?

She'd reached the end of the driveway, but instead of continuing toward the house, she stood there admiring the cedar shakes, the box-woods that Wyatt had kept trimmed, the brass bell she'd polished herself just the week before, and beyond the house, the beach they both loved to walk along.

The house would always be Luke's. But it was Wyatt's, now, too.

And hers, she realized.

She would give him the place if he couldn't bear to share it with her. Maybe even legally, although she'd have to talk to Roger to figure out how that would work. In the meantime, she could and would leave if that's what Wyatt wanted.

But as she walked around to the back of the house and sat in one of the chairs on the patio, she knew she didn't want to do that.

Before she could talk herself out of it, she pulled her phone out of her bag and called James.

"Aly?" he answered. "Everything okay?"

"Yes." She stared out at the water, which was gray and calm. "Actually, no."

"You heard Meagan left," he said. "Don't be worried about the transition—we have a meeting on the books for Tuesday to talk through what this will look like for you, and our team is already looking for someone to fill in as interim editor in chief."

Days earlier, she would have been incensed that he wasn't telling her she could have her job back. Now she didn't care. "That's not it, James," she said. "I saw the video. You probably were unaware of this, but I couldn't remember what I'd said in the heat of the moment—apparently forgetting conflict is a symptom of PTSD."

"I see."

"Now, before you run to Linda to tell her that I have PTSD so she can make sure you have all your legal i's dotted and t's crossed, that's not what I'm calling about."

James laughed nervously. "What is it, then?"

"I'm not returning to the magazine. I'm not returning to Innovate, either. I quit." She exhaled the breath she hadn't even realized she was holding.

"You don't mean that, Aly. I've nurtured your career for twelve years. I've mentored you and given you every tool available to help you succeed. And we need you now more than ever."

"Not so much that you're going to give me my job back. It floors me that you're more concerned about the company's image than honoring the work I've put in. You had to have known that I didn't want to be shuffled offstage even as you expected me to handle the entire production."

He cleared his throat. "I have to tell you, I'm really taken aback by what you're saying."

"I understand that, and I don't blame you. But James—the two tools you didn't give me were transparency and a fair wage. Even after my title change, I'm making less than the *Sporty* senior editors." She'd looked up the other magazine's salaries on an anonymous message board for people working in the media. "To be entirely clear, we both know that making me editorial director isn't a promotion; it's a demotion. And I'm not willing to let you continue to use my talent without fairly compensating or crediting me."

"The editorial director position isn't a permanent decision. Let me talk to my team before you make any big moves."

Her eyes followed a pair of gulls circling overhead. "There's no need. I don't even want to be editor in chief anymore." It was true. What Aly had been trying to keep wasn't the position; it was her identity. But a title would never make her exceptional, or even normal. It would never make her feel accepted or loved. All of that had to come from within her . . . and to a lesser degree, from the people she loved. "Without that desire, I won't be any good."

"What happened, Aly?" he asked quietly.

"My life happened," she said. "I'll email the staff to let them know I'm not returning. But James?"

"Yes?"

"Do everyone a favor and fire one of your assistants and use that money to pay a decent wage to a smart and savvy editor in chief that will help *All Good* create a digital presence and stay out of the media graveyard. If you're not sure where to start, Google the word *influencer*, okay?"

James laughed nervously. "I'm not sure what I'm going to do without you, Aly Jackson. I'll miss you."

She wanted to say that she'd miss him, too, but it wasn't true. He hadn't been a bad boss. But she wouldn't miss his early morning texts, or the mental gymnastics she'd had to perform in order to justify the financial and editorial decisions he made, knowing deep down that they were at odds with the long-term success of the magazine she loved. In fact, she already felt like someone had lifted an enormous weight off her shoulders. "I appreciate all you've done for me, James."

"Our door is always open if you change your mind," he said.

After she hung up, Aly took a deep breath. She felt good. Not quite relaxed—she hadn't fixed things with Wyatt—but not conflicted or cloudy. And maybe that was why she dialed Seth's number next.

"Aly?" he answered. He sounded confused.

"I'm sorry I didn't call sooner," she said.

"Oh. Uh. It's okay."

Neither of them spoke. Then Seth said, "Honestly? I wasn't okay with it. You just . . . cut me off, Aly."

"I know, Seth. I'm sorry," she said, leaning back in her chair. The sun felt good on her skin. "I was trying to protect myself. I've been doing a lot of thinking during my time off, and . . . I was a lot more messed up than I ever let you know."

"About us? I tried to be a good boyfriend, Aly."

"I know you did. That's not what I mean."

"Then what do you mean?"

"My childhood, Seth." He'd so rarely asked about her past, and she'd been happy not to volunteer information about it. "It was traumatic. I think that's why I had the meltdown with Meagan and Ashleigh."

"Oh. I'm sorry, Aly. I wish you'd told me."

"It's alright. It's not your fault I didn't. I just wanted to close the loop between us, I guess, and tell you I feel bad about how I ended things."

"I forgive you," he said.

She believed him.

"How do you want to handle this?" he asked. "Since you'll be back in the offices soon, we'll probably see each other. I don't want it to be awkward."

Of course James hadn't told him yet; she'd only broken the news to him minutes earlier. Aly examined her nails. Next month's issue had an article about kitchen staples that doubled as beauty aids, and apparently a dab of olive or canola oil was just the thing to soften cuticles. It was strange to think that soon she'd have to wait until *All Good* hit the newsstands to read it, just like everyone else. "I won't, so no need to worry about things being awkward. I quit."

"No." Seth sounded stricken.

"Yes!" Even *she* was surprised at the glee in her voice. "I'm done being an editor." Aly knew as soon as she said this she would need to email Meagan, too, and tell her that there was zero possibility that she would be working for her. Aly needed to find out who she was when she wasn't bent over pages with a red pen.

"What are you going to *do*?" asked Seth.

"I'm not sure," she admitted. Whatever it was, it wouldn't involve teaching people how to fit in. It wasn't that there was anything wrong with *All Good*'s message. Really, it had gotten her through so much of her life. But now she saw a different way—a path that didn't require a map to navigate.

Maybe her new career would involve helping people see that trying to be normal was overrated.

Aly sighed the sigh of someone who had lived several lifetimes, which was pretty much how she felt. "I really am sorry."

"Me, too," he said. "Don't be a stranger, okay?"

Aly doubted she'd ever speak to him again. But she could appreciate the sentiment all the same. "I honestly wish you all the best, Seth." Just then, a couple of gulls swooped down and started fighting over something in the sand.

"Where are you, anyway?" asked Seth.

She looked out at the water. "Home."

Aly felt relieved after she hung up, but depleted, too. The truth set you free—but first it wore you out.

Even so, she had one more thing to do before she called it a day. "Roger," she said to his voice mail, "it's Aly Jackson. I just want to know what I'd need to do if I wanted to transfer the deed to my brother's beach house to Wyatt Goldstein."

THIRTY-NINE

Wyatt did not come home that night, and Aly tried not to think too much about where he was laying his head, or why he hadn't called. Of course, she hadn't called him, either. She wasn't sure if he'd pick up if she did. But mostly, she wanted to talk to him face-to-face.

That wasn't the only conversation that wasn't meant for the phone. So after breakfast the following morning, Aly invited her mother over. Cindy sounded surprised to hear from her, and Aly almost didn't expect her to come. But forty minutes later, she was at the door, holding a bouquet of wildflowers.

"How are you holding up?" she said, examining Aly much in the way Aly used to examine Cindy when she was trying to figure out how loaded she was.

"Better than expected," said Aly. She hesitated, then leaned in to give her mother a hug. "Thank you again for the other day."

"No need to thank me," said Cindy, but she held on to Aly longer than she normally would have.

"Well, come in and make yourself comfortable," said Aly, taking the flowers from her mother. "Can I pour you a cup of coffee?"

"Sure," said Cindy, sitting on one of the stools at the island.

Aly put the flowers in a vase and filled it with water. Then she poured Cindy a mug of the dark roast she'd just made. "Here you go," she said, passing it to her. "It's not as good . . ." It occurred to her that she didn't need to censor herself—not anymore. "It's not as good as Wyatt's," she finished.

"If it's hot, it's good enough for me," said Cindy, lifting the coffee to her lips. She took a sip, then said, "It's perfect. Speaking of Wyatt, any word?"

"No," said Aly, who couldn't help but look through the double doors to see if a tall man with terrible posture happened to be roaming the beach. Alas. "There's something I need to tell you, Mom," she said, turning back to Cindy.

Cindy smoothed her T-shirt before meeting her daughter's eyes. "I'm listening."

After the truth bombs she'd dropped the day before, Aly hadn't expected to have trouble telling her mother the whole story.

And yet.

"Luke didn't just leave the house to me," she said quietly. "He left it to Wyatt, too—that's why we've been living together. We weren't dating yet when you stopped by that day."

"Not dating?" Cindy shook her finger playfully. "Could've fooled me."

Aly blushed. "Yeah, well, it did turn into something."

"I should think so! That is one good-looking man, and the sparks flying between you two—whoo boy!"

"Yeah," said Aly, who had to smile. "It was really good until I messed it up."

"Then you haven't made up with him yet?"

She glanced out at the water. "No. But I might leave the house to Wyatt, Mom. He loves it here."

"And you don't?" said her mother, raising an eyebrow.

"I've come to," Aly admitted. She would miss walking on the beach in the morning, and the coffee shop downtown, and being able to see Mari.

"Then why are you leaving?" said her mother. "Summer's the best time to be here. Though fall's not so bad, either, and winter's pretty idyllic with all that snow. But spring?" Cindy made a face. "Ack! I'm sure you remember how wet and gray it is in this part of Michigan. Everyone's itching to get it over with and get back to the beach. So if you can leave in, oh, March, I'd say you're golden."

Aly laughed. "I didn't know you were trying to sell me on staying."

Cindy looked embarrassed as she glanced out the windows. "It's just nice having you around is all. I know you have your job to get back to, but . . ."

"Actually, I quit."

Cindy whipped around to look at her. "You? Left the magazine?"

Aly nodded. "Yeah. Being here has given me a chance to think about what I want. And . . . it's not that anymore. Luke left me some money, so I'll be okay. I might head to Chicago to be near Harry."

Cindy stood and began to pace. "Aly Jackson, I just don't think you should leave this place. Your brother left it to you, too. And didn't you give me an earful about letting Billy move into my bungalow?"

Well, yes—she had. But this was different. "Is he still there?" she asked.

"You know that's not what I'm getting at."

"Sure, but did you tell him to leave?" asked Aly.

"Not yet."

Cindy and Billy were both yellers, but Aly didn't know him to be physically aggressive. That didn't mean her mother felt comfortable kicking him out. "Well, I think it's time, don't you? I could help you. Or if you want, Luke's lawyer is really good—I bet he'd know how to handle it. I'd be happy to give him a call."

Cindy looked down at her coffee mug. "You know I don't have money for that."

"No, but I do," said Aly.

"You don't have to help me. I don't deserve it."

"That's not the point, Mom," said Aly. "I'm offering because I can. And because it's what Luke would have wanted."

"That means more to me than you can know." Cindy blinked hard a few times. "I didn't think the other day was the time to go into this, but I'd like for us to try to have a relationship. A different one than we had before. If you'd be willing."

Aly wasn't so sure she was willing. Her mother did seem different, but who was to say it would last?

"I want you to know that . . . I did love you, Aly," said Cindy quietly. "I do now, course, but I did then, too. I'm sorry I didn't know how to show it. I want a happy family again, more than anything in the world."

It was impossible for Aly to hide her astonishment. "No offense, Mom, but we were *never* a happy family."

Cindy stared back at Aly like she'd just sprouted antlers. "Well, sure you were. I wasn't a part of it, and neither was your dad. But you and Luke were as happy a family as I've ever seen. I don't know any younger sister whose brother wanted to hang out with her, even when they were kids—do you? And you worshipped the ground he walked on, which only made him try to be even better for you. Neither one of you would've come out the way you did without the other one."

Aly turned away. She'd already cried in front of her mother, but at that point she really did need to be alone.

Cindy seemed to understand this because she excused herself to the bathroom. When she returned several minutes later, Aly asked, "Why are you telling me all this now?"

"Making amends is part of my program," said Cindy, wringing her hands. "But . . . I guess what happened the other day got me thinking. I want you to forgive me."

"I forgive you," said Aly.

"Thank you," said Cindy, sniffing.

"It might take some time for us to . . . figure out how to make this work," Aly said. "I'm going to be honest with you, Mom—I don't know if I can just pretend the past didn't happen, and sometimes being around you triggers me. But I'm willing to try."

"That's all I ask," she said, and the next thing Aly knew Cindy was hugging her. Her face was still wet on Aly's shoulder when she added, "Listen—don't you let this house go. Okay?"

Aly pulled back. "What? Why?"

"Well, I'm thinking about your brother. Remember that time your dad broke our television when he was mad?"

Aly shook her head; she didn't remember that. In fact, she couldn't recall a lot of incidents with her father—because as she knew now, her brain shut down, trying to protect her.

"Your brother was so upset that the two of you weren't going to be able to watch Saturday morning cartoons that he traded our tablecloth for a glazed ham, and then traded the ham for a boom box, and then found someone to swap the boom box for a small TV. I think the whole ordeal took him less than three days," said Cindy, grinning.

"I do remember that," said Aly, smiling at the memory of Luke hauling the TV home in a borrowed wagon.

"And of course, you were too young to remember this, but this one time when you were maybe a year, eighteen months at most, we had this crazy overnight storm that dropped a boatload of snow. Your dad and I were asleep, but Luke got up early, just like he always did, and bundled you up in your snowsuit, put you on the sled, and pulled you around the neighborhood like a beauty queen on a parade float. When I spotted him out front, I was mad as a hive full of hornets and told your brother to use his head. You know what he did?"

"What?"

"He looked at me with those clear eyes of his and said, 'I *did* use my head. I knew you and Dad weren't going to take Aly out today and that she'd want to see the snow. So I changed her diaper and made sure she was warm and got out before the snow got too deep.' I was so dumbfounded I had to laugh."

Through her tears, Aly laughed, too.

"Point being, your brother never did anything he didn't think through, even when it didn't make sense to everyone else. He was just like you that way: always had a plan. I'm not saying that it worked out every time—otherwise he'd be here right now."

"True," said Aly, who couldn't help but wonder if Cindy suspected what she now knew about her brother's last trip.

"Now, don't you think Luke left this house to you and Wyatt for a reason?" Cindy smiled at Aly. "I bet he knew all along that you two were good for each other—and that it was just a matter of time before you figured it out yourselves."

FORTY

Crying was exhausting. Really, sometimes life was exhausting, even when you weren't trying to convince everyone that there was nothing wrong with you. After Cindy left, Aly lay down on the sofa, intending to rest her eyes for a few minutes. When she woke, the sun was low in the sky.

She rose and washed her face, then dabbed on some concealer and a little blush. That mostly mitigated her skin's splotchiness, but there was nothing she could do about the light that had left her eyes. Just as she began to turn away from the mirror, though, she caught a glint of something in her reflection. It was a tiny spark, yet it ignited a realization—

She hadn't forgotten her fight with Wyatt.

Either fight, come to think of it. She could remember what they'd both been wearing each time, as well as the confusion and hurt in his eyes. She could recite, nearly verbatim, what each of them had said.

I am done having other people hurt me, she heard herself say.

Except Wyatt hadn't hurt her—not intentionally, and maybe not even at all. She'd hurt herself by not giving him the benefit of the doubt, by overreacting and cutting him off.

But in remembering, Aly had proved herself wrong. Because her intuition, maybe even her psyche, knew what her lizard brain had failed to notice: she was safe with Wyatt.

And yes, loved.

"What have I done?" she said aloud as she retrieved her phone from the coffee table.

Roger had left her a voice mail while she'd been sleeping. She could transfer the deed, he'd said, but it would be a complicated process, particularly because Wyatt was the executor of the estate and said estate wasn't settled yet—Aly assumed this last part referred to the life insurance that was still in limbo. But yes, if that was really what she wanted to do, he could help.

Fine: Aly knew how to do complicated. She would call him back tomorrow and tell him to set it in motion.

Now she just had to tell Wyatt about her decision.

Her hands trembled as she hit his number, but the call immediately went to voice mail. She hung up before it began recording and tossed the phone on the sofa.

As Luke said, when you couldn't think straight, you could still read—except in her state of mind even reading seemed completely out of the question. But when you couldn't read, you could still walk. Aly smiled to herself as she slipped on her flip-flops, because Luke would've liked that addendum to his aphorism. There were so many things she wanted to say to him; so many moments and memories that he would not be a part of. Even after all the grieving she had done over the past month, the thought of life without her brother felt unfathomable.

And still Aly threw open the French doors and stepped onto the patio. Luke might be gone, but she was still here. And while she was, she would go down to his beach and enjoy it for him.

She'd just begun to descend the stairs when she saw the boat in the water. Though she hadn't yet seen a body beside it, she immediately broke into a run.

Seconds later, Wyatt came into view. He waded in the water, which was up to his thighs, doing God only knew what beside *the boat*—the one that Luke had taken out in Florida, which had returned to Michigan in tatters, without him. Except it wasn't in tatters anymore. It was polished a deep brown and looked nearly as good as new.

"What are you doing?" she cried, still kicking up sand as she ran toward him.

At the sound of Aly's voice, Wyatt turned slowly, lifting a hand to shield his eyes from the sun. He didn't call back to her, and she felt her stomach drop: he was still upset.

But why had he sailed Luke's boat here? Was this some sort of mariner's revenge? A symbolic gesture to signify that he was really and truly done with her?

"Hey," he said, walking toward her through the shallow water. "Sorry, had to make sure it was anchored."

"Hey yourself," she said, sounding roughly 108 percent more confident than she truly felt. "I called you."

"You did? When?"

"I don't know, ten minutes ago?" she said.

"Sorry—I must have missed it. I've actually been out here for almost an hour, but I was on the phone with my mother," he said, looking sheepish.

"You *were*?" She wanted to hug him—she knew calling his mother was a huge step. But she didn't have a right.

"Yeah. It was time. You didn't see me?" he asked.

She shook her head. "I was napping."

His smile wasn't so faint that she missed it. "But you never nap."

"Apparently I do now," she said, letting her own lips curl up.

They looked at each other.

"Aly—" he began, just as she said, "Wyatt—"

"Go ahead," he said.

"No, you," she said, but her eyes had just landed on the freshly painted navy script on the back of the boat.

As Luke Would Have It

She wasn't sure whether to smile, laugh, or burst into tears. Maybe all three. "A terrible pun. Luke would've loved it," she told him.

"A terrible *nautical* pun," said Wyatt, grinning at her. "His favorite kind. I thought about painting *Frayed Knot* on it again, since it wore off the last time, but I felt like maybe it was time for something new. You're not angry, are you?"

"Not even a little." She examined him. He didn't look upset, but maybe her eyes were playing tricks on her. And in spite of everything, she still had the impulse to put her hands on him, to run her fingers along the flat plane of his stomach, the curve of his bicep, the stubble on his jaw.

But that was how she'd messed things up in the first place.

"Wyatt, before you say anything else, I am so sorry."

"Aly," he said.

And then he wrapped his arms around her and he kissed her and oh—how he had ruined all other men for her.

"*I'm* sorry," he said after he finally pulled his mouth from hers. "I should've called. I wanted to give you space after telling you about Luke, but I think I gave you too much. Am I wrong?"

"You're right—but I don't care. You did the best you could. Luke . . ." She was about to say that he had made a mistake, but that wasn't really true. "He did know what he was doing. I never should've blamed you for his choices. I messed up, but I'm going to transfer the deed to you. It's the only way I know to show you that I truly am sorry."

Visibly rattled, Wyatt held her at arm's length. "What? Why would you do that?"

"I know I ruined everything between us. I don't need the place, and you—you love it." It was nearly the golden hour, and the house glowed in the sunlight. Aly couldn't help but think that Luke must have seen it exactly as she was seeing it now when he'd decided to buy it.

"I do love this house," said Wyatt, who'd pulled her closer to him again. The vibration of his voice made his torso rumble against hers. "But I love it because of *you*, Aly."

She stared up at him, unable to speak.

"I was dead inside when I got here. But then you showed up and—well, I'm alive again, in a way I never have been before. I know this probably isn't what Luke had in mind when he left us this place."

Or maybe it was, she thought.

Wyatt continued. "I tried hard not to, but I love you, Aly. I can't help it, but I do. Now, I know your plans don't include me—"

"Wait," she said, lifting a finger to his lips. "I love you, too. And my plans *do* include you. Or at least they will if you'll forgive me."

"Forgive you? I'm not even upset with you. Wrecked that you told me to leave, yes—but I'm not mad at you, Aly. I would've reacted the same way if I were in your shoes. But I need to show you something." He reached into his back pocket and pulled out a plastic sandwich bag. In it was the wrinkled, folded envelope Luke had addressed to him, which he handed to her. "I think you should read this."

Aly wasn't sure she wanted to—not after so many unpleasant surprises. But she thought about the video, and how that had shifted her perspective, and knew she had to be brave this time, too.

Her eyes ran over Luke's handwriting. Like so many other things about him, it was relaxed, yet precise.

The first thing she noticed was that the letter itself was not just addressed to Wyatt.

It was for both of them.

"Keep reading," said Wyatt, who stood behind her with his arms around her.

> *Dear Aly and Wyatt,*
> *If you're reading this, I obviously didn't make it to Cuba and back.*

I'm sorry. I'm sure it must look bad, but I need you to know that I wasn't trying to end my life; that was never, ever my goal.

I was simply trying to live it.

You both know I'd always wanted to make that trip, and no matter what, I will have been glad to have had the courage to do what I really wanted to do.

I hope you don't both hate me. For all I know, you do (just kidding—neither of you do, because I'm dead and who hates a dead man?!). By now you've probably had time to come to terms with my being gone.

Knowing the two of you, it probably took you a year to go anywhere near my bedroom, and another six months to open the drawer of my nightstand. Wyatt, I figured you'd get there first and would actually open it, which is why I addressed the envelope to you.

I'm really hoping you've found an arrangement that involves both of you enjoying the house, and maybe even living in it or at least splitting your vacations. But just in case it hasn't worked out, I want to tell you why I left the place to both of you.

I know you have nothing in common—well, except me.

I also know you're my two favorite people on the entire planet, and that's no coincidence.

Wyatt, Aly has that weird thing that you and I never did—an ability to look across endless water and see land. You and I have talked a lot about how you can feel aimless, and you know I've been there. But she'll never let you lose your way or steer you off course. And I guarantee that while Aly will have some trouble with your housekeeping (or lack thereof, ha!), she'll still accept you for who you are, fully and unconditionally. That's just who she is.

Aly, Wyatt is the beacon in the storm—and I'm guessing your life might feel a little stormy right now. I'm so sorry that I left this world before you, and I hope you'll understand that as much as you can. Sis, I love you more than you'll ever know; you've made my life worth living, even if I wish it had been a little longer. But with Wyatt, you won't be alone. As I'm sure he's told you, he knows what you're going through right now. And he'll do anything for the people he loves. Anything. *And of course, you're going right in the (admittedly small) group of people he'd walk over hot coals for, because to spend time with you is to love you. That's why I made sure you both ended up under the same roof, at least for a while.*

Even if you don't like each other right off the bat, I have truly no doubt that you'll learn to love each other. And call it a hunch, but something tells me that by the time you read this, you already have.

I miss you both already. Say hi to my beach for me.

All of my love, always—

Luke

Aly's cheeks were drenched as she looked up from the letter. "Oh, Wyatt."

He slowly lifted his hand to wipe away her tears. And this time, Aly didn't flinch.

"What do we do now?" she whispered.

"When I'm not sure what to do, I ask myself: What would Luke do now?"

She widened her eyes in surprise. "I do that, too."

"Great minds." He leaned to kiss her tenderly, then said, "I think Luke would want us to take his boat out."

"Yeah, about that," she said, glancing over at it.

"I've been working on restoring it for months—I wanted to surprise you, and to honor Luke's memory. I wasn't trying to hide that I was working on the boat at the children's center, but I didn't want you to come by before I was finished. That's why I didn't tell you I was there," he explained.

"I know we should, but . . ." She made a mental note to tell him about what had happened the other day, when her mother had pulled her out of the lake. "You know I'm afraid of boats. I don't think going out on the open water will be good for me."

"Should we try the bathtub, then?" said Wyatt, and she pretended to swat him. "Look at that," he said, gesturing out to the lake, which was not placid, but not choppy, either. "Conditions are perfect. We'll just go a little way from shore."

Aly looked back down at the letter and considered what Luke had said about living while he had the chance. She owed it to him to do the same.

She owed it to herself, too.

"Or," she said to Wyatt as they waded toward the boat, "we could just go where the wind takes us."

"And then can we go home?" said Wyatt, looking toward the house.

Aly laughed. "Then we can go home."

Wyatt helped Aly climb into the boat, then hoisted himself inside. He handed her a life preserver. "Just in case. I can't believe I haven't asked you this before, but can you swim?"

She nodded. Luke had taught her at a friend's pool. "Swim, Aly! Swim!" he'd said, a few fingers below her torso as she kicked furiously and windmilled her arms the way he'd shown her. He'd cheered her on the entire way. "You're swimming! You're doing it!"

She hoped Luke knew that she was still doing it. Her inner shark may have slowed considerably, but she was swimming all the same.

Wyatt lifted the anchor, and the boat began to drift away from shore. "Before we set sail, I thought we'd take a moment," he said, sitting beside her. "You okay?" he asked as he wrapped his arms around her.

"Better than okay," she said, gazing up at him. She smiled and kissed him again, then looked back out at the lake. It was a wonder—so vast a person could easily mistake it for an ocean. The sunset painted the water in pastel shades, and she couldn't help but wish Luke were there to see it.

Maybe he was the sun, warming her skin. Maybe he was the wind at her back, or the tiny glittering star she saw in the distance.

But as she closed her eyes and remembered, Aly knew exactly where Luke was.

With her—just as he'd always been.

ACKNOWLEDGMENTS

First and foremost, thank you to my readers, including you—you are the reason I continue to write.

Maria Gomez, working with you has been an absolute dream, and I'm ecstatic to call you my editor. My deep gratitude to the rest of the Lake Union and Amazon Publishing team, including Danielle Marshall, Mikyla Bruder, and Gabriella Dumpit. Jodi Warshaw, it was a joy to work with you in a new capacity; thank you for helping strengthen this story as well as my writing. Elisabeth Weed, thank you for your friendship and guidance, and for representing me all these years. Michelle Weiner and the entire team at CAA, thank you for continuing to champion my work.

Kathleen Carter, Paige Hazzan, Suzy Leopold, and Lucy Silag, I can't tell you how much I appreciate your spreading the word about my novels. Likewise, a big shout-out to the entire #bookstagram community, especially my early readers. You make launching and publishing so much more enjoyable.

To my fellow authors—especially Chris Bailey, Anne Bogel, Lisa Barr, Katherine Chen, Katie Rose Guest Pryal, Kelly Harms, Sarah Jio, Kyunghee Kim, Kerry Lonsdale, Barbara O'Neal, Zibby Owens, Lori Nelson Spielman, Jane Stinson, Laura Vanderkam, and Rochelle Weinstein—your friendship and support means the world to me.

Thank you to Laurel Lambert, Shannon Callahan, Darci Swisher, Jacob Lambert, Joe Lambert, Janette Sunadhar, Suman Sunadhar, Stefanie Galban, Michelle Stone, Nicole Perrin, Jennifer Lamb, Stevany Peters, Craig Galban, Mike Stone, Tim Peters, Jeff Lamb, Matt Sampson, Jamie Berman, Sara Reistad-Long, Lauren Bauser, and Pam Sullivan for always having my back.

And above all, thank you to JP, Indira, and Xavi Pagán—who have given me the kind of happy family that I once believed only existed in fiction.

ABOUT THE AUTHOR

Photo © 2022 Liv in the Moment Photography

Camille Pagán is the #1 Amazon Charts and *Washington Post* bestselling author of nine novels, including *Everything Must Go, I'm Fine and Neither Are You, Woman Last Seen in Her Thirties*, and *Life and Other Near-Death Experiences*, which has been optioned for film. Her work has also been published in the *New York Times*; *O, The Oprah Magazine*; *Real Simple*; *Time*; and many others. When Camille's not working on her next story, you'll usually find her with her family, talking shop with other writers, or at the beach—with a book in hand, of course. To learn more about her work and subscribe to her newsletter, visit www.camillepagan.com.